No One to Hold

ARELL RIVERS

NO ONE TO HOLD
Book 1 of **THE HOLD** series
Copyright ©2016 Tarnished Halo Publishing LLC
Published by Tarnished Halo Publishing LLC
2016 Edition

ISBN print: 978-0-9982844-1-5

Editing: Angela Polidoro, www.polidoroeditorialservices.com
Proofreading: Jennifer Leisenheimer, Beyond the Cover Editing, www.beyondthecoverediting.com
Formatting: Cassy Roop, Pink Ink Designs, www.pinkinkdesigns.com
Cover design: Kari Ayasha, Cover to Cover, www.covertocoverdesigns.com
 Author Photo: Elzbieta Kaciuba Photography LLC, www.elzphoto.com

Dedication

For my husband, my very own sexy rock star.

No One to Hold

Prelude

No One to Hold

All my fame
And my awards
Couldn't help my mom
Can't embrace me now
Where is a hand for me to hold?

Looking around, I'm surrounded
Screaming, pleading, begging
Yes, oh please
But never for keeps
Who is my hand to hold?

Appearances can be faked
To give you what you want
But I'm so hollow inside
This can't be my forever – Oh No, Oh No
Please don't leave me with No One to Hold

Lyrics and music by Cole Manchester

One

Somehow I endure the first hour of the party.

No. Not party. Wake.

Two hours ago I placed a blood-red rose atop my mother's casket on this freezing February day. Now, I'm trapped in my parents' house, choked by a tie, listening to stories about her while pretending everything is okay. It's *not* fucking okay.

When I can't take it anymore, I collapse onto the step at the foot of the stairs, looking at all the people milling around the family room. They are eating catered food off Mom's good china. Swilling drinks from her favorite wine glasses. Photos of her are displayed everywhere, some in frames and others in the scrapbooks that she spent hours creating.

Reaching between the spindles of the banister, I pick up a frame off the closest table. It's a photo of Mom and me at the Grammy Awards a couple of years ago. She's beaming, clearly enjoying herself. I trace her beautiful smile with a calloused finger.

A bunch of Mom's high school students surround me like yipping hyenas, giving me little choice but to put down the photo, stand up and join them. They're on the cheerleading squad Mom coached. They all seem to be talking at once, making it impossible for me to follow their conversation, and a few of the girls seem star struck to be near me. Some even cast what they obviously think are flirty, seductive glances in my direction. Seriously?

One girl points her cell phone at me while the others titter. My hand flies to block my face in a gesture I've perfected after years of protecting myself from the paparazzi.

Rose Morgan, my ponytailed and bespectacled account rep with the Greta VonStein PR Agency, appears at my right. I take my first deep breath since being surrounded, knowing Rose will take care of the girls.

"Ladies, a word," she says. She's wearing what she always wears—a skirt and blazer—this time in black. Ushering the group deeper into the family room, Rose says something that I can't hear and then takes the would-be photographer's cell phone. After pushing a few buttons, she returns it to the girl, who mouths the word *sorry* to me. Quickly, the cheerleaders disperse. Rose to the rescue. Again.

Returning to my side, Rose places her hands on my cheeks. My breath catches at the contact.

In a low voice, she says, "It's all taken care of, Cole."

Behind her glasses, her blue eyes are filled with compassion and some other emotion I can't identify. They seem like they belong to someone much older and wiser than me, not to a woman who's a few years younger than my thirty-two.

I close my eyes to block out everything except the feeling of her hands on my skin and the comfort they're pouring into me. The intensity of the sensation startles me back to the present, causing my eyes to pop open. Clearing my throat, I say, "Thanks for the save. It's kinda weird being fangirled here."

Rose drops her hands and I immediately crave her soft warmth. "I'm so sorry for your loss," she finally says. "Your mom is—was—a wonderful lady. I remember the first time I spoke with her, right after you'd signed with

Greta. She couldn't believe you had a publicist." She shakes her head. "Her exact words were, 'I can't believe other people will really follow what my Cole does.'"

I laugh. It's a rusty sound. "I can hear Mom saying that."

Smiling, Rose says, "After you took her to your first Grammys, she sent me a lovely thank you note and gift basket. She was so proud of you."

"Mom never got tired of talking about when she met Adam Baret there." Mom's teenage heartthrob sent a very nice arrangement to the funeral. I'm sure she's looking down on us from above, blushing.

"Take some time and stay here with your father and brother."

My gaze follows hers to the kitchen, where Jayson and Dad are hugging. It's just us now. And Jayson's boyfriend, Carl. "I plan to."

"Family is so very important. Lean on each other." Her tone leads me to believe she's speaking from experience, although I wouldn't know. Up until now, all of our conversations have been strictly business.

I nod. Swallowing past the lump in my throat, I say, "Thanks for making the trip from Los Angeles, Rose. And I appreciate how much you've kept the paparazzi away from us."

"I wanted to be here for you." She reaches out like she's going to touch me again, which sends a flicker of anticipation through me, but her hand stops and returns to her side. My disappointment shocks me.

She continues, "And don't worry about all the cards and gifts your fans are sending to the office. We'll make sure everything receives a response, and the stuffed animals and other presents will be distributed to children's hospitals."

I shake my head at her use of "we." That idea has Rose's signature, not Greta's, all over it. "My fans are really sending stuff?"

"You mean a lot to them." Her lips quirk into a small smile, and I feel my mouth move upward in response.

"I left a card from Josh with the others over there." She motions toward the front hallway table. "I thought you'd want to see it."

"Thanks." I first met Josh four years ago at a meet-and-greet. His love of music reminded me of myself at his age, so passionate. His single mother was unable to pay for a violin coach, so I arranged for him to have private music lessons. He must be fourteen by now.

She nods, sending her ponytail swinging. For the second time today, I find myself ensnared by her blue eyes. They're an icy blue, yet they're bright with emotion behind the thick lenses of her glasses. How have I never noticed their remarkable color before?

After a beat, she says, "Let me know when you're planning on returning to LA, and we'll set up some appearances for you. In the meantime, Greta wants me to issue a release on your behalf, thanking your fans for their support and letting them know you'll be spending some personal time with your family." She gives me a quick hug and walks off in Dad's direction.

Business never stops for long.

My agent, Russell Waldock, and his wife fill the void left by Rose. At fifty-five, he's one of the most powerful men in LA, yet he's also very down-to-earth, which drew me to him. "I appreciate your coming all the way to New Jersey for Mom's"—my voice breaks—"funeral."

Russell claps me on the back. "Julie was a great lady, Cole. Always looking out for you. And she was fierce. The way she scolded me about your music video for 'Prowling' made me feel like I got caught rifling through my father's *Playboy* collection." His wife smiles at him.

I chuckle. "She always called it my 'racy' video."

"Well, she wasn't wrong there," Russell agrees. No, she wasn't.

His wife picks up a photo of Mom and Dad holding hands on a beach in Hawaii and then returns it to the side table. She asks, "How's your father holding up? This has to be hard on him."

I glance over at Dad. "He's okay. It's been . . . rough."

How *is* Dad going to handle this? Mom's touch is everywhere in this house, in his life. They were married for so long they used to complete each other's sentences. "I'm trying to do whatever I can. Of course, Jayson and Carl live nearby."

"Let me know if you need anything, okay?" Russell says.

"Thanks. I'm grateful you arranged for the label to give me an extension on recording my next album."

Russell nods. "Call me when you're ready to go back to LA. No rush."

They each give me a hug. "Thanks again for coming," I say. "Will do."

I circulate around the room, numbly making small talk with acquaintances I haven't seen in years. I'm standing in the dining room with some family friends the next time Rose crosses my line of vision. She's in the front hall, running her fingers over the framed photo of Mom holding me when I was a baby. She wipes a tear from her cheek and looks up.

Our eyes meet.

We both freeze.

After a long pause, she retrieves her coat and walks out the front door. I catch a breath as if my heart just restarted.

I continue circulating and reminiscing about Mom. Around nine, Jayson and Carl leave to take care of their new puppy. Just Aunt Doreen and her family remain. "How are you doing, Cole?"

"I'm okay," I lie. Yanking off my tie, I ask, "How about you, Aunt Doreen?"

"About as well as I can be. I want you to know you can always count on me, whatever you need."

"Thanks."

We discuss mundane things, like how beautiful the funeral was and our amazement at how many people came to the wake. After a pause, she says, "You know, I swore to my sister that I would keep an eye out for you. She really wanted you to settle down." She picks invisible lint off of my blazer.

Can't she give this a rest? Even today? I sigh. "There's no one in my life at the moment. Frankly, I'm not interested."

"I understand. But getting through tough times is easier when you have someone by your side. And celebrating the good times is better, too. I intend to hold you to the promise that you made to your mother and me before your career took off." She looks deep into my eyes. Her green gaze mirrors mine. And Mom's.

Trying not to squirm, I say, "I've kept my promise, Aunt Doreen. I don't have a bad boy reputation."

"That's true, thanks to your publicist, but we both know that running through women like tissues is not exactly living up to the spirit of your pledge." I stifle the urge to roll my eyes. "Just think about what I said. And let me know if I can help you in any way, honey. I love you." She gives me a peck on the cheek, and after another rounds of goodbyes, leaves the house with her family.

Aunt Doreen's comments remind me of my last conversation with Mom—how can it be that I won't have another one with her? I try to swallow the lump in my throat. Mom made me promise that I would settle down. And I can't deny that Aunt Doreen's words have struck a chord. At the cemetery, everyone had a hand to hold. Even my younger brother. I had Dad's, and he needed me. But it's not the same.

Taking off my blazer, I walk into the kitchen and roll up my sleeves. Grateful for something productive to do, I join Dad in packaging up all the leftover food and arranging it in the refrigerator. It looks like casseroles mated in there.

I'm exhausted, but suspect neither one of us is quite ready to face going upstairs. As has become our nightly custom since I flew back home, he pours two fingers of scotch for each of us. Tonight, I bring the stack of sympathy cards from the hallway to the dining room table before sitting down.

"Want to look at these?" I ask.

He shrugs. "Sure."

I hold up the first card and glance at the scribbled signature. "This one's from Josh."

Dad smiles at the card with the violin on the front. "You still paying for his private violin lessons?"

"Yeah." I squint, trying to read his chicken scratch. "He sends his 'condulances.'" We both smile at his attempt and clink our scotches.

Jessie Anderson's distinctive handwriting catches my eye. "Jessie and Amanda sent a card."

"Another one in the long line of ladies you've dated." He uses air quotes around "dated."

"Yeah, well that didn't end up how I expected." Jessie is gorgeous, and when Rose set us up on a publicity date, I thought we'd be in bed within hours. Shaking my head, I trace her girlfriend's name on the card. The two of them are great together. Like Mom and Dad are. Were.

Clearing my throat, I say, "Jessie's filming her TV show, so they couldn't be here. They send their love."

"Jules—Julie—your mother," his voice catches. I reach over and pat him on the shoulder while he collects himself. "She never missed one episode of Jessie's show. She had a group of friends over every Thursday night for a viewing party." He smiles. "I made myself scarce those nights. To be honest, they scared me a little."

We both laugh, then stop short as if we did something wrong. Maybe it's too soon for laughter. Dad knocks back his scotch, then stares blankly into his empty glass.

I reach out for another card, but drop my hand. I can't concentrate any longer. "Let's call it a night, Dad."

Sad brown eyes meet mine. He looks so tired. "I'll put the glasses in the dishwasher and you get the lights."

Our chores completed, he slowly leads the way upstairs. On the landing, Mom's perfume lingers. Dad pulls me in for a long hug and whispers, "Goodnight, son. I love you."

"Love you, too."

Walking to the doorway farthest from my parents' room, I enter my childhood bedroom. The room is as I left it ages ago, filled with all the stuff I once considered important. Posters of musicians—some of whom I'm privileged to call friends now. That makes me smile. Posters of models, generally glistening wet. Seems like my tastes haven't changed much over the years. Just my access.

I sit down on my old twin bed, feeling horribly alone, wishing a woman were here to put her arms around me and tell me everything will be okay. I'm thirty-two fucking years old. Shouldn't I have someone special in my life by now?

Images of Rose from today replay in my mind. The connection I felt when she touched me was . . . What am I thinking? She works for me. Besides, she's all business, all the time.

Shit, I'm living the life most guys only dream about. I have money, fame, millions of fans across the globe, houses on both coasts, people to do my bidding at the snap of my fingers and a very steady diet of gorgeous women. There can be nothing wrong with my lifestyle if it's the American dream. Right?

Looking up to the ceiling, lyrics start to form. Grabbing my trusty notebook, I scribble down the words that are tripping over themselves to come out.

Two

PULLING INTO MY BEST FRIEND'S DRIVEWAY, I shut the engine and look around his corner of LA. Down the street, kids ride their bikes wearing helmets. A father teaches his young son how to skateboard. A mother jogs on the sidewalk behind my car, pushing a stroller. Just another lazy June Sunday in sunny California. Tamping down the pang of nostalgia, I exit my car and make my way to the front door.

"I'm so glad you're here, buddy," Dan says, ushering me into the family room. "Emma's been crying all morning. We've tried everything, but can't get her to stop."

Though I'm not accustomed to being around babies, I try to commiserate. "Have you tried singing to her?" My best friend apparently takes that as an offer on my part. The next thing I know, Dan's wife thrusts my four-month-old goddaughter into my arms. Thoughtfully, she puts what looks like a diaper on my shoulder.

"It's called a burp cloth," Suzanne declares with a smile in her brown eyes.

Well, hell. I look down into the baby's little face, all scrunched up with red blotches from her crying. "Emma, sweetie, what's the matter?" I ask in a low-pitched, hopefully soothing voice. She continues to wail.

I look up for help from Dan or Suzanne, but both have disappeared, presumably to change for the christening. "I guess it's just you and me, Emma." This is not good. Emma emits a particularly loud note. Not good at all.

"C'mon, sweetie. Stop crying for your Uncle Cole." Yeah, like that'll help. I might as well take my own advice and try singing. At the very least, my voice should drown out some of her screams.

I can't think of any kids' songs except for the one about a spider. Then my eyes land on a framed picture of Dan and Suzanne's wedding, and I decide on the song I wrote for them, "She's Your Happy." I prepared it as a surprise for their wedding, and sang it after my best man toast.

Emma miraculously stops crying after I sing the first verse. By the end of the song, she's staring at me with this adorable look on her face. It's almost as if I wrote the song with Emma in mind even though she came along years later.

"I can't believe it. You wrap females of all ages around your finger with that tenor voice of yours," Suzanne says from the threshold.

I look up, smiling. "She likes your song." Gratefully, I hand Emma back to her mother and return the diaper burp thingy to her as well. Straightening my tie, I wink at her and say, "Play one of my albums for her the next time she starts crying like that again."

"No daughter of mine is going to be a Cole groupie," Dan states flatly. "She's way too smart for that, even at four months."

"Oh, I don't know, Danny-boy. She looks pretty enthralled to me," I say. It feels good to tease him.

Making a fist, he says, "You'd better keep that dimple away from her, if you know what's good for you." Laughing, we head out to the church.

Following the christening, we go to a restaurant on Mulholland Drive for a small celebration. I carry Emma into the private dining room, and give her to Suzanne to be fed. Thankfully, she hasn't cried since I sang to her. My goddaughter sure knows how to turn on the charm when it comes time to perform.

"You look good with a baby in your arms," Dan whispers loudly. He lowers his voice. "Maybe one of the tabloids will run a photo of you with Emma, saying she's your love child. Imagine the frenzy."

"Screw you." I give Dan a punch. "I don't think Rose needs another mess to mop up. Besides, you and Suzanne would have to come down from your television ivory tower to set the record straight. And I know how much you executive types hate to leave the safety of that tower."

"Simply because we don't crave the spotlight like some other people I won't name, does not mean that we live in an ivory tower."

"Yeah, whatever." The waitress comes over to take our order, effectively ending our friendly banter.

Back at their house, Dan and I relax with a couple of beers while a baseball game plays on the television. Suzanne is in the other room with Emma. It's nice to hang out with my former roommate, even if it's only a few hours.

"So, how are you doing, Cole? I'm still so sorry that we couldn't be there for your mom's funeral."

"You didn't have much of a choice. Emma was ready to make her appearance. If I never mentioned it before, it means a lot to me that her middle name is Julie." Emma was born the day after Mom's funeral.

"Your mom was very special to me. I wanted to honor her."

We both take long pulls of our beers. Mom took an immediate shine to Dan when we roomed together at New York University, and the fact that he'd already moved to LA made her feel better about me doing the same when I signed with my label.

I clear my throat, causing Dan to look at me. He knows I do that when I'm about to bring up a particularly difficult subject, but I doubt he's prepared for what's going to come out of my mouth. "I've been thinking a lot lately, as you can imagine. It's been rough. One thing that Mom made me promise is that I'm going to settle down."

Dan snorts.

Ignoring him, I continue. "Yeah, yeah. I know I've had more than my share of women, but sleeping around feels hollow now. When Mom called to tell me about her diagnosis, I was in bed with a model. I was barely holding it together when I shared the news with her. You know what her response was?"

He shakes his head, and I continue, "She said, 'Oh, that's too bad. Want a blow job?'"

Dan's eyebrows meet his thinning hairline. "That's messed up."

"I know, right? I told her to leave." I sigh and run my hand through my hair. "Jessie and I are real friends, you know? I think she's my first female friend. Of course, there's no romantic interest considering she's with Amanda, but I do enjoy hearing her take on things, even if I'm mystified by some of her logic."

"Oh boy, do I get that. But don't let Suzanne hear you say that."

"Hear you say what?" Suzanne comes into the living room holding Emma, dressed in her footie pajamas.

"Nothing," Dan and I both say in unison, trying to look innocent. Suzanne taps her foot.

"I'm putting Emma down for the night. Daddy, kiss your baby girl good night." Dan gives his daughter a kiss, and Suzanne brings her over to me. "Kiss your goddaughter, Uncle Cole." I dutifully give her a kiss too, and they leave the room.

I figure now is as good a time as any to make my request. Sucking in my breath, I blurt out, "Dan, do you know any women who might be good for me. You know, long term?"

Dan's eyes get wide. "Are you seriously asking me to fix you up on a *date?*"

"Don't let this go to your head, asshole. It's just, you know, I don't meet a lot of down-to-earth women. Most of the ones I go out with are for show, set up by Rose. Or groupies. I have yet to meet anyone who holds my interest beyond the bedroom. Or back room." I snicker to relieve some of my tension.

But then I picture Rose sprawled across a bed, and my smile fades. These thoughts have to stop. It's bad enough she's been popping up in my dreams. She's my employee, for fuck's sake.

Dan says, "I get it. Congratulations, man, you're finally growing up."

"I wouldn't go that far, buddy. I'm not ready for the white picket fence and 2.5 kids. But I would like to have someone to share my life with."

"Any particular requests? Blonde, brunette, tall, short?"

"You know me. She doesn't have to be a model or anything. I've been with enough models and starlets to know that beauty can only take a person so far. Usually, they're most interesting when they're on their backs or their knees."

Dan snorts. "You're right, you're not growing up."

"Cole, growing up? Ha!" Suzanne comes back into the room carrying a tray holding the baby monitor and another round of beers. She joins us on the couch with her iced tea.

"Our boy here wants us to fix him up."

"On a date?" Suzanne asks excitedly. Dan nods while I slump back into the sofa with my new bottle. "That's great, Cole. I have a few women already in mind for you. Let's see, you'll need a career woman because you're always on the road. Someone who can keep you on your toes, yet give you the pampering you need. Smart and funny, 'cause you like to laugh a lot."

She continues for a solid fifteen minutes, but I've totally tuned her out. I glance over at Dan, whose eyes are equally glazed over. I'm brought back into the conversation when Suzanne says, "Do you want kids?"

Thankfully, Dan fields this one. "Not right away, honey. I think we know Cole well enough that we can come up with a few good candidates without badgering him."

Oops, judging by the way Suzanne's eyes turn into slits, Dan's choice of the word "badgering" is going to get him into some hot water. Seeing how I might have inadvertently caused this little tiff, I try for some humor. "What a great song title. I can name my next song 'Badgering.'" Lame, but we all laugh anyway, and it breaks the tension.

I stay for a few more hours, watching my NY Mets lose, again, and catching up. It's nice to have a quiet evening in with friends, away from spotlights, cameras and eager fans. I know how important my fans are to my career, but it's difficult to be "on" all of the time. Especially lately, when they step all over themselves trying to "comfort" me.

Fishing my keys out of my pocket, I give Suzanne a hug. "I had a great time seeing you and Emma. I'll take my godfather duties very seriously, I promise."

"I know you will. Emma's a lucky girl. She'll be the envy of all the other girls in her day care." Suzanne says, smiling.

"Not to mention the moms," Dan chimes in.

"Asshole."

"Better watch it. This asshole is going to be setting you up on a date in the very near future."

Well, shit. What did I get myself into?

Three

I PUT THE FINISHING TOUCHES ON THE music for "No One to Hold." Mom's warm presence surrounds me, as if she's wrapping me in a thank you hug for the song. It's taken months to get it right, but it may be the best one I've ever written. Not sure how I'm going to be able to perform it live, though, because so many of my emotions are packed into it. I'll play it for Russell to get his take. As I pull out my cell phone to call him, it beeps with a text from Dan:

Don't forget you're meeting Alicia tonight.

As if I could. My nerves are tingling like they do right before I hit the stage. I shake my head at the absurdity. I'm simply meeting this woman for dinner. Who knows if we'll even have chemistry?

All set. Will let you know how it goes. I hit send.

According to Dan, first dates are usually at a coffee shop or a bar—low pressure and easy to escape. However, those options simply are not available to me. So, Dan thought a nice dinner in a quiet restaurant would be a good idea. The reservation's under his name, and we're arriving separately.

Don't let the paparazzi catch wind of this covert operation, I whisper to myself. If they do, Rose will have to do clean-up. For some reason, the thought of Rose finding out about it makes me queasy. I tamp down the heat coursing through my veins at the mere thought of Rose. Focus, Cole.

My date is Suzanne's colleague. Alicia is a news reporter with Suzanne's station, which means she's had her own issues with celebrity. At least she can sort of understand what I deal with daily.

I've caught a couple of Alicia's news segments. She's pretty, smart and does her job really well. Dan has warned me that she's a vegetarian. Armed with this information, I'm as ready as I'll ever be for my first blind date.

Coming to a stop in front of the restaurant, I toss my keys to the valet and walk inside, keeping my head down and cap on. No flashing lights, and no one's calling my name. So far, so good. The perky, red-headed hostess shows me to a table in a dark corner. Though she doesn't make any inappropriate comments, I recognize the look in her eyes. If she sensed any willingness from me, she'd offer up anything I might like for an appetizer. Or dessert.

"When Miss Jones arrives, please escort her to my table. Your discretion is much appreciated." I slip her a hundred-dollar bill, which she takes but looks disappointed I didn't slip her something else.

Sitting down, I remove my cap off and order a bottle of champagne. I'm about to take my first sip when Miss Perky Hostess returns with Alicia. I stand to greet her.

"So nice to meet you in person," I say, giving her a kiss on the cheek. "You're even more beautiful than on TV."

"Thanks, Cole. I'm so happy that Suzanne set us up."

"Please, sit. Would you like some champagne?" She nods her assent, so I pour her a glass.

"A toast. To a wonderful evening." We clink glasses. "I enjoyed watching your reports last week about that rash of burglaries."

"Thank you. The ring is nasty and the police have few leads. Hopefully the reports will lead to some useful tips."

I nod. The waiter comes with the menus, and runs through the specials.

"So, have you been here before? Dan recommended this restaurant to me. He says the fish is to die for."

"I bet. Those poor fish had to die a terrible death just to end up on a plate served with lemon."

Well, crap. "I thought vegetarians eat fish, but not meat."

"Pescatarians do, but I'm a vegan," she announces.

Damn. This is already going south. "Well, I hope you find something on the menu that suits your diet."

"When I go out, I usually tell them what to make for me. It's rare that there's anything appropriate on a menu."

Rare. She said that word, and now all I can think about is ordering a steak: Rare. Shit, if I do that, will she be offended? Even more offended than she already is? Might as well ask. "Oh. Well, um, do you mind if I order a steak?"

Her look of revulsion is answer enough, so I quickly add, "Or fish?" No way in hell am I eating tofu or dandelions or whatever the hell she considers "appropriate" food.

Alicia sighs. "I can deal."

I decide to go with the potato-crusted mahi-mahi. At least that's half vegan. I hope.

Desperately trying to change the subject, I ask, "How long have you known Suzanne?"

"She's the producer for my news program. I met her when I got this job in LA, about six months ago."

"Where were you before?"

"I was in Philadelphia. This is a stepping stone for me; I really want to get to the NY market. That's where the real action is."

"Oh." I wonder if Suzanne knows this. I guess ambition is pretty common in their cutthroat business. We go on to discuss her career, in depth. She's *very* into it. I'm getting pretty bored hearing about ratings, asshole reporters, camera men with wandering hands and story pitches, but every time I try to change the subject, she veers it back. It's like playing the guitar with a broken string.

She picks up her water and starts to chew on the ice. This is my ultimate pet peeve—like nails on a chalkboard. My hands ball into fists under the table. If I could yell out for the check, I would. I silently cast my eyes about, actually hoping to lock eyes with a fan who'll disrupt our dinner. Where are the fangirls when you need them?

Somehow, I get through the rest of the entree and profess to be too stuffed for dessert. The women in LA rarely eat dessert anyway. "Alicia, I had a nice time."

"Thank you, Cole. So did I. It's too bad you're such an avid fisherman. I had no idea." We both smile. I figured it would be better to feed her a white lie than to tell her there's no way I'm interested in dating a militant vegan, career-obsessed ice chewer. I'll be a little blunter with Dan and Suzanne.

"I would walk you out, but I don't want to cause a commotion. If there are any paparazzi out there . . ." Letting the sentence hang, I take her hand and kiss it. The last thing I want to do is piss off a reporter of her caliber. "Get home safe." I watch her navigate through the tables and leave the restaurant.

I sit down, loudly exhaling, then I motion for the waiter. "I'd like a ribeye, rare."

Four

TWO WEEKS AND A FEW MORE disastrous dates later, I'm sitting in a meeting about my upcoming album with my manager Russell and Jon Merkin, my A&R rep from Platinum Records. One bright spot is that Greta the Gruesome is sick and couldn't make this meeting, so at least I don't have to put up with her passive-aggressive shit today. Rose is here in her place, dressed in her usual skirt and blazer combination—navy blue this time.

I repress a shudder as memories of my first meeting with Gruesome come unbidden to the forefront of my mind. Within minutes of arriving, I was ordered to stand up and take off my shirt. She proceeded to circle around me, commenting on my physique like I was a contestant in a gigolo contest. Then she ordered Rose to make me appointments to highlight my hair, whiten my teeth and get a style makeover. Ugh. The worst was when she pulled me aside to tell me that she'd be willing to bend the agency's strict non-fraternization policy for me. Thank God I averted that disaster, since she is the best in the business.

Planting that meeting with Gruesome firmly in the past, I tune back into the present as Jon says, "I agree with Russell. It's time to go on a world tour. Your fans in Europe and Australia have been sending in way too many requests. We can't keep ignoring them."

Yes. Now I'll get to see the world while doing what I love. My life rocks. "I've never been to Europe. I'm so down with that. I only have to tweak a couple of songs before I'm ready to record."

"You're scheduled for studio time in a couple of weeks." Jon says.

I nod. "I have enough material now. I recently finished a song that I wrote for my Mom. Russell's heard it."

"The song's great," Russell says, nodding. "I think it should be the first single."

"Care to give us a preview?" Although Jon phrased it as a question, I know better. The label has been generous with my deadlines since Mom died, but they're starting to get itchy.

"Sure. Can you get me a guitar?" One good thing about meeting at Platinum Records' office is that there's always an instrument around. Pretty soon, one is handed to me.

I take a deep breath, and slowly exhale. Looking up to the ceiling, I whisper, "Here you go, Mom." I start "No One to Hold." When the song ends, both Russell and Jon are smiling. They're seeing dollar signs—it's their job—but Rose's eyes look watery behind her glasses, and the tenderness in them causes my breath to catch.

My attention is diverted from Rose to Jon, who says, "Gotta hand it to you, man. That song is phenomenal. I agree with Russell, it has to be the first single to drop. Without a doubt. And I haven't even heard all of the other tracks yet."

I smile in relief. The song takes a lot out of me, but I'm proud of it. I make a mental note to run it by Dad and Jayson.

Rose snags my attention again when she brings her hand up to her ear and starts playing with her earring. She says, "I'll work up a publicity strategy for the song that centers on your mother and how much she meant to you. I can pull up some footage from the Grammys, and maybe you could supply some other photos. It'll be nice to give your fans the chance to connect with you on a more emotional level."

Her suggestion hits me in the gut. It makes sense as a publicity strategy, but I don't want people to think I'm taking advantage of Mom's passing. It would destroy me.

Rose continues, "Of course, I'll have to run the idea by Greta."

Russell pipes up. "Rose, that sounds like a very good idea. Cole's fans were so supportive when she passed. It'll be a way to honor both Julie and the fans."

I can't keep silent any longer. "This song is very personal to me," I say. "I don't want it to seem like I'm capitalizing on my mother's death."

The room goes silent for a full minute. Rose, still fiddling with her earring, wades into the silence. "Perhaps your profits could be donated to the American Cancer Society."

I suck in my breath. "Yeah. That's good. That's right. Thank you, Rose." Mom always said Rose was the "secret sauce" of Gruesome's operation. Over the past few months, I've come to think she was right. I offer her a smile of appreciation.

She looks down at her notebook, but her cheeks seem to be a little pink. I don't have time to ponder Rose's reaction, though—the topic has already shifted to the logistics of recording the album. Afterward, we start preliminary outlines for the world tour. I'm going on a fucking world tour. If only I could call Mom to share the news with her.

Another hour and a half later, the meeting comes to a close. Jon and Russell have other projects to discuss, so Rose and I head down to the lobby alone. In the elevator, I turn to face her. "Your ideas were brilliant in there."

Rose looks down and a blush colors her cheeks again. She adjusts her glasses and says, "I really liked your mother, Cole. She was a great lady, and I think your song is a wonderful tribute."

Now it's my turn to flush, and the heat in my cheeks takes me by surprise. After filming music videos half-dressed and having panties thrown at my face at nearly every concert, it takes a lot to faze me. Needing to lighten up this mood, and fast, I joke, "I'm beginning to think you're the brains of Greta's operation."

Rose's eyes grow wide with . . . fear? Trying to put her at ease, I lean down to her and whisper, "Your secret's safe with me, Miss Morgan."

We arrive at the lobby and walk out to the valet station to get our cars. Rose and I hand in our tickets. A couple of guys stand near the side entrance, and one pulls out a pack of cigarettes. My whole body clenches.

Stalking over to them, I growl, "Don't do that." I throw the repulsive thing on the sidewalk.

"What the hell, man?"

"My mother died of lung cancer, asshole. Don't do that to your family."

Rose places her hands on my arm, gets on her tiptoes and whispers in my ear, "You've done a good deed, but now it's their decision. Let's leave them to it."

Rose's words, or maybe the calm tone in which she delivers them, diffuse my anger. Recognition flashes through the eyes of the guy whose pack I tossed. He knows who I am, so he probably knows what I've been through. It was well publicized, thanks to Rose, that I quit smoking the day Mom got her diagnosis. He throws the pack into the garbage. I nod and walk back to the valet station with Rose.

Taking deep breaths to calm down, I say, "Thanks. My temper gets away from me lately."

"I understand," she says softly. I believe her.

My car arrives, but I decide to be a gentleman and wait for Rose's car to pull up. After a few minutes, her valet returns on foot. "I'm sorry, miss, but your car won't start. I tried to jump it, but it's not turning over."

Rose's eyes flicker from her watch to the valet to me, then back to the valet. She mumbles, "I have another meeting in thirty minutes."

"Where?" Turns out, she's going to a building across the street from Dan's office.

"I'll take you."

Her blue eyes widen in surprise. Shit, I'm sort of surprised, too. But she's done so much for me, and I want to do this for her. Something deep inside me *needs* to do this for her.

Rose shakes her head. "No, that's okay. I'll call a taxi."

"Rose, you and I both know that a taxi will take twice as long. Let me take you to your meeting. My best friend works right across the street. I was planning to touch base with him anyway."

Maybe because my solution is practical, she relents. For some reason, it's like I climbed Mount Everest. Twenty minutes later we're in front of the building. "Call me when you're finished, and I'll pick you up. How long do you expect the meeting to take?"

"Two hours. But you don't have to pick me up. This is my last meeting of the day, so I can get a car service."

"No arguments, Miss Morgan. Call me when you're done." With an exasperated look, she nods and leaves the car.

Once she's safely inside the office building, I call Dan. Luckily, he hasn't eaten yet, so we arrange to meet at a nearby café for a late lunch.

I've only just sat down across from Dan when I hear someone shriek, "*Oh my God. It's Cole Manchester!!!!*"

I sigh. So much for a quiet lunch. Dan shakes his head good-naturedly, muttering something about ivory towers, and sits back to watch the show.

Five women crowd around our table. They are all chattering at once, and it's obvious they have no intention to leave without talking to me.

"Ladies, my friend and I are *starving*." I fake hunger pains. Dan turns his head and I swear I hear him snort. "If you have anything for me to autograph, or if you'd like a photo, I'm all yours for the next five minutes." I say this with a wink in their general direction. Luckily, they take the not-so-subtle hint. After I pose for a group shot and sign a few napkins, a take-out menu and a bra, they go on their way, giggling.

"Dude. I seriously need to get you on my network pronto. You're a natural!"

"You're a dick, you know that?"

"Well, this dick holds your dating life in his hands. How did it go with

Gretchen?"

"You mean the giggler? She made those five look like amateurs. That was one long date."

"Better or worse than Alicia?"

"Are you and Suzanne keeping score of who sets me up on the worst dates?"

Dan gives me a wicked smile. "No, dickhead. We're in competition to see who sets you up with the girl who steals your heart."

"So far, Emma's winning."

"Stay away from my baby girl. It's bad enough that your songs are the only thing that'll calm her down when she's on a crying bender."

"That's awesome."

Dan throws a straw wrapper at me. "So, how's work going?"

We start discussing my meeting and plans for a world tour.

"Guess your dream of world domination is coming true," he teases. "I remember that you used to talk about studying abroad in Spain when we were rooming together at NYU. At least you'll get your chance to visit."

"Yeah, I love performing live anyway, and now I'll finally get to see Europe and Australia."

We continue chatting while eating our sandwiches. After a while, Dan checks his watch and says, "I hate to break this up, buddy, but I have to get back to the office. Some of us work for a living."

It's my turn to snort. "I'm going to stay put. I need to make a couple of calls, and it's pretty quiet in here now." We stand and give each other what my brother Jayson has termed our patented man-hug.

After Dan leaves, I grab my cell and call my mechanic. "How's the car that was towed to you?"

"It needs a new part that I don't have in stock. The fastest I can get it here is two days."

I hope Rose is okay with this. "That's fine."

"Are you sure you don't want to get a new car? This one is almost nine years old, and it's been patched up quite a bit already."

"It's not mine. Go ahead and order the part, and put it on my bill." The fact that her car is so old surprises me, as I pay Gruesome's firm quite a hefty sum.

Since Rose is going to be without a car for at least a couple of days, I don't stop to question my protective instincts toward her and call a rental company. "What car did you have in mind, Mr. O'Connor?" I have a credit card in Dan's name for times like these when I don't want to give out my true identity.

"I'd like a BMW hard top convertible."

"Sure thing. What color?"

I think for a second and respond, "Light blue." It'll match her eyes.

"Do you want to pick it up, or should we deliver it?"

"Deliver, please."

"No problem, Mr. O'Connor. What's the address for the car to be dropped off?"

That question pulls me up short. I want it dropped off at her house, but I don't know her address. "I'll call you with the address later."

Now that the car issues have been mostly settled, I order another coffee and a bottle of water while I wait for Rose to call. A blonde woman comes over and asks for my autograph, but other than that small interruption, no one pays me any attention. My phone finally rings. "Cole, I'm so sorry, this meeting ran way over. I literally just finished. I understand if you gave up and went home."

"Rose, I told you I'd wait. I'll be there in five."

She sighs. "Thank you." Wow. No fight? That must have been some meeting.

Five minutes later, I pull up to the curb and Rose scrambles into the front seat. The hem of her blouse comes untucked as she juggles paperwork, notebooks and her purse. I've never seen her look so frazzled.

"Thank you," she repeats, rubbing her hand along the back of her neck. I'm glad I thought to buy her a bottle of water. She gratefully accepts and drinks about half of it in one gulp.

"Where to?"

"Venice." My eyebrows raise, but I steer toward that part of LA without saying a word. It's a mixed neighborhood, with some luxury homes next to streets filled with much less desirable ones. Her car's a beater, but hopefully that's only because she spent her money on one of those luxury homes. She leans her head back against the headrest and winces.

The ponytail probably gave her a headache. It looks painful to me. "Why don't you take your ponytail out?" I suggest.

"Greta doesn't like anyone to be out of uniform with a client."

Wait, what? "Does her dress code actually dictate how you wear your hair? Well, Greta the Gruesome isn't here, and I promise not to tell," I whisper conspiratorially. I throw in a wink for good measure.

Rose bursts out laughing. "Greta the Gruesome? That's hysterical!" She catches herself and turns to me, wide-eyed. I chuckle to set her at ease.

After a brief pause, she pulls her hair loose. I realize it's the first time I've ever seen her without that signature ponytail. Her thick, brown hair looks nice around her shoulders. It's not a flat color; reddish highlights dance in the sunlight. Somehow my hand finds its way into her hair and I wrap a lock around my fingers. Her eyes close for a minute before she jumps forward. "Turn here!" she exclaims way too loudly, pointing to my right.

Returning both hands to the steering wheel, I turn. Something about the way she looks with her hair down niggles at the back of my brain, but I can't figure out the connection it's trying to make. "Have we met before?"

Rose gives me a quizzical look. "Um, we've been working together for the past five years."

Smart ass. "I just had this feeling of déjà-vu, like I might have met you before that."

Rose turns and looks out the window. "I'd remember meeting you."

Shaking my head, I change the subject. "I had your car towed to my mechanic. He says you need a new part, and it'll take a couple of days for it to arrive. I've already arranged for a rental car to be delivered to your house tomorrow morning. Unless you need it sooner?"

"Cole, you didn't have to go so much trouble. I can take care of it. Tell me where my car is, and I'll get it to my guy. There's no need for a rental."

"Do you have a second car you can use?"

"Well, I might be able to borrow my roommate's. If not, I can take the bus. I've done it plenty of times before."

"Listen, Rose, we're in LA. Having a car is a must."

"I don't need a rental." She sounds pissed. At least her headache seems to have gone away.

"You do. Let me take care of this for you. It makes me feel good to be able to fix something for you, since you're always mopping up my messes."

"That's my job."

"Well, I've made your transportation my job."

"Have your mechanic send me the bill. I don't need the rental."

"No, and you do. How do you plan on getting to Gruesome's office tomorrow? I don't remember seeing a bus stop near her office." Rose cracks a smile at the nickname, just as I hoped she would.

"I can use a car service."

"You're being ridiculous."

Stubbornly, she raises her chin, her blue eyes blazing through those coke bottle glasses she wears. Once again, I'm plagued by a feeling of déjà-vu. "Send me the bill."

"Fine." I agree, but only because she won't let it drop. No way in hell I'm letting her pay. After all, she's an essential member of my team. I should be covering her expenses.

In a huff, she turns on the radio. The tail end of my first single, "Prowling," is playing. After it finishes, the female DJ remarks, "That was Cole Manchester. Rumor has it that he's getting ready to record a new album. It will be nice to hear some new songs from him, right, ladies? Speaking of ladies, remember that he was dating Jessie Anderson a while back? Well, I know someone who saw Cole and Jessie together at a local restaurant the other day. In a quiet back corner, very friendly-like. Maybe they're rekindling their romance? I, for one, hope not; I don't want to lose my chance with that hottie!" The DJ laughs and throws to a commercial.

I glance at Rose, who has a pensive look on her face and is once again fondling her poor gold hoop earring. Somehow I find that trait endearing. "Did you do that?"

"No. I guess Jon leaked the news about your new album. At least he was smart enough not to mention the world tour."

"I meant about Jessie, not the album." Intrigued by her line of thought, I ask, "Though, why would it be bad for him to have spilled about the tour?"

"The tour will take a lot more finesse than a simple call to a radio station. The venues need to be lined up first, so we can go in and get your fans worked up for your shows. We'll need to do advance press online, work with local media, hype it up here in the US so that your fans can choose their favorite city and arrange flights, develop contests, that sort of thing."

I get it. Again, I wonder how much Greta actually contributes to her own publicity operation. "Okay, makes sense. Now, what about Jessie and me?"

"Were you out with her recently?"

"No. We've talked about getting together, but her schedule is so tight while her show is filming." I pause. Maybe someone saw me out with one of my blind dates? "Maybe they just saw me with someone and assumed it was Jessie."

"Is there something more to that story, Cole?" she asks, frowning. "Do we need to do damage control?"

"Nope."

"You're sure?"

No fucking way I'm going to tell her I've been out on blind dates. "Positive."

Fingers firmly wrapped around her earring, she says, "Maybe it would be a good thing for you and Jessie to get back together, so to speak. It might be a way to ramp up the public interest in your new album, especially since the rumor mill is already running. Jessie's been seen out with her co-star recently, and a love triangle always plays out well in the media. It's something to think about."

"Do you want my opinion?"

Rose turns and looks at me, as if only then realizing she had spoken her thoughts out loud. "What?"

"Do you care what I think about this whole publicity stunt?"

"Not really." I glance over at Rose, who's trying to hide her smile by looking at her lap. So, she wants to play?

Smirking, I quip, "Too bad, missy, I'm going tell you anyway." I turn off the radio. "Jessie's a great friend, and that asshole co-star you've linked her to drives her nuts. Anything I can do to help her and Amanda out, I will."

Rose's head snaps around at me. "You know about Amanda?"

"Of course. What did you think Jessie and I did on all those publicity dates you set up? We certainly didn't fool around. We talked, like normal people. She told me all about her girlfriend, and the three of us have had dinner together several times."

"Wow. I'm impressed."

"See, I can keep a secret. You should be happy about that, since I think I'm up to keeping two for you."

"Good to know. Oh, turn right at the stop, and my place is on the left."

I pull to a stop in front of a modest house with an attached garage. The landscaping out front could use a green thumb. I'm taken aback at her neighborhood, which most definitely is not the part of Venice I was expecting, but I keep my mouth shut.

"Cole, really, thank you for the save today. I meant it when I said that I want your mechanic to send me the bill."

"You're welcome, Rose. Oh, and enjoy the convertible."

I laugh as she slams the door shut. I swear, she's probably the only woman who has ever been mad about the free use of a convertible. I'm finding the prickly side of Rose fascinating.

Not to mention her cute ass.

Five

A WEEK LATER, PLATINUM HAS SIGNED OFF on all the songs for my third album. I need to be in the studio on Monday to start recording *Moving Forward Slowly*, as session musicians have already been brought in for the drum and guitar tracks. Before I start recording, I want to give both Dad and Jayson a heads up about the first single.

I walk into my music room and sit down at the piano. Once I'm settled, I dial Dad on FaceTime. "How are you doing, Dad?"

"I'm okay. Work is keeping me busy, and I'm going out to dinner with friends almost every night. Plus, your Aunt Doreen has me, Jayson and Carl over for Sunday afternoon dinners." Other than having lost a little weight, he looks pretty good.

"Sounds like you're keeping busy and out of trouble."

Dad chuckles, which puts a smile on my face. "Dad, I called because I wrote a song for Mom that's going to be on my upcoming album. It's actually going to be the first single. I wanted to play it for you first."

"What's it called?"

"'No One to Hold.'"

Dad's eyebrows shoot up but he doesn't make a comment, so I sing the song for him. After the last note on the piano fades, I ask, "What do you think?"

He nods. "It's good, Cole. It's really good. Your mom would love it."

I exhale a cleansing breath. "Thanks. We're donating the profits to the American Cancer Society."

Dad rubs his hand over his mouth. "That's appropriate," he murmurs.

I nod. "It was Rose's idea." *Her kindness adds to her allure. Allure?* "Oh, I'm going to need some photos of her to include in the video. I'll come home and go through them soon, okay?"

"It'll be great to see you in person," Dad says, smiling.

The front gate bell rings. "Sorry to do this Dad, but I gotta go. Someone's at the gate. I'll call you again soon."

"Be safe, son. I love you."

As I walk over to check the security camera, I reply, "Love you too, Dad." Disconnecting the call, I check the feed. A delivery person waits at the road.

Pressing the intercom, I say, "I didn't order anything. You must have the wrong house."

"You Cole Manchester?" the teenaged delivery boy asks.

"Yes."

"That's who the package is for, at this address."

"All right. Come on." I buzz the gate, then wait at the front door for him to come up the driveway. After I sign the receipt and give him a good tip, I bring the package to my living room and sit down on my black leather sofa.

Who would have sent me a package? It's not my birthday. I rip it open to find *NYC Legends*, a coffee table book depicting the music scene in New York City through the years. I flip through the pages and see great photos of legendary musicians who got their start in NYC, just like I did.

This gift is awesome. I still don't know who sent it to me, so I search through the packaging until I find a card.

It says:

Cole,

Thank you for all your help with my car. I hope this book brings you some happiness. I look forward to another edition with your information included.

Thanks again,
Rose

My first thought is to wonder if I'm reading it correctly. I never imagined Rose would send me a gift. My next response is to feel flattered that she thinks my name belongs in here. Wow, what a thoughtful gift.

Before I get the chance to start reading my new book, my cell rings. Jayson's profile appears on the screen. "Dad loves it and I want to hear it. *Now!*"

I smile even though he can't see me over the phone. "Well, nice to hear your voice too, bro. How are Carl and your puppy?"

"We're all fine. *Now!* I can't wait another second!"

"Ever the drama queen, huh, Jayson?"

"You don't want me to go all nuclear on your ass, do you?"

"Fine." I sigh. I've missed this. It's hard being so far away from my family, especially now. "The song's called 'No One to Hold.'" For the second time today, I sing the new single, this time a cappella. It still takes a lot out of me each time I perform it, but it's getting easier.

I wait a full ten seconds for Jayson's reaction. I can't see him, so this is killing me. He finally says, in a quiet voice, "Cole, no wonder Dad was nearly in tears when he called me."

Dad was in tears? He didn't look upset to me. "Dad didn't like the song? Why didn't he tell me? I won't release it."

"No, he loved it. I love it, too. It's just, so, I don't know . . . personal. Are you okay?"

"Yeah."

"No you're not. I can hear it in your voice."

"Seriously, I'm fine."

"Right. And I'm the Queen of England."

"Well, you're the Queen of something," I joke.

"Damn straight!" We both laugh. "Cole, have you taken Mom's advice to heart? Is this what the song is about?"

I'm amazed that my brother can still read me like a book. "You're a pain in the ass, you know that, right?"

"Spill."

"Fuck you."

Silence.

"Fine. Yes. I've asked Dan and Suzanne to fix me up on some blind dates. I think it's time I looked for someone seriously."

"Cool. Have you been on any yet? Any good prospects?"

"Well, so far I've been out with a militant vegan, a giggler, a woman who only wanted to use me to meet another singer and a reality show hopeful."

"Wow. My carnivore brother out with a vegan? I can picture how well that went!"

Jayson laughs for a solid thirty seconds while I strum my fingers on the cover of my new book, waiting for him to catch his breath. It feels good to hear him laugh, so I'll let him do it, even if it's at my expense.

"Are you done yet?" I finally ask.

"Cole, this is too rich! You should write a song about your dating experiences!" He continues to chortle.

"No way."

"I got it! Let me put you on an Internet dating site. I'll write you a great profile. It'll go something like I love music and going to concerts. I will rock your world, literally. And I'll use my green eyes and dimple to tempt you into my back room." Jayson gasps for air, he's laughing so hard.

"Glad you're finding this so funny, asswipe." I'm smiling too, but only because he can't see me.

"Don't like that idea? I think it would get you tons of dates. Oh, wait,

I know! You should do a television dating show. Doesn't Dan's network produce one? I'll call him up and tell him to put you on it. Imagine the ratings!"

"Fuck you." I quickly hit mute so he doesn't hear me laugh.

"Such language, Cole. For shame. What would your future wife say?"

Taking him off mute, I respond, "She'd say, 'Who's that prick you're talking to on the phone? Come back to bed.'"

"Well, first things first, you gotta find a woman you like. From the sounds of your recent dates, I'll bet you haven't been knocking boots with anyone lately."

"Knocking boots? Really? Does anyone say that anymore?"

"Well, I just did. Okay, now that I've gotten all that out of my system . . ." He trails off into another fit of laughter before getting himself back under control, then clears his throat. "I'm done now. Okay. Were your dates really that bad? I'm surprised Dan and Suzanne didn't set you up with better people."

"They're always amazed when I tell them about my dating disasters."

"Maybe they're nervous being around you?"

"All of them? I don't think so." I walk over to the wet bar and pull out a bottle of beer. "I don't get it. I have over a million fans on Facebook, and twice that many followers on Twitter. More than half of them are women. Have you checked out my official Facebook page, bro? I get proposed to on there a few hundred times a week. Why can't I meet one woman who I want to take out on a second date? What the hell's going on?"

"Seems like you're the common denominator here, big brother."

"What the hell is that supposed to mean?" I open the beer and down half of it in one gulp.

"You know that your fans literally worship the ground you walk on. Most would prostrate themselves to have sex with you. But just because you're some famous singer doesn't mean you can snap your fingers and your friends will magically produce the perfect woman for you. Although . . ."

I'm a little pissed at his attitude, but he has me intrigued. In spite of my reservations, I hear myself fill the pregnant pause by saying, "Although, what?"

"Is that little Rose still on your team?"

"Rose Morgan? Yeah." My eyes travel to the beautiful coffee table book. "In fact, I helped her out of a jam last week and she sent me a nice thank-you gift."

"What did she send?"

"A book about the New York City music scene."

"Wow. Now *there's* a woman who would keep you on your toes. You know, Mom always spoke highly of her. Dad likes her, too. He's had a sweet spot for her ever since she suggested that you take Mom to the Grammys. That night was one of Mom's best."

"Yeah, we had a great time." I smile, remembering her acting like fangirl with Adam Baret. My mind shifts to Rose. "I'm not sure if Dad told you, but she came up with the idea to donate all of the profits from 'No One to Hold' to charity."

"That's cool, man. Why don't you ask Rose out?"

It's not like the thought hasn't occurred to me. It has, and way more than once. I've been noticing her lately – the way she plays with that damn earring, the expressiveness of her eyes, her quiet strength, her intelligence. But I tell him what I've been telling myself. "Not a good idea. She works for me."

"So what?"

"So that's the type of huge line you never cross."

"Says who?"

"How old are you, Jayson?" I take another sip of my beer. "I can't blur the lines between professional and personal. She knows more about my bad habits than I'd want any woman to know early on in a relationship. Besides, Gruesome has a strict non-fraternization policy—which applies to everyone but her, apparently. No way would Rose cross that line."

"She's sharp, funny, beautiful and thoughtful."

"So are a million other women who don't work for me." I pause. "You think Rose is beautiful?" She had looked a lot more relaxed after she took her hair out of that damn ponytail. And her eyes are a very pretty shade of blue behind those glasses. Who am I kidding? She's beautiful. Plus, she's definitely smart and kind. She also has a good sense of humor, but she's too professional to let it shine through all that often. Then there's that odd feeling of connection with her. I can't deny that getting to know the real Rose appeals to me.

"Cole? Are you still there?"

His words snap me out of my reverie. "Sorry, Jayson. Someone, er, is at my door. Gotta go. Glad you like the new song. Hi to Carl and your puppy. Love you."

"Bye, Cole. Love you, big bro."

I disconnect the phone and sink down on my sofa, in front of my coffee table. I thoughtlessly flip through the pages of the book Rose sent me.

Am I seriously considering asking her out?

Well, shit.

Six

"Come on, Cole, concentrate."

I'm on my second rep of twenty toes to bar in my circuit-training workout with my personal trainer. I can't fault him for chiding me about not being all there today; I'm not. My mind keeps wandering back to my date last night.

It was unique in that there was nothing wrong with Lori at all. She seemed like a good match for me, and I enjoyed our date. Just not enough to ask her out again. I finally met the kind of woman I should be interested in, and there was no spark. Nada.

"Go run 200 meters, and then do 500 meters on the rowing machine. *Now!*"

I drop from the bar, grab some water and hit the treadmill. The worst thing about it was that I kept comparing her to Rose. Lori had brown hair, but it didn't have any reddish highlights. Her eyes also were blue, but not the right shade. Shit. Am I really this far gone? Over someone on my team?

"Are you going to keep messing around, or are you actually going to work out today?"

I switch to the rowing machine, renewing my effort.

"You do want your fans to drool all over your hard body, rather than look sad every time you drag your dad bod onto the stage, right?"

Damn. That's hitting below the belt. I finish the set. Back to the bar. Three more reps to go. I refuse to let my mind wander any more during this workout. Fifteen minutes later, it's over. I'm drenched.

"Man, where was your mind at the beginning of our workout?"

I like Zak, but I am not about to share my dating situation with him, so I keep it light. "Sorry. I was thinking about a chick I met last night." Not a total lie.

"She must've been something. You're usually a lot more into training."

"She certainly gave me a lot to think about."

"Well, go hit the shower and sauna. You'll need the heat for your muscles."

"Thanks. See you in two days. I'll be ready for you on Friday."

I head to the shower. Towel around my waist, I make my way into the sauna. I usually skip this step, but heat sounds really good to me today. As an added bonus, no one else is in here right now, so I'm left to my own thoughts, which take me to Rose.

On Friday, after my work out, she and I are going on a photo shoot. I think it's just plain wrong when musicians and actors have professional photos on their social media accounts, so I managed to convince Greta the Gruesome that Rose and I can handle taking the photos for all my accounts. Of course, my fans believe I'm the one writing those posts and tweets, which shows what a great job Rose does. Some of her posts even fooled Mom.

This time's different, though. It's going to be my first date with Rose. Only she doesn't know it's a date, which is fine by me. If she had an inkling that I'm thinking about dating her, she would probably freak out. Not to mention bring along a photographer, some extras for the photos, a driver and probably a pit bull. I still can't believe I'm taking Jayson's advice.

I shake my head, and beads of water fly everywhere, which makes me think of Rose in a much more intimate setting than the photo shoot. She's so buttoned up on the job that she has to let loose sometime, right? No one can be that prim and proper. Hell, no. I've seen glimpses of a different Rose when Gruesome's not watching. Someone needs to break her the rest of the way out of her shell, and I'm just the guy for that task.

Now that my mind has gone down that path, I can't stop. I picture her naked, her glasses off and her hair free from that damn ponytail. She's going to look spectacular in my bed, with her nipples all pink and distended from my lips and her legs wrapped around my waist while I pump into her. I can't wait to see the look on her face as she comes for me.

Damn, I'm starting to get a hard-on, and anyone can walk in here at any moment. I better get a grip. I'd like to get a grip on her nice ass, though. *Okay Cole, stop it.* I shake my head to try to clear the images that are bouncing around in it.

The door opens and two guys walk in. That's my cue to leave. I don't want to be stuck in the sauna with two Academy Award winning actors while sporting a woody. And I haven't even kissed that girl yet. Damn.

Seven

F RIDAY AFTERNOON FINALLY ARRIVES. I put on a pair of jeans and a white T-shirt and then check my stubble to ensure it has the required two-day look. Grabbing my sunglasses, board shorts and keys, I head out to the Santa Monica beach where Rose and I agreed to meet. En route, Rose calls and tells me where she parked.

I pull into a parking space and look around for her car, which I identify based on my mechanic's description. Turning off the ignition, I take a deep breath and remind myself to play it cool. After a slow, steady exhale, I'm ready.

Rose isn't in her car, but I catch a glimpse of her near the beach. She's watching a volleyball game. Her ponytail is blowing in the breeze, and she's pushing her glasses up the bridge of her nose. A camera hangs from around her neck. She looks adorable, yet out of place, in her blouse and skirt. At least she ditched the blazer.

I start walking over to her, but as soon as she sees me, she motions for me to stay in the parking lot and walks over to join me. "I've been watching the volleyball game for a while and thought it might make for some interesting shots if you joined in. What do you say?"

I smirk. "Ever the professional, huh, Rose?"

One of her eyebrows rises. "I just thought your fans would like to see you score." Both of her eyes widen and she puts her hands in front of her mouth to hide her laughter, exclaiming, "I can't believe I just said that!"

I burst out laughing, too. "I promise to remind you every chance I get!" Smiling broadly, I put my arm around her and give her a one-armed hug.

She smiles up at me, her cheeks a gorgeous pink. "Thanks, Cole. A true gentleman would have helped me remove my foot from my mouth instead of rubbing my face in it."

"Now that's a mixed metaphor if I ever heard one." I decide to cut her some slack. "So, where to?"

Rose glances back at the volleyball game, but it seems to be breaking up. "I guess my idea of the game is out. Let's wander around and snap some candids."

"Sounds good."

We walk away from the beach, moving toward the street and its high-end shops and restaurants. Rose snaps some photos of me along the way, trying to be careful not to give away our exact location. Plus, we don't want to give free advertising to the stores, especially if I can't vouch for them.

"You know, I brought my board shorts if you want me to go on the beach for more shots later." We've been having a great time, but I want to turn things up a bit. See if she's interested in me, or, at least, could be interested.

"I've been having such fun today that I almost forgot we should get some photos on the beach. I'm sure your fans will eat them up." She wiggles her eyebrows at me.

"I'd hate not to get credit for all my time in the gym."

"I'll make sure to put your trainer's name in the post."

"Let me run back to my car and get my shorts. Why don't we meet in the café over there?" I suggest.

"Sounds good," she says.

My mind is racing as I turn and head back to my car. I'm enjoying today, and I'm pumped that she seems to be, too. Dating Rose is a scary line to cross, but shit, I've laughed more with her than I have with all my other blind dates combined. She gets me. Yeah, I'm falling for Rose Morgan.

When I get to the café, I head straight into the bathroom to change into my shorts before joining Rose at the table. Time to turn things up another small notch.

"Hey, beautiful," I whisper into her ear. I take my seat, putting my sunglasses on the table and jeans on the chair beside me. "Thanks for getting me coffee."

She nods but keeps her eyes angled downward. Shit. Did I go too far? But before I can do or say anything, a blonde-haired woman comes over to our table. She looks vaguely familiar, but that's par for the course.

"Cole Manchester?" the blonde squeaks. Rose's eyes snap to the woman's face and she discreetly hides the camera on her lap.

I lean in toward the woman, pitching my voice low. "Yes, but I'd appreciate it if you would keep your voice down. I'm trying to keep a low profile today."

The blonde looks blissfully happy to share a secret with me. "Your secret is safe with me, Cole," she says, like we're best buddies.

"Thanks." I wink at her, hoping she'll go away quietly so I can get back to Rose.

"Can I get an autograph?"

Forcing a professional smile, I reply, "Sure, darlin'." She pulls a pen and a piece of note paper from her purse, which I sign.

"Here you go. Thanks for keeping my secret."

The woman, thankfully, takes the hint and leaves. It's just Rose and me again. I clear my throat, trying to assess Rose's mood.

"I'm surprised she's the first person to recognize you."

"Well, she's the first one to approach me today. Doesn't mean that others haven't recognized me."

"True enough. She seemed nice, though. Not pushy or anything."

"They can be annoying at times, especially when I'm trying to drink a hot coffee in public," I blow on the hot liquid and take a sip. "But, for the most part, they're respectful. I owe everything to my fans, so I always take time for them."

Rose nods. "I've noticed. You're a good man, Cole."

Wow, a compliment. I stifle the urge to do a fist pump at the table, but I'm not as successful at containing my smile. My dimple might even be showing. "Watch it, or I'll think you're flattering me."

We finish our coffees chatting about her plans for the photos. Rose gathers her things and we make our way to the beach, stopping off at the car to stow my jeans in the back seat. Once we're by the water, Rose's bossy streak comes to the fore. *Stand there, turn here, put your arm this way. Smile. Don't smile.* Geez. I know that she wants to get a variety of shots for my social media pages, but did the woman ever hear of spontaneity?

It's time to take control. Ignoring Rose's latest set of instructions, I strip off my T-shirt and tuck it into my back pocket. From the corner of my eye, I catch her checking me out. I'm going to give Zak a big tip at my next personal training session.

Doing a 180, I start walking toward the ocean. Rose has no choice but to follow. I turn around and see her stumbling in the sand, tripped up by the sandals she's still wearing. Does she ever loosen up? Well, I'm going to make her.

Striding back to Rose, I stop right in front of her. I can tell from the look on her face that she has no idea what I'm about to do. Dropping to one knee in the sand, I reach for her right foot while directing her hands to my shoulders. Her ankle feels so delicate in my hands. I love the feel of her hands on my shoulders, although I wish they were holding on tighter. A few heartbeats pass before I look up at her, silently asking her permission. She inclines her head, and I remove her sandal and then watch as she places her bare foot in the sand. I repeat my actions with her left foot.

Holding both of her sandals in my hand, I stand up and enjoy the feeling of her hands sliding down my arms, like a long crescendo. Rose looks up at me, mouth open. Smiling, I trace her lips with my finger.

"Let's get some more photos, Rose," I murmur. Anticipation is good.

I grab her hand and we stroll to a secluded spot at the water's edge. She takes some shots of me out there, but I want more. Of her. Taking the camera out of her hands, I turn the lens on her and become the photographer.

Mimicking her attitude from before, I start barking orders. "Turn left." "Look at me over your shoulder." "Yeah, that's great Rose!" At first she's camera-shy, but soon she's smiling and sassing it up for me. Oh yeah, I'm really enjoying this side of Rose.

The sun starts to go down. It's now or never. Invading her personal space, I release her hair from that damn ponytail. Her gorgeous locks float around her head and shoulders. Her eyes dart left and right. I say, "Gruesome isn't here to see you out of uniform. Relax. Enjoy. I know I am."

Rose's posture is rigid again, so I step back and keep playing with her as my model. "Smile!" I click several shots in a row. "That's it, Rose. Pretend I'm a journalist and you're trying to convince me to write a good story. How would you get me to do your bidding?" She smiles, and it reaches her eyes. I suck in my breath. "With that smile, I think you've gotten me wrapped around your little finger."

I put my arm around her shoulders, positioning the camera to take a selfie of us. But as I'm about to take the photo, I shake my head. Reaching over, I take off her glasses and click the shot.

"Why did you do that?"

"Because I want this picture to capture the real us. No barriers."

Rose sucks in her breath and I can't hold back any longer. The brilliant colors from the setting sun bring out the beauty of her blue eyes and silky reddish-brown hair. Her gorgeous body is like a siren calling my name. I must taste her. Wrapping her in both my arms with the camera off my shoulder, I look deeply into her ice blue eyes. Desire and anxiety seem to be at war in them.

"Don't be nervous, Rose. I've wanted to kiss you for a long time."

Add surprise to the list of emotions blasting from her eyes, right before they close. I can't prevent this kiss any more than the waves can avoid crashing into the rocks. I stop a hair's breadth from her lips and inhale her unique scent. My mind registers the smell of flowers and the ocean. Her face tilts up toward mine in silent assent. I'm lost.

Finally, our lips meet in soft exploration. I move my hands down her back, pulling her soft body against mine. Her lips yield to my demands without hesitation. Her hands hesitantly climb up my naked chest and encircle my neck. She emits a low moan.

That little sound encourages me to deepen the kiss. Her mouth opens. Soon our tongues are exploring and caressing. My cock hardens as passion erupts between us. Needing to feel more of her, my hands move lower on her back until they meet her ass. Her body is molded to mine. Cupping her luscious cheeks, the final bit of my restraint is gone. I crush her against my body, knowing full well she can feel my rock hard erection against her stomach. Her boobs rub against my chest in time with her erratic breathing. She moans again. Or is that me?

All too soon, our lips break apart, foreheads touching, each of us panting for air. That odd sense of déjà-vu I experienced the other day, the first time after I saw her with her hair down, flits through my mind again. "You're amazing, Rose."

I'm a little shocked at my body's reaction to her. I've known her for five years, but this kiss changes everything. It has totally put me out of my depth.

Still clutched in my embrace, Rose says, "Wow." She lets me hold her for a few staccato beats. I can feel the second she comes back to herself. I wish professional Rose would stay away longer, but a part of me is relieved she's back.

"Let's go back to the cars," I offer as a graceful way to end this amazing interlude.

Rose nods, and we walk up to the virtually empty parking lot, each of us looking in different directions and carefully not touching. When we reach the pavement, I hand her back her sandals and camera. While she's busy putting on her sandals, I put my own sandals on and pull the T-shirt over my head. We continue walking toward the cars in silence.

It's like we're denying the magic of what happened.

I don't want that. Hell, I might not know exactly what I'm doing, but there's a spark between us. A bigger one than I expected.

When we reach her car, I turn to face her. Looking into her eyes, I say, "Rose, thank you for today. I had a wonderful time."

"I did too, Cole," she responds, her voice a little breathy.

"Please send me that photo of the two of us."

"I will." After a brief pause, she begins, "Cole, about what happened back there . . ."

"It was a kiss, Rose. And if you're waiting for me to say it was a mistake, you'll have a long wait."

"Oh."

"Yeah, oh."

Her swollen lips call to me, but I tamp down my desire. For the moment. Opening her car door, I give her a quick kiss on the cheek. "Now you'd better get home before I do something totally outrageous."

Eight

I DRIVE BACK TO MY PLACE WITH A shit-eating grin on my face. I can't stop thinking about Rose and that kiss. She arouses me like no woman has in a long time. If ever. And I know it's not solely physical. I enjoy talking with her. I admire her wit and humor when she lets them shine through, and her insights never cease to impress me. While I certainly want to fuck her senseless, for the first time in my life I want something more.

For our next date, I'd like to get her to relax more. I want to coax out more of her fun side. It doesn't seem like Rose has too much fun. Other than work, I'm not sure what she does. She certainly doesn't spend money on her car or housing. Her wardrobe doesn't look cheap, but it's also not top of the line. From the ponytail to the glasses and the matching suits, it's the type of wardrobe that's designed to blend in rather than stand out. Not for the first time, I wonder what Gruesome pays her.

As I'm powering up my tablet to research some options, my cell rings and Rose's face pops up. With a smile, I answer the phone. "Couldn't stay away, huh, Rose?"

Rose doesn't answer. The line is filled with loud background noise. Did she butt dial me? I try to get her attention. "Hey, Rose."

Still no response from her, but now I hear sirens in the background. I'm instantly on alert. "Rose, tell me what is going on," I demand.

Rose's voice comes over the line, although she's not talking to me. "No, I don't want to go to the hospital."

Grabbing my keys, I race out to my car. Hospital? I've moved from high alert to borderline panic. I shout into the phone, "*Rose!*"

But the phone must still be in her pocket. Her voice has a higher pitch than usual when she says, "My place was trashed when I got home." A man asks her a question that I can't make out, and she responds, "No, I didn't see anyone except for my roommate." She catches her breath and continues, "Do you have any word about him?"

What the hell happened? She was fine when we left the beach not even an hour ago. More sirens join the background cacophony, then the line goes dead.

Fuck! I knew when I dropped her off at her place that she wasn't living in the best of neighborhoods. But this? My car once was broken into while I was living in New York City, although all the thief did was break a window and take my GPS unit. I can't even imagine how violated Rose must feel. Thankfully she wasn't home when it happened. It sounds like her roommate might have been, though. *A guy.* I tamp down a sudden spike of jealousy toward her roommate. I just need to get to Rose, and press down on the gas pedal.

Twenty-five minutes later, I pull up to her place. Barely taking the time to put my car in park, I spring out of my seat and race toward her front door. I stop abruptly upon seeing police tape surrounding her front lawn. At least five police cars, a fire truck and an ambulance are parked haphazardly on the street, and guys in uniform are milling about everywhere.

I dial Rose's number while scanning the crowd. When she doesn't pick up, I walk over to a gathering of a bunch of people in civilian clothes, presumably Rose's neighbors. I approach a friendly-looking grandmotherly type. "Excuse me, have you seen Rose Morgan?"

The older woman eyes me up and down. "You're a right pretty one, aren't you? Good for Rose. She could use someone like you in her life. She's over there." The woman points to a police car. I smile in relief, although my heart rate accelerates. Before I can leave, the woman grabs my arm and pulls me down to whisper in my ear, "Now don't you go hurting my little Rose, or you'll have to answer to Grandma Gertie. Got it, Hot Stuff?"

I smile at the protectiveness emanating from this cute elderly lady. It's nice to know that Rose is well liked by her neighbors. Even though they won't be her neighbors for too much longer, if I have my way. "I'll take good care of Rose, Grandma Gertie. I promise." She nods her white head and releases my arm.

I make my way to where Rose is standing, talking with the police. It feels like weeks since we were taking those photos on the beach, sharing our first kiss. Rose looks exhausted, but at least she's unharmed.

"Rose."

She turns and her eyes find mine. They look liquid blue, not their normal icy shade. The fear and sadness isn't what catches me off-guard; it's the sense of defeat. I swear to myself that I will do whatever is humanly possible to rid that emotion from her world.

I open my arms and she walks into my embrace without hesitation. Her body trembles against mine. Holding her close, I murmur, "You're safe now, Rose. I'm here for you."

She looks up at me. I'm surprised that she hasn't shed a tear. Any of the other women I've dated would have mascara tracks all down their faces, and probably every police officer in the county would be trying to console her. But not Rose. Somehow, she's managed to hold everything together, at least on the outside. Inside, I'm not so sure.

"You're not alone anymore, Rose."

She takes a step back. "How did you find out about this?"

I half-smile. "You butt dialed me."

Her eyes widen, then she looks down and shakes her head. "You didn't have to come all the way. I'll take care of this."

"Rose, there is no place I'd rather be." The look on her face tells me she doesn't believe me, but it's not some line—it's true.

"Thank you for coming, but you can go back to your plans. I need to go to the hospital to see my roommate, and then I'll need to start cleaning this mess up." She gestures toward her house.

An officer standing nearby joins us and chimes in. "Actually, Miss Bloomer, you can't return until forensics does a thorough examination of your home. We don't expect that to be completed until sometime tomorrow afternoon. Is there somewhere else you can stay?" He looks directly at me.

"I—" Rose begins.

"She will stay with me." My tone brooks no argument, from her or the cop.

Nodding his head, the officer takes out his notebook. Looking at me again, he does that double-take people do when they recognize me out of context. "Are you Cole Manchester?"

"Yeah." *Don't cause a scene, buddy.* Because I raced out of my house so quickly, I forgot any semblance of disguise. I don't even have a baseball cap with me.

Luckily, the cop is cool. "I thought I recognized you. Sir, I need to take down your address and contact information." I give him my information, all the while rubbing Rose's back to try to calm her. Her body stops trembling, which I take to be a good sign. Her breathing seems to have evened out, too.

"Do you have any clues?" I ask.

"There's been a string of robberies around here lately, and it looks like the same group was responsible for this break-in. But this time was different because her roommate was home. They hurt him, but not too badly. I think he'll be released from the hospital tomorrow." I nod my head, remembering my discussion about this crime ring with my first blind date, Alicia the vegan reporter.

"Mr. Manchester, I have a teenage daughter."

I raise my lips into a tired smile. He's trying to be professional, but he doesn't have to draw the lines for me. He'd have hell to pay if he tells his daughter about meeting me and doesn't bring anything back for her.

"Do you have something you'd like me to sign? Or would you like to take a photo on your cell? I don't want to get you into hot water at home."

The cop gives me an embarrassed shrug. "Can you write her a note? Her name is Erica. She'll be over the moon to get something from you." He hands me a blank police report.

"No problem." I flip the pre-printed sheet over, write a quick note telling Erica what a great dad she has and sign it. He takes it back to his cruiser.

Rose turns to me and says, "Cole, I appreciate the offer, but I'm fine. I'll spend the night in a hotel after I go check on Tommy. I'm sorry to have bothered you."

"No. I'll drive you to the hospital and then you're spending the night at my house. I have four bedrooms and there's only one of me."

Why does she have to be so stubborn? Something tells me she plans on sleeping in her car right here on the street, and I can't let that happen.

"I'm not a child. I can take care of myself." Her chin goes up.

"Rose, I don't think of you as a child. I know you're an independent woman." Boy, do I ever. "But it's okay to accept help sometimes. And right now is one of those times. Besides, I told the cop that you'd be with me. He said he'd call me when your place has been cleared for you to return."

"He has my cell too, Cole."

We're at a standoff. Rose is staring at me with a belligerent look, the kind of look that says she knows she's lost this argument and she's not happy about it. Her chin wobbles, but remains in place. Damn, all I want to do is wrap my arms around her, hold her tight and get her the hell out of here.

"I think I see Cole Manchester over there. Cole, what brings you to this area of town?"

As if this evening couldn't get any more complicated. Somehow I didn't notice Alicia and her news crew setting up for a live report. No way am I going to be trapped in an interview with my former date.

"Rose," I say in an undertone, "the reporters are starting to get here. If you're not ready to have your photo plastered everywhere with mine, it's time to leave."

That statement gets through to Rose. "I need to get to the hospital to see Tommy."

Her roommate. "Fine, I'll drive. Is your car in the garage?" She nods yes. I hand her my keys. "Good. Leave it there. I'll take care of the reporters and meet you in my car, okay?"

Silently, Rose takes my keys and walks off in the direction of my car, her head down. Thank fuck she didn't fight me on this.

I make my way toward Alicia. "Hey, Alicia. It's nice to see you, even under these circumstances." *Please don't harbor any bad feelings toward me after our one and only date.*

"You too, Cole. We heard that the burglary ring struck this house tonight. What brings you here?"

I swallow. Think fast. I'm suddenly happy that Rose's roommate is a guy. He's the perfect cover, and should overshadow the fact that I'm at my publicist's house. "My friend was home when the robbers broke in. I figured I'd try to get an update from the police before visiting him in the hospital." I hold my breath, hoping that Alicia doesn't pick up on the lie.

"So your friend was hurt? That's a new twist. No one's ever been hurt by this group before."

Seems like she's buying it. Better get out while I can. "Yeah, he's in the hospital overnight. Sorry I don't have any more information for you. I hope your report tonight gets the police some good tips." I pause, watching Alicia take in everything I told her. "Alicia, I would appreciate it if you could keep me out of this story."

"I won't mention your name, Cole."

Murmuring my thanks, I leave Alicia with her news crew and make a beeline for my car. Rose sits in the passenger side, just like I had asked her. "Let's go to the hospital."

Tommy, Rose's roommate, is in pretty bad shape regardless of what the police told us. Two broken ribs, two black eyes, too many bruises to count. The nurse confirms that he'll be released in the morning, which perks Rose up. I stand outside the room, giving Rose and Tommy some privacy. How could a day that started out so lightheartedly turn into this? I resolve to make sure that Rose's night finishes on a positive note.

A little while later, Rose leaves Tommy's room, her shoulders drooping. "Okay, I'm ready to leave. Thank you for driving me here and for offering to take me in tonight. I really appreciate it."

I never want to see her this dejected again. "No worries, Rose. Let's go home."

I like how that last sentence sounds. Shit, I'm in deep, but it feels so *right* to be with her.

Rose falls asleep in the car on the way to the house. I'm sure she's exhausted now that the adrenaline has worn off. Pulling into my driveway, I look over at her. She's absolutely gorgeous. For once, her hair is loose. She looks so heartbreakingly tiny, but I know that she's 100% grit and determination.

The car's stopping rouses her. "We're here," I whisper. Her sleepy eyes lock with mine. "Do you want me to carry you inside?"

I'm all for picking her up and walking into the house with her in my arms. Rose's eyes widen, as if she can read my thoughts. At least she doesn't look repulsed.

"I'm awake. You don't have to carry me, Cole."

Too bad.

She follows me into the house, up the stairs and into a guest bedroom at the end of the hall. Thankfully, my cleaning lady was here the other day and everything looks tidy. "There's an extra toothbrush in the adjoining bathroom. Let me grab you a T-shirt to sleep in."

"Thanks. I can't believe I didn't even take an overnight bag from my place."

"I don't think the cops would have let you take anything from the house.

It's fine, I have plenty of extras."

I quickly walk to my bedroom on the other side of the house, and return with an extra-large T-shirt from my first tour. Mom had insisted that I keep a bunch of shirts from the *Meet Me In The Back Room* tour.

"Here you go, Rose. Do you want anything to eat? Or drink?"

"I'm good, thanks."

"Let me know if you need anything else." I turn to go, even though all I want to do is put my arms around her and hold her all night long.

"Cole?"

Looking back at her, I quirk an eyebrow, and say, "Yes?" Whatever her question is, my answer is yes.

She takes a deep breath. "You're a lifesaver. Thank you."

I can't stop myself. Without saying another word, I walk over and wrap my arms around her. Shifting my hands to her cheeks, I tilt her head up and give her a reassuring kiss on her forehead.

"You're safe here, Rose. Pleasant dreams."

Nine

I LOOK OVER AT THE CLOCK FOR THE hundredth time since leaving Rose in my guestroom. Finally it registers seven, so I figure I can get up. Rose may be sleeping in a totally separate area of the house, but I didn't want to risk making noise any earlier.

I go into my bathroom and brush my teeth. Despite the early hour and my lack of sleep, my eyes are bright with anticipation. I'm looking forward to spending more time with Rose today, even if we have to spend it working through this awful mess. Oh, and I have about a million questions for her. Like who the hell is Tommy? From what I could tell in the hospital, her roommate doesn't seem gay. An unexpected spike of jealousy and protectiveness races through my bloodstream. Something else niggles at the back of my brain about her, but I can't put my finger on it.

Shaking my head, I turn on the shower and step into the spray, letting the water cascade over my body. In my mind's eye, I picture Rose in here with me. She's naked and glistening with water. Damn, it's enough to make me hard in an instant. I want to push my throbbing cock into her and watch as she comes undone. I can almost hear her making all sorts of sexy noises while I pump into her tight pussy, my hands roaming between her boobs and ass.

I curse my vivid imagination and grab my cock in my right hand, so turned on that I can barely stand. I widen my stance and slowly move my hand up and down my hard shaft, picturing Rose's mouth doing that for me. The water droplets hit my body, heightening my pleasure. My hand moves faster; my breathing accelerates. I'm so fucking close. With a few quick movements of my hand, an orgasm surges through my entire body. My hips jerk as come shoots out, and I place one hand on the wall for support.

I better get a grip on myself or else Rose will think I'm a minute man. But what that Fantasy Rose does to me . . . I wonder if I can survive the real woman.

Catching my breath, I soap up and finish my shower. Dressed in a pair of ripped jeans and a T-shirt from my friend Ozzy Martinez's last concert tour, I head downstairs to the kitchen to make breakfast.

A few minutes later, a slightly disheveled Rose wanders into the kitchen wearing the T-shirt I gave her last night, which hits her nearly at her knees, giving me an unobstructed view of her bare legs.

To stop my mind from picturing all the delicious things I would like to be doing with those legs, I ask, "Would you like some coffee? I have a Keurig and plenty of choices over there."

Her gaze finds the coffee machine. "Thank you, Cole. I can't seem to say that enough to you."

I pull a coffee mug out of the cabinet and hand it to her before returning my attention to the ingredients I've been prepping. "I'm putting a ban on the words 'thank you' for the rest of the day. You've said that enough, and I've told you that I'm more than happy to be helping you out. Now, what would you like in your omelet?"

Rose looks startled. "You're making omelets?"

"What, did you think I couldn't cook?" I clutch my chest, pretending to be offended. "There's more to me than singing. And a killer bod." I wiggle my eyebrows in her direction.

She looks down, tugs on the T-shirt and walks over to select her coffee. "I didn't mean anything by my remark. Sorry."

I'm not going to let this mood continue. "Rose, I was teasing. How would you know I'm not one of those guys who always orders in? I like to cook because it centers me. Now, look at all the stuff I have here and let me know what you'd like in your omelet."

Rose smiles at me, but it doesn't reach her eyes. "I'm duly impressed, Mr. Manchester. I'll take mushrooms, spinach and some of that grated cheese, please. It all looks delicious."

"Sounds good. Let me put my apron on and your omelet will be right up." I go into my pantry looking for that crazy-ass apron Jayson gave me last Christmas. I'm sure it will help Rose loosen up a bit. Tying it around my waist, I saunter back into the kitchen. Rose is taking a sip of her coffee.

"What do you think?"

It's touch and go for a minute, but Rose manages to swallow her coffee instead of spitting it all over. Tears stream down her face, she's laughing so hard. *Score!*

"Where on earth did you ever get an apron that says *that?*"

Putting on my most innocent face, I look down at my apron and back up at her. "What? Don't you like it?" Rose keeps on laughing.

The front gate bell interrupts us. Chuckling to myself, I check the intercom and then answer the front door. "Jessie, Amanda, I'm so glad you could get here on such short notice. Come on in, Rose is in the kitchen. I'm about to make us some omelets."

Both of the ladies have a good laugh about my apron as we enter the kitchen. They rush over to Rose and give her a big hug.

"I'm so glad you weren't there when they broke in."

Rose tugs the T-shirt down with one hand while running her other hand through her hair. *At least she doesn't look pissed at me for inviting them over.* "Thank you, Jessie. Me too," Rose says, slanting me a look because she used the banned words. I nod in acknowledgement and give her a smirk.

"I bet you're going to be very happy when you see what's in this bag," adds Amanda. "Although, I'm not so sure your host will agree."

After shooting me a quizzical look, Rose takes the proffered bag and opens it, revealing a heap of new clothes. I hope she's okay with Jessie and Amanda doing this for her. I texted Jessie last night, and she eagerly agreed to my request. Judging from the size of the bag, they've gone above and beyond.

"Jessie, Amanda, you guys shouldn't have done this. I'm sure I'll be able to get back into my place soon." Rose tries to return the bag to them, but Amanda stops her.

"Rose, after everything you've done for Jessie and me, this is the very least we could do for you. Please don't insult us. Keep the clothes and wear them in good health."

"You both are so kind."

Grabbing the bag from Rose's hands, I sort through the clothes, saying, "I hope there's something sexy in here. I'm taking Rose out tonight, and I want to make every guy jealous!" Triumphantly, I pull a light green dress out of the bag and pretend to model it, making the women laugh.

Smiling, I set the bag down in the corner. "C'mon, ladies," I say, pointing at the fixings, "it's omelet time. What'll it be?"

While I'm making the omelets, they set the table. Rose disappears into another room and comes back out wearing leggings. *Ruined my view.* Jessie and Amanda brought some bagels and fruit to accompany my omelets, so we have a feast. Rose's laugh resonates with me like keys on the piano.

Breakfast is exactly what Rose needed. She's so lighthearted and upbeat. I'm surprised when Rose brings up Jessie's current "stage" boyfriend and the comment that DJ made a couple of weeks ago. We discuss inserting me in a "love triangle"—an idea Jessie loves—and Rose promises to bring up the idea to Greta. Amanda catches my eye and gives me a look that says Rose is the real miracle worker, not Gruesome. I nod in silent agreement.

After our meal, I escort Jessie and Amanda to the front door while Rose insists on putting the leftovers away. "Do you know what you're doing?" Jessie whispers, her head motioning toward the kitchen.

"It's innocent, I swear," I reply. *Well, maybe not so innocent.*

Amanda's skeptical look stops me in my tracks. "We like her. A lot." Both ladies nod. Amanda gives me a kiss on my cheek. "Thanks for brunch. Please be careful with her."

Jessie kisses me good-bye. "She works for Greta. Things could get complicated."

Don't I know it. "Like I said on the phone last night, I wanted to help Rose out after the robbery. And," I take a deep breath. "I'm not toying with her."

Jessie stares at me for a long moment, right into my soul. "You're different with her. Just make sure you're both on the same page, okay? She could lose her job over this."

Jessie's words repeat on a loop as I return to the now tidy kitchen. Rose looks at me, her eyes nearly drowning me in their icy blue depths. "Cole. What you—" Her cell rings, diverting her attention. *Damn.* She takes a deep breath and answers it as she leaves the kitchen. "Hello, Greta."

Figuring that the call may take a while, I dry and put away the brunch cookware while replaying my last conversation with Jessie and Amanda. Chore completed, I turn on the TV to see how the news is covering the break-in at Rose's. I catch Alicia's report, which does not mention either Rose or me by name. The crime scene shot does have me in it, but my back is to the camera, so I don't think anyone will notice. *Good.*

Rose walks silently into the kitchen and grabs the bag of clothes Jessie and Amanda brought over. She turns to go to her room, obviously to shower, but her demeanor has taken a drastic left turn. Placing my hand on top of the one that's holding the bag, I ask, "Rose, what's wrong?"

Refusing to look up at me, she murmurs, "Nothing, Cole. I want to get cleaned up. Thanks for the delicious breakfast."

"We're done with that word today, remember?" I say, giving her hand a little squeeze. "We were having a great morning with Jessie and Amanda. Tell me what Gruesome said to upset you."

"She didn't say anything, Cole. She saw a report on TV and pieced together that it was in my neighborhood. She wanted to make sure I was okay. It shocked her to hear my place was the one that got hit."

I'm suspicious. Those sentiments do not seem to be in line with what I know of Gruesome. "I call bullshit."

Ice-blue eyes collide with mine. "What?"

"You heard me. What is the deal with you and Gruesome? What does she have on you?"

"She doesn't have anything on me. Why on earth would you think she does?"

Indignation on her behalf bubbles to the surface. "Oh, I don't know. Maybe it's the way you jump to fulfill her every ludicrous order. Maybe it's how you seem to be managing both Jessie's career and mine but always give her the credit. Don't think we haven't noticed."

The bag of clothes drops to the floor. Rose looks everywhere but into my eyes. It's time for me to get to the bottom of this one mystery. I soften my tone, not releasing her hand.

"Please, Rose, let me in. You have to know that I have real feelings for you. I want to help you, but I need to understand. Tell me about Gruesome."

"Cole, I love being a publicist. And I love Greta's clients." She pauses, as if realizing what she just admitted to me. I'm not arrogant enough to think she means it literally. *Yet.* "I mean, I love the opportunity to work with her A-Listers. It's amazing. You all keep me on my toes." She gives me a half-hearted smile.

"Look, I get it if Gruesome has structured her business so that she brings in the clients and has you do all the work. But why are you afraid of her? You do excellent work."

"I'm not afraid of Greta. I just really need this job." Rose sighs, obviously hoping I will drop the subject. When I raise an eyebrow and gesture for her to continue, she says, "I don't have any back-up. My mom raised me basically by herself, and it was tough for her to keep food on the table." She takes a deep breath and plunges ahead. "When I was a teenager, her daycare business failed and she had to file for bankruptcy. I was lucky enough to get a full scholarship to NYU, and promised myself that I'd never end up in a similar financial situation. So, I live well within my means. And I learned from Mom, who's much happier being an employee at a daycare center than she ever was as a business owner, so I make sure to do whatever Greta wants in order to keep my job."

I ponder what she's told me. Did I know that she went to my alma mater? I can't remember ever discussing it with her. "What happened with your father?"

"He never was in the picture. He had money, but he never paid my mom any child support," she responds quietly.

"Your mom sounds like a strong woman. She certainly passed her work ethic on to you. Did you get your independent spirit from her, too?"

"I wouldn't call it that. But, yes, she taught me how to take care of myself."

I nod, remembering how she reacted when I helped her with her car. "So that explains why you live in Venice, with a roommate."

"Tommy moved in about a month ago. I was living with Sharon for the past two years. She got engaged and moved out. Tommy is her fiancé's friend."

"Are you and Tommy involved?"

Her head shoots upward. "What? No."

"Good."

Rose shakes her head. "I don't think he's going to be living with me for much longer. The poor guy is in bad shape."

"You shouldn't stay there either. The neighborhood isn't great. Grandma Gertie can't keep you safe. I know you want to live within your means, but there has to be somewhere else that you could stay."

"I've looked around, Cole. For the space and the price, it's the best place for me."

"It's a long way from downtown. The commuting time and money must eat into your budget." Practicality seems to be the most sure-fire way to appeal to Rose's sensibilities.

"Time is not an issue for me. I've budgeted for the commute and my car upkeep. It's still the best deal."

I purse my lips, deciding to table the discussion for now. There'll be plenty of time to regroup later.

"Speaking of time, what do you do when you're not working?"

"Sleep."

"Ha, ha. I'm serious. What do you do in your downtime?" My interest is piqued. "Do you have a boyfriend?"

"No."

"So what takes up your free time?"

"I'm boring."

"Oh, come on," I say. "Indulge me. Everyone has hobbies."

"I don't have that much free time. I work eighty hours a week, which doesn't leave too much time for fun. I watch television, spend time with Grandma Gertie, or read to unwind."

I've clearly delved deeper into her personal life than she would like. I can't ask her straight up how much money she makes. But the issue of where all her money goes won't disappear from my brain. Then it hits me. "You send money to your mom, don't you?"

Rose looks taken back. I wasn't supposed to guess that. Following a long pause, she says quietly, "Yeah. It's the least I can do."

That admission endears her to me more than ever. "You're really special, Rose. I don't think I've ever met anyone like you. I'm lucky to have you in my life."

"I'm sure you do the same thing, Cole."

I did help out with Mom's medical bills, but my family has refused all my other offers of financial help. Then again, they don't need the money.

Watching her tug at the hem of my T-shirt again, I pick up the bag of clothes and hand it to her. "Why don't you go shower and change? Maybe by the time you're ready, the police will have called with an update."

She smiles at me. "I won't be long. Oh, and Cole, it's been a while since someone has taken an interest in my life story. I want you to know that I didn't want for anything growing up, and had the most important commodity . . . love, in abundance." She gets on her tiptoes and gives me a chaste kiss on the cheek.

Ten

ROSE LOOKS LOVELY AS SHE comes down the stairs in one of her new outfits. She's wearing a black skirt that could be a bit shorter, and a blue print top that shows off her curves but isn't overtly sexy. Her hair is loose and still wet from her shower. She looks good enough to eat, and I love that she didn't put her hair in that damned ponytail.

I inhale her clean scent when she stops in front of me.

"Yes?" I say, raising my eyebrows.

"I heard the phone ring," she says with a devilish smile. "Can I go home?"

Deciding to torture her a bit, I reply, "Oh, so you heard the phone ring and assumed it was for you? Did you think that maybe someone was calling to speak with me? Maybe Jayson or my Dad? Or one of my friends?"

"I'm sure you have a long list of people calling you non-stop." She squints at me through her glasses, as if trying to read my mind. "I know that smirk, Cole! You're deliberately teasing me. It was the police on the phone, right?"

How can I resist this playful side of Rose? "Maybe."

"When can I go home? Can we go now?"

"It would seem I have information that you want. Badly. Hmmm, what's the price of admission?"

"There's a price?" she squeaks.

"Oh, yes. If you want to know who was on the phone, it'll cost you." I know what price I'd rather extract, but I'll settle for this. "One kiss."

Rose looks at me, dumbfounded. She clears her throat and responds, "Cole, I'm flattered, but you know we can't keep doing this. I work for you."

At least she isn't saying her feelings for me are strictly professional. Besides, I'm not surprised by her argument. It's why it took me so long to explore my interest in her. "I know it's crazy. If we get involved, we'll be breaking all sorts of rules. But you're taking up more and more real estate in my head, and I don't want to evict you."

"Greta has an absolute no fraternization policy. Zero tolerance. I can't risk my job over . . ." She pauses, chewing on her bottom lip.

"Over what, Rose?" I'm genuinely interested in how she intended to end that last sentence. I'm also a tad bit scared of where her mind was wandering.

She blushes and looks down. Now I absolutely need to know what she's thinking. "Tell me."

In a rush, she whispers, "I can't risk losing my job over a fling that you'll forget all about by next week."

I suck in my breath. Well, I had insisted that she tell me. "Wow, what exactly do you think of me?"

"Cole, I really like you. You're smart, funny and crazy-talented. You have a wonderful family. I just don't see you as the settling down type. And you're my client. Greta—"

"I know. Gruesome forbids her employees from hooking up with her clients. Too bad that same edict does not apply to her." Rose gasps.

"Not what you're thinking!" I say. "She propositioned me the first time we met. It was all I could do not to gag."

"It's her company. She can break the rules, but no one else can."

"Fuck that, Rose."

"You know I'm right."

"Also, I'm not looking for a fling, as you put it." I continue, ignoring her justification for Gruesome. "I've had more than my share of those. Not that you have any reason to know this, but ever since Mom died, I've been reevaluating my life. One thing she always wanted for me was to settle down. I've found myself wanting that, too."

Rose looks stunned by that admission. "I didn't mean to offend you. We already talked about why this job is so important to me. I can't cross that line."

"Do you want to?"

"I *can't*. It doesn't matter what I do, or don't, want."

"So I guess we're at a stalemate. For now." I pause. "I'll defer your price of one kiss and let you know that yes, the police did call me."

Rose doesn't seem as excited as she did before. "Can I go home now?"

"Yes. But Rose, I want to help you when we get there. You may need my strength moving furniture and I want to be a shoulder for you to lean on." She looks skeptical, so I add, "A friendly shoulder."

"I'd like that," she finally admits.

She goes back upstairs to gather her few belongings and the bag of new clothes. I take the time to try to figure out how I can break down the wall Gruesome put up between us. I don't want to be the cause of her losing her job if we don't last past a week or two, but I don't think that will be the case. My feelings for her are venturing into uncharted territory. I decide to try to spend as much time together with Rose as possible, and let nature take its course. I can be patient. To a point.

"I'm ready, Cole," Rose says with a shy smile.

"Great, let's go fix up your place. I do want to repeat that I don't think you should stay there."

"Duly noted."

From the outside, no one would ever know her place had been robbed. If she refuses to move, at the very least I will insist that she install an alarm. No, I'll do it for her. It'll be my re-housewarming present to her, so to speak. She won't like it, but I'll hate it more if she stays here without one.

Rose gets out of the car and squares her shoulders. No one would ever accuse her of being timid, that's for sure. She walks straight up to the front door and pulls out her key. I want to take it from her and open the door; fuck, I want to make this whole thing go away. But I know that she needs to reassert some sense of control over her own home. Take back what was violated.

We enter the living room and she sucks in her breath. The place is trashed. Papers, broken glass from picture frames and misplaced furniture are everywhere. The insurance company's website had a form that Rose printed out to inventory the items that were stolen.

Leave it to Rose to have renter's insurance for her contents.

I pull her into my arms and whisper, "I'll help you get through this, Rose." To my relief, she lets me embrace her. "Let's throw away everything that's broken and put the furniture back into place. Then we can fill out the form from the insurance company."

Rose looks up at me and I'm surprised to see she isn't teary. No, her blue eyes are steely with determination. "Sounds like a good plan, Cole."

We get to work.

About an hour later, we've restored the living room to order. Well, mostly. "I need to use your bathroom. Where is it?" Distractedly, Rose points to the hallway and says, "First door."

I open the first door and realize it's not the bathroom. No, it's Rose's bedroom. Her inner sanctuary. Which some group of thugs ransacked as thoroughly as the living room. Knowing that I shouldn't go in, I hesitate for a split second, but I can't stop myself. We'll be cleaning this room soon anyway. I'm starving for information about her.

Her room is painted a light green and has flowered curtains, which surprises me. Despite her name, I didn't take Rose for the chintz and flowers type of girl. Her furniture is unremarkable except for a vanity that looks antique. Of course, the drawers are all on the floor with their contents strewn about. Her bed is messy, too, with something bright pink right in the center. I walk over to take a closer look and my eyebrows rise sky high. It's a pink vibrator. *Well, well, Rose has a naughty side?* I smirk and turn to leave her bedroom before she catches me where I shouldn't be.

"Wow, they did a job of it in here, too," says Rose from the doorway.

"Yeah. I guess they figured you'd keep all your valuables in your room," I say, walking toward her.

Meeting her at the doorway, I say, "Uh, I'm sorry I invaded your bedroom. You said the first door."

"That's okay. The bathroom is that room," she says, pointing.

"Thanks. Be right back."

I take a step to move around her, but stop when she mumbles something that sounds like, "Oh, my."

I turn and follow her line of sight to the bed. Damn. She probably won't take kindly to being teased about it, especially since the thugs left it right in the middle of her bed to let her know they found it.

"Uh, Rose?"

She looks at me with a question in her eyes.

Be a man, Manchester. It's not like you've never seen or used a vibrator before. I walk back to the bed and pick it up. "I'll throw this out for you."

Rose turns a brighter shade of pink than her vibrator. I take it with me and throw it into one of the many trash bags before making my way to the bathroom. Someday I will tease her about it, but today is not that day.

When I return to the bedroom, Rose is going through her jewelry box. We both knew that her jewelry would be gone, but from the slump of her shoulders, I could tell she'd still hoped. I walk quietly over to her.

She looks up at me when I place a hand on her shoulder. "They took all my jewelry, but at least they left this box. Most of my jewelry was costume, except for one piece, but my grandmother gave me the box. She died when I was nine."

And the tears I've been expecting start to fall.

I go down on my knee, offering her what little comfort I can. She grips my shoulders, sobbing, and I run my hand up and down her back, trying to alleviate her pain.

"You still have your jewelry box, Rose. We can fill it with other jewelry, but the box is more important." It would gut me if someone took anything my mother had given to me, so I can share in her gratitude that she still has this piece of her grandmother.

A couple of minutes pass before she stops crying and pulls back. "I'll have plenty of time to cry later. I need to get through this." With a few sniffles on her part, we tackle the rest of her place, minus Tommy's room.

As we're finishing up in Rose's office, my cell phone rings. It's Dan. I excuse myself and answer the call. "Hey, buddy."

"Hey, buddy yourself. What's going on? Who's this *good friend* of yours, Tommy, who was beaten up by thugs?"

Wow, news travels fast. "Don't get your panties in a twist, Dan. How did you hear about Tommy?" As I say the words, the answer comes to me: Alicia.

"Alicia mentioned it to Suzanne. I've never heard of him before. What's the deal?"

"I don't know Tommy, but he's Rose's roommate. It's a long story, but their rental was hit by a robbery ring. He happened to be home at the time, so they roughed him up. I pretended that Tommy was my friend to give Rose and me a cover. It worked."

I can almost see Dan's eyebrows going up. "So, it's like that, huh?"

"Yeah, it's like that."

"Okay. Well, now I understand. Guess you want me to put your next date on hold?"

I sigh. "I'm pretty into Rose, but she doesn't think it's a good idea. Gruesome has a no-fucking-the-clients policy that covers everyone except herself."

"I have to agree with Rose, it's never good to swim in the company pool." My heart starts to sink, but then he adds, "I also know you, and I don't think you're just taking her out for a test drive. Tread lightly, Cole."

"I intend to. Listen, I need to get back to her. We've been cleaning up her place for the last few hours, and I don't want her to shoulder this alone. I'll call you later."

"Sounds good. And Cole, be careful."

"Always." I disconnect the call and return to Rose's office. She's in the process of tying up a garbage bag.

"Can you gather all of the garbage bags in the kitchen? I'm going to start bringing them out to the garage."

I nod my head in agreement and she takes a bag out.

I'm heading for the kitchen with four bags in tow when I hear Rose scream from the garage. Dropping the bags, I race out to her. She's standing at the back of her car, looking madder than hell.

My heart's racing. "What's going on, Rose?"

She turns and looks at me. Hurt, disbelief, anger and a myriad of other emotions, all at once, cross her face. "Look at this. I can't believe it."

I join her at the back of her car. "What the fuck?" We look at each other. "When did you park your car in the garage, Rose? You must have parked it after the robbery, right?"

"Yes. I parked it in here when I got home from the beach. I went inside and found the mess and Tommy like . . . that . . . and called 911."

"So, someone did this to your car after the thugs had already left."

"Yes."

"We have to call the police now." Rose sighs, but she takes the hand I hold out to her and we head back inside together. She finds the card of the officer who's investigating the robbery and places the call.

Needing something productive to do, I ask her if she wants anything to drink. As I begin to boil water for her tea, I wonder when this nightmare is going to end. Why would anyone write "Stay Away Bitch" on the back windshield of her car?

I walk into her living room with the steaming cup of tea. "Here you go, Rose." She takes the cup from me and puts it on the coffee table without even taking a sip.

"Why do that to my car, Cole? I don't get it."

"Let's hope the police can shed some light on it. They should be here soon, right?" Rose nods. "In the meantime, go pack a bag. There's no way I'm letting you stay here tonight." I'm proud of myself for stopping with tonight. I'd be a lot happier if she left today and never returned.

"You may be my client, but you're not the boss of me," she snaps, showing me I wasn't nearly as suave as I thought I was. In a softer voice, she continues, "Cole, you can't order me around. I'm perfectly capable of handling this situation."

"I didn't mean to imply that you couldn't. It's just that I want you to be safe, and obviously this place isn't safe. Someone did that to your car *after* the robbery. Until the cops can find out who did it, I would be more comfortable if you stayed somewhere else. You know I have a guestroom at my house that you can use. Please, Rose, I want you to be safe."

Rose closes her eyes. She's been through so much over the last twenty-four hours. For someone who's used to controlling everything down to the smallest detail, I can't imagine the toll this must be taking on her.

"Greta can't know."

I smile. If that's her only objection to staying with me, I can handle it. "No problem."

She looks at me like she's looking straight into my soul. I've never felt such intense scrutiny. Apparently, I've passed some sort of test because she gives me a quick, clipped nod and stands. "I'll go pack a bag. Can you please let the cops in if I'm not done by the time they get here?"

"Of course. Pack a bathing suit, too."

Eleven

HOW THE FUCK DID I GET MYSELF into this situation? When I let Rose choose the evening's activities, I had no damned clue she would want to do this. Seriously? Who goes to a *planetarium* except for teenagers who have no other options?

Shaking my head, I glance at Rose. Well, shit. Her ice blue eyes glitter in anticipation. I'm caught up in her smile. I could gaze at her all day and all night, especially with that look on her face.

I manage to focus and actually enjoy the next half hour. I'm holding Rose's hand, which makes me feel like I'm on top of the world. She's starting to accept that we're an "us." I'm positive of that.

The finale starts, catching me off guard.

It's set to one of my songs.

Rose's head turns toward me, and she squeezes my hand before returning her gaze upward. I probably should have known this was coming, and in retrospect, I vaguely remember Russell mentioning something about this to me a year ago.

As the music ends and the lights start to flicker back on, I quickly put my baseball cap on my head. People here may be more inclined to recognize me since my music was just blaring over the loudspeakers.

"From that smile, can I assume you enjoyed yourself?" she whispers.

"Let's just say that this was a unique experience for me," I respond directly into her ear. I love that she shudders when my breath reaches her lobe.

Over the loudspeaker, I hear, "We hope you enjoyed the laser light show at the Planetarium Theater. Thank you for visiting."

While everyone in the theater is busy gathering their things, the same two ushers who originally greeted us appear at our side. They lead us out through a side door so I can avoid being seen by my fans in such a public place.

Several of the Planetarium's employees are loitering in the hallway. I pull Rose toward me and whisper, "Let me say hello to these good people, and then I'm taking you out for dinner." She nods in agreement and slips into the back of the room.

Being my publicist, it would be okay for her to be seen with me, but her job is to get me noticed while remaining in the background. I resolve to make some changes in the near future, but it has to be this way for now.

Nearly an hour later, Rose and I finally return to my car. "Thanks for being so patient back there."

"No problem. The Planetarium's employees seemed so excited to meet you." Her forehead crinkles. "Did that one blonde near the end seem familiar to you?"

"To be honest, they all blend together for me after a while."

"Oh. Well, she reminded me of the woman who asked for your autograph at the café in Santa Monica. I'm probably mistaken. Anyway, how did it feel watching the show set to your music?"

"Obviously, I had forgotten about it. But it was cool. Thanks for suggesting it." I smile at her and she beams back at me. "Are you ready for dinner? I've thought of the perfect place to complement the Planetarium."

"Uh-oh. I've seen that twinkle in your eye before. What do you have up your sleeve?"

I give Rose a disbelieving look and mouth, *Who, me?* Her laughter wraps around me, drawing out my own.

"You'll see," I tell her with a grin.

We pull up to Pink's, and Rose lets out a snort. I laugh so hard that the people in the surrounding cars all look over. "C'mon, let's get on line," I tell her, opening her car door.

"I can't believe you brought me to Pink's!"

"Yeah, well, I figured a hot dog dinner is the perfect end to an evening at the Planetarium." We both laugh as we join the throngs of people waiting for the best hot dogs in all of LA. This is perfect. We're not agonizing over the robbery or Rose's car. We're simply hanging out and enjoying each other's company.

Some people in line recognize me, but they're cool. So many celebrities come here that my presence isn't particularly noteworthy. I don't consider myself a celebrity anyway; I'm a working musician. Rose and I chat easily in line, and our conversation only stalls while we're eating. For me, a twelve-inch hot dog with chili, cheese and guacamole and a side of fries. For Rose, a "Mushroom Swiss Dog."

As we make our way back to the car, satiated, I can't help but laugh at Rose's comment about how much I'm going to have to pay at the gym for tonight's dinner. "What about you, Rose? No extra workout for you?"

She smiles. "Oh yeah, but it was totally worth it. Thanks for the dinner. I've always wanted to get out to Pink's."

"Glad to have taken you out for your virgin trip."

Damn. Why did I say that? She's clearly noticed my verbal stumble, so I change the topic as quickly as I can.

"Are you game to sit back and check out the LA lights? It's the perfect ending to a night at the Planetarium and Pink's."

She looks over at me, her eyes registering surprise. Did she think I was going to try to seduce her? Then she clears her throat and responds, "That sounds like a great way to end the evening."

Soon I'm pulling into a parking spot that has a gorgeous view of the valley. Rose sucks in her breath. "Cole, this is extraordinary. I've been to some celebrity parties up in the Hills, but nothing with this vibe. It's like we're the only two people here. LA looks almost peaceful, with all its lights."

I stop myself from saying some cheesy line in reply. Instead, I tell her the truth, "I'm glad you like it up here. Sometimes I drive out here by myself just to think. I've composed songs up here. It's special to me."

"Thank you for sharing it with me," she says softly.

I half-smile, and cup her cheek in my hand. She looks at me, but she's not totally in the moment. I can see she's starting to think about all the crap going on at her house. Maybe if we talk about it, she'll be able to relax.

Running my fingers through her hair, I ask, "Do you agree with the cops' theory that one of Tommy's exes did that to your car?"

Rose chews on her bottom lip. "I don't know. I guess anything is possible."

"We need to let the police do their jobs. When did they say you'd get your car back?"

"Hopefully, I can get it Monday afternoon," she sighs. "Cole, thanks for letting me stay at your place again tonight. I appreciate it."

"Ro," I stop short, sounding out my first nickname for her. "Ro, you know how I feel about you. I want to be here for you. You don't have to deal with this whole mess by yourself."

She shakes her head. "We talked about this before. You're my client . . . we have a business relationship. I can't cross that line."

"Have you ever done anything wild, Ro? Really crazy? Let your hair down and did something just because it felt good or took your breath away?"

"Of course." Her words are belied by her body language. She's staring out into the Valley and each of her fingers is flicking her thumb sequentially.

"I don't believe you."

"I can be as spontaneous as the next girl. Why do you care?"

"I care, Ro, because you matter to me. I want to know all about you. I want to know what makes you tick, what ticks you off, and what makes you howl with laughter." I lean in to her, placing my hand on her shoulder, "I also want to know what makes you scream."

"I can scream right now if you want me to. You're making me want to scream right this second."

Flopping back into the driver's seat, I reply, "Fine. Share with me one crazy thing you've done, and I'll let you off the hook."

I'm not going to say another word until she does. Is she making up a story in her head? Or is she trying to summon the courage to tell me something truly personal? Either way, I'm intrigued.

I get out of the car, walk around to her side and open the door. I take her hand and walk over to an empty bench at the tree line. Admiring the view, I wait in silence.

Finally, Rose turns to me and speaks. "I had a one-night stand once. There. That's wild and crazy."

Well, that admission scores maybe a one on my wild-and-crazy meter, but for someone as buttoned-up as she presents herself to be, that must have been some night for her. I want to know more. "When was this, Ro?"

"In college."

"Were you drunk or high?"

She gives me a look. "No." She looks down and amends, "Well, a bit tipsy."

Now this is getting interesting. "Fine, you were a bit tipsy. Did you know his name?"

"Of course!"

"Did he know yours?"

"Well, uh, I told him my name."

"Was that before or after you were naked?"

"This is juvenile! I told you one crazy thing I did. We're not going to play twenty questions about it."

"I'll take that was *after* you were naked." Rose makes a very unladylike sound and crosses her arms over her chest. I fight to keep my lips from curling up. "So, you had drunk sex one night with some dumb frat boy you wanted, but up until then the doofus didn't even know you existed. Did you take the walk of shame the following morning, or did he?"

"Neither."

My eyebrows go up. "Well, well, Ro. Did you meet at a party and go into the bathroom?"

"Something like that."

"Okay. On my crazy-o-meter, I'll give that maybe a five." I've upped the rating to make her feel better. I bet she's never done anything more outrageous than this, but that only means I'll get to help her release her wild side.

"The frat boy was an ass," I add. "He couldn't see how special you are."

"Thanks, I think." Rose frowns at me. "Your turn, Rock Star."

Expecting her to ask about my most wild adventure, I search through my memory banks for a rather tame episode. So, I'm taken aback at her question. "When did you lose your virginity?"

"Wow. I didn't see that one coming," I tease. "I was eighteen." Taking in her look of disbelief, I continue, "I'm not lying. I was a late bloomer. It was in the backseat of my car at a scenic overlook." I smirk at her, recognizing that we're in a similar situation right now.

"Oh." She must realize the same thing.

My mind wanders back to that momentous evening. "It happened after the last performance of our high school musical."

She raises her eyebrow.

I shrug. "I played Danny Zuko in *Grease*. Anyway, I intended to ask the girl I'd been dating for a few months, the head cheerleader Steffy, out to Prom after the performance. I was head over heels for her. But she walked up to me on the arm of her ex-boyfriend, claiming my performance had brought them back together. I later found out she'd only used me as a placeholder until she could get that guy back. Later that night, I met my first groupie."

She was an older woman, a college sophomore, who went all fangirl over me. In an effort to forget the cheerleader, I took her to The Lookout. That's where it all started, or stalled, for me. Sex without any strings or emotions to get trampled became my motto, starting that night.

Snapping her fingers, Rose clears her throat. "Earth to Cole." I offer her a lopsided grin of apology.

"Seems like you've made up for lost time," she says.

I try to figure out if she's making an honest observation, or is jealous. Of course, I'd prefer jealousy.

Turning to her and holding her gaze, I say, "Yes, I've had a lot of meaningless sex. You, unfortunately, have had to clean up after me on way too many occasions, so I can't deny or hide my past. But I'm ready to change. I don't want that lifestyle anymore."

I reach out and grab her hand, bringing it up toward my lips. As her hand nears my face, I turn it over and kiss the inside of her wrist instead.

Sucking in her breath, Rose murmurs, "Your mom would be very pleased to hear you say that."

Smiling, I reply, "Yes. I think she would be even more pleased to know that I want you to be my first girlfriend."

Rose yanks her hand from mine and looks away. *What the hell did I say this time?* "Rose, what's up? Tell me why you went all cold on me."

"Cole, one thing I can't abide is lying. Putting aside our professional relationship, if, and that's a very big if . . . *if* I were crazy enough to consider the possibility of being with you, if I ever get the whiff of a lie, I'm done. Through."

"Okay, I get that. But I haven't lied to you."

"Really? Then what's all this crap about wanting me to be your *first* girlfriend?" She nearly shouts the word "first."

I blink, speechless. "Rose, I've never had a real girlfriend." Steffy came the closest, but she had never really wanted me in the first place. "Yes, I've hooked up with women, but I never considered any of them girlfriends." I say the word "girlfriends" in air quotes.

"A girlfriend is someone I'd be proud to introduce to my family and friends. Someone to go on adventures with and share the happy and awful times. Someone to challenge me to be better, act silly with me, make me laugh, and have off-the-charts amazing sex with me." My voice drops. "A girlfriend should be someone who could turn into a wife."

Catching my breath, I look over at Rose to gauge her reaction. Tears are streaming down her face. *What did I do?* Then Rose launches herself into my arms. She's repeating my name and holding me tightly. I breathe in her floral scent and tighten my arms around her. I love having her in my arms, even if I don't understand what brought this on.

I start stroking Rose's back, and pretty soon she calms down. She yawns. I smile down at her, tilting her chin up so I can look into her eyes.

"What brought on the tears, Ro?" I ask gently.

"I've always thought you had it all. I just realized that I was wrong. You've never experienced romantic love."

I clear my throat. "Well, I haven't exactly been looking for it. And I certainly haven't felt like I was missing something in my life, until recently. Have you ever been in love before, Rose?"

"Twice."

"Lucky bastards. I hope they're both fat and bald now."

She offers me a small smile. "My first love was my high school sweetheart. His mother still is my Mom's best friend."

"He was an idiot to let you go."

She whispers, "We were young and stupid."

Rose rests her head against my shoulder, the subject of her prior boyfriends clearly closed. I cradle her in my arms and we stay like this for a few minutes, until I hear her yawn again. "We've had quite a day. We're both shot. Ready to go home?"

Her sleepy eyes look into mine. "It feels like today has been years long, but I'm happy that I spent it with you." She reaches up and places a tender kiss on my lips.

"There's nowhere else I'd rather be than with you," I reply honestly. She looks shattered. "Let's go home."

As I drive back to my house, Rose falls asleep. I'm beat, too. We certainly hit some major highs and lows today. No wonder she's passed out.

I glance over at her, sleeping peacefully on the passenger side. I can't believe it's taken me years to actually see her. I need to make up for lost time.

Tomorrow, I'm going to suggest that we go for a swim in my pool after breakfast and charm her out of her bathing suit. She's nervous about crossing the imaginary line, but that ship has sailed. She's different from all the rest. And I'm ready to prove that I'm different from the two other losers she once loved.

We reach my house and Rose doesn't stir when I pull into the driveway. Trying not to wake her, I get out of the car as quietly as possible and walk over to her door. She doesn't rouse when I pick her up and bring her into the house. She feels perfect in my arms.

Where should I bring her? I want her in my bedroom, not the guest room. Maybe I should leave the decision up to her? Looking down at her, I whisper, "Ro, is it okay if we sleep in my bed?"

Rose turns her head against my chest and mumbles something that sounds like "um-hum."

I enter the house, go up to my bedroom and carefully place her on my bed. After removing her shoes and dress, I ease her under the covers. She barely registers her new surroundings before her breathing tells me she's back in a deep sleep.

I quickly strip down to my boxer-briefs and slide on top of the comforter. I kiss her cheek and fall fast asleep.

Twelve

I WAKE UP TO AN UNFAMILIAR, yet welcome, feeling. I'm not alone in my bed. Rose's leg is thrown over me, her arm is around my torso and her head is snuggled in the crook of my neck. For my part, my hand is on her bra-covered boob. Well, I certainly can get used to this. I squeeze, savoring her perfect weight in my palm, and her breath accelerates against my neck. I quickly tuck my hand under my head, letting her think she was more intertwined with me than I was with her. No need for her to know that I copped a feel.

When her gorgeous blue eyes open, I ask, "Morning, Ro. Sleep well?"

She looks up at me, clearly disoriented. "Cole?"

"Hmmm?"

"Um, Cole, what happened? How did I end up here?"

"Well, after I drove us home, you practically begged me to sleep with you. It was pretty embarrassing, to tell the truth. You were not taking *no* for an answer." I'm proud that I managed to get that out without laughing out loud.

Still struggling to fully wake up, she moans and buries her head against my chest. I take that as a good sign that she's coming around to my way of thinking about us. I smile broadly, knowing that she can't see me, and pull her in tight.

A minute later, she leans back, her eyes drawn into slits. "Why am I still wearing my underwear? I mean, if I was so hot and bothered for you and all?"

"You fell asleep?" I deliberately let my voice rise to a question. She hits me squarely in the chest with a pillow. I can't help but laugh.

"Very funny. You're getting a lump of coal in your stocking for Christmas." She says that with an answering smile as she unwinds her body from mine.

I don't want to lose the contact with her, so I wrap my arms around her, drawing her back to me. "It won't be the first time," I say with a chuckle. I lean forward to give her a kiss, but she turns her head so that I kiss her cheek instead.

"I haven't brushed my teeth, Cole. That's gross."

"So? I haven't brushed either, so we're even." I lean forward to kiss her other cheek. She's right, morning breath is gross, especially after dinner at Pink's. But there's no way I'm missing this opportunity.

I lean in again and capture her lips. This time, she doesn't resist. I take my time kissing her, molding our lips to one another. My tongue seeks and gains entrance. Leisurely, I explore her mouth, nibbling at her bottom lip. She's learning my mouth, too. We have all day to get to know each other's bodies, so I'm in no rush. Damn, the chemistry between us is off the charts.

I move down to her neck, trailing kisses along my path. My hands have moved lower as well, and are cupping her luscious ass. As I knead her bottom cheeks, she moans softly. Her hands travel to my shoulders. Encouraged, I draw her to my erection so that only her panties and my underwear are keeping me from driving into her. She moans again, louder this time.

I shift one of my hands from her ass, but only to move it up to her back and unhook her bra. Rose's eyes are closed, but there's a voluptuous smile on her face. My lips move down farther and trace her collarbone, which I find to be one of the sexiest parts of a woman's body. I linger there a while removing her bra from her arms, then continue on to my prize. Her boob. Like I did before she woke, I weigh it in my hand. She's the perfect size. And real. I haven't found one fake thing on her body, which matches her personality.

I lick around the areola, avoiding her nipple. Rose arches her back under me, whimpering. Her movement brings her pussy ever closer to my straining cock. I'm the one who lets out a moan this time.

I look down at her flushed face and half-closed eyes. My gaze moves down to her nipples. They're hard buds, begging for my attention. "Your nipples are almost as hard for me as my cock is for you, Ro."

In response, Rose grinds her pussy against my cock and grabs my ass— all without saying a word. I latch onto her nipple, giving it tiny bites that make her hips jerk against me in a matching rhythm.

Not wanting her other boob to feel left out, I move over to her left nipple and give it the same treatment. At the same time, I strum her right nipple with my fingers. Rose is writhing against me. "Do you like that, Ro? You're so responsive to me."

She murmurs something that sounds like "oh yeah," but it's so low I can barely make it out. She's like a guitar hand-crafted only for me. Pinching her nipples lightly, I recapture her mouth in a ravenous kiss. Rose's hands climb up to encircle my neck, and one threads into my hair. I love when a woman runs her hands through my hair.

Rose applies just the right pressure on my scalp. "That feels so good, Ro. Don't stop," I direct her. She complies, and what little control I had left slips even further away. That earlier feeling of having all the time in the world is a distant memory.

Lady Gaga's "Telephone" breaks my concentration. What the hell? Only pleasure and Rose exist in my bedroom. Where is that music coming from?

Under me, Rose stiffens. Fuck. She's pushing against me, trying to scramble upright in my bed. "Where's my purse, Cole?" she asks urgently.

I shake my head to try to clear the passion from it. Is she seriously going to answer that phone?

"Let it go to voicemail. We're busy," I respond, trying to recapture her.

"No, I have to answer it! Where's my phone?"

Sighing, I roll over and land on my back. Rose manages to find her purse on the nightstand and pulls the phone out. I hear her say, "Good morning, Greta."

Of course. Gruesome. Who else would call at the ass crack of dawn on a Sunday? I glance over at the clock and realize it's actually 11 a.m. Well, she's still calling Rose before noon on the weekend. I smile when I realize that Rose must have purposefully assigned her boss that ringtone. I love her sense of humor.

Rose is sitting up against the pillows, half naked. Well, I certainly appreciate the view, although I much preferred her grinding against me. Her voice sounds a bit breathless; I wonder if Gruesome picked up on anything? Sounds like she's calling about our trip to the Planetarium last night. Apparently some photos of me with the employees have been posted on the Internet. It doesn't seem that Rose was connected with me, so we're still flying under the radar. Good.

Rose catches my eye and mimes for a pen and paper. Damn. Grumbling, I sling my legs over the side of the bed and walk over to a table with a scratch notepad on its top. When I hand her the pen and paper, I catch her checking me out. My boxer-briefs are doing nothing to hide my excitement, although the call did diminish it somewhat. Smirking, I slowly turn around and make my way to the bathroom, making sure to flex my ass before I enter. I turn and look back at her. She's staring at me like I'm the last piece of chocolate cake. I give her a wink and leave her to her conversation.

I brush my teeth and take a cold shower, then wrap myself in a towel and re-enter my bedroom. Rose is still on the phone. Is this normal? Can't it wait until tomorrow?

Rose says, "And Jessie?"

Taking the long way to my walk-in closet to give Rose a show, I ditch my towel and pull on a bathing suit. Ro probably won't be in an amorous mood anymore after talking so long with Gruesome. Cockblocker. I might as well make breakfast. From the doorway, I nod downstairs, and she lifts her chin in response.

Rose walks into the kitchen as I'm plating a batch of French toast that looks to be one of my best. She's wearing her bathing suit and a cover-up, so she obviously took my lead. Good. Pulling out the leftover fruit that Jessie and Amanda brought over yesterday—was that really only yesterday?—I walk over to the table.

"I hope you like French Toast."

"Thanks, it looks amazing."

Her response brings a smile to my lips. Before taking my seat, I indulge in a sweet kiss. Minty. She must feel better now that her teeth are brushed, given how concerned she was earlier.

After the kiss ends, Rose leans into me, placing her forehead to mine. We stay like this for a minute, until her stomach rumbles.

Laughing, I take my seat. She's blushing. Damn, this woman is just too cute for words. "Eat, Ro. Let me know if you like it."

She takes a tentative bite from my proffered fork and looks at me. "Cole, this is really good. What other hidden talents do you have?"

I laugh and say, "Oh, you'll find out soon enough. But eat, you're going to need your strength to keep up."

She makes a big production out of stabbing a blueberry with her fork. Figuring that I should get it out of the way, I ask, "So, what did Gruesome want to talk about so early on a Sunday?"

"Actually, we usually talk about this time on the weekends. We touch base about any um, problems our clients managed to get themselves into the night before. We do immediate damage control if need be, as you well know."

Yes, now that I think about it, I do know. It never dawned on me that my extracurricular escapades would force Rose to work over the weekends. I only knew that the messes I created were always cleaned up right away. "I'm sorry I was so selfish. Do you ever get a free weekend?"

Rose looks at me and takes my hand. "Cole, don't feel that way. I knew what I was signing up for when I became a publicist. Sometimes clients do stupid things and need somebody to fix it so that the general public doesn't find out. That's my job, and I love it."

Although skeptical, I let it go for now. "I heard you mention the Planetarium. Does Gruesome have a problem with our visit there last night?"

"No, it's all positive press. I'll work up an angle for social media and maybe we'll connect the trip with your upcoming world tour. Something like going global and seeing the universe. Obviously that's a rough idea, but the visit wasn't a problem at all."

"Was there a problem?"

"I shouldn't discuss it with you. It's about another client."

"Is it about Jessie? Because she's my friend too. If something's wrong, I want to help."

Sighing, she responds, "Please don't mention this to anyone, especially Jessie." I nod in agreement and she continues. "Her co-star, you know the actor that she's seeing publicly, got a DUI last night. His mug shot is going to be plastered all over the gossip sites by nightfall."

"So? Brandan is an ass."

"He was with someone."

"Oh."

"Yeah. Luckily, no one got hurt. . . that's the good news. But now we're going to have to deal with the fallout over this mystery woman who was with him, and how it might affect his public romance with Jessie."

"What a clusterfuck." She nods. "Have you decided how you're going to handle it?" I deliberately leave Gruesome's name out of it. I'm pretty sure her boss just dumped the facts on Rose and told her to figure it out.

"Well, I'd already brought up the idea to have you, Jessie and Brandan form a love triangle. I think it just became a quadrangle."

If that's the way they decide to go, I'm fine with it. I really like Jessie, so spending time with her won't be a chore. Plus, she knows about Rose and me, and I love Amanda. "What was Gruesome's response?"

"She gave it the go ahead, and has officially added me to Brandan's team. But we have to get the scoop on this mystery woman he was with in the car. I don't know if she's Brandan's girlfriend or some random fan he picked up."

"I take it he didn't spend the night in jail?"

"No. It was his first DUI, so his license is suspended and he has to pay some fines and take classes. After breakfast, if it's okay with you, I need to call him and get the details."

"No problem, Ro. I'll meet you at the pool when you're done. Now, eat before the French toast gets cold. I don't want all my hard work to go for naught," I tease.

She smiles and picks up the maple syrup. It's nice that she eats. All of the models and actresses I've dated weigh under one-hundred pounds sopping wet and refuse to eat anything more than a piece of lettuce.

With breakfast done, I show Rose to my office where she can comfortably make that call to Brandan and figure out the next steps. I grab the book she sent me from the coffee table and head out back to the pool.

I'm sitting on the side of the pool with my feet in the water, reading, when Rose walks out. She's returned to her professional mode, all calm, cool and collected. I look forward to helping her shed that façade as well as her bathing suit. Smiling, I walk over to her. "All set?"

"Yes. I think it'll be fine. Turns out Brandan was with his older sister in the car, so we're going to play it like the DUI was the last straw for Jessie. You'll be waiting in the wings, ready to scoop her back up."

"Ha. As if. How was The Ass?"

"Look, I know you don't like Brandan much, and he and Jessie don't get along that well, but he is Greta's client. He actually isn't a bad guy." She ignores my raised eyebrow and continues. "I think he's lost his way out here in Los Angeles. His sister was out trying to remind him of who he used to be. This arrest has shaken him up. I hope he can get it together."

Damn. She's made him into a real human being instead of just some jackass who annoys Jessie. "Well, even if he isn't so bad, he's been an ass to Jessie. Maybe it'll help him grow up when I steal her away." She nudges me with her shoulder and gives me a small smile.

Again, I'm hit with a feeling of déjà-vu, but her delectable body doesn't let me linger on a mysterious past. "Now, let's get you out of that cover-up and into the pool. The water's great."

Not waiting for her to answer, I grab the bottom of her cover-up and pull it over her head. The way she quickly shrugs out of it tells me that we're going to be crossing that professional line very soon. Who am I trying to kid? We left tire marks on that line a while ago.

I toss her cover-up on a chair and grab her hands, stepping back to enjoy the sight of her body encased only in her bathing suit. Clearly the suit was her choice and not one purchased by Jessie and Amanda, as it's a two-piece but not a bikini. What is that type of suit called? Oh yes, a tankini. It's cute enough but doesn't expose nearly enough skin for my taste.

"Very cute bathing suit, Miss Morgan. I can't wait to get you out of it."

She looks down, biting her lower lip. "Cole, I know I didn't stop you this morning, but—"

Placing my finger on her lips, I silence her. "It's just us."

"You're still my client."

"Actually, I'm Gruesome's client. I'm like a client once removed or something."

She studies me for a long moment, then replies, "Well, since you put it like that."

Licking my lips, I step backward to thoroughly inspect her body. Something at her hip draws my attention. "What do we have here? Do you have a tattoo? That would register on my crazy-o-meter, you know."

Instead of laughing, she looks up at me wide-eyed. What's that reaction about? Curious, I step closer and bend down, moving her bathing suit bottoms to the side slightly to get a better look. "This isn't a tattoo, is it Ro? It's a birthmark. It looks like . . ." I squint and cock my head from left to right. "It looks like a flower."

She steps back and puts her bathing suit back in place.

Suddenly, a hazy memory of a back room and a college girl with this exact birthmark flashes behind my eyes. I remember saying something to the chick, but what was it? Concentrating, I remember something like, "It was a very good night, Rose Bloomer with the flower birthmark."

Rose *Bloomer*. Didn't the cop call her Miss Bloomer that night her house was robbed? What the hell is going on?

"Oh my God. *I* was your one-night stand."

Rose goes still. Her eyes dart everywhere but to my face. That's all the confirmation I need.

"What the *fuck?*" Red colors everything in sight.

"I—"

"What's this all about?" I shout.

"It's—"

"Have you been laughing at me behind my back all this time?"

"What? No—"

"Is this some sort of sick, twisted revenge plot? I can't believe you didn't say anything to me. You made such a big fucking deal about honesty ... well, what the hell is this?"

"But—"

"You know what, I don't care."

I ignore the stricken look on her face. "You hear me, Rose Morgan, Rose Bloomer, or whatever the fuck your real name is? *I don't care!*"

"Cole—"

Turning to leave, I shout back at her, "I need some air."

She gasps and staggers toward a chair, but I don't stop. Storming into the house, I grab my keys and head for the driveway. My tires squeal as I peel out onto the street.

Rose, who I thought was so genuine and honest, is as fake as all the models and starlets I've dated, if not worse. They, at least, know that they are selling an illusion. Rose peddled honesty and sincerity, all while manipulating me. Well, she is a publicist, so she can't be all that honest, can she? How could I be this gullible?

I stomp harder on the gas pedal.

Thirteen

AFTER AN HOUR OF AIMLESSLY DRIVING, I find myself parked in Dan's driveway. I'm still fuming, but if I don't talk with someone, I'll explode. Gathering myself as best as I can, I get out and ring the bell.

Luckily, Dan answers. His smile slides off his face once he gets a good look at me. "Come in, buddy. I'd say it's good to see you, but I can tell that something's seriously wrong."

"You can say that again," I respond, entering his house and making a beeline to his fridge. Taking out a beer, I drain it in one gulp.

As I'm reaching for a second beer, he says, "Whoa there. What's going on? I haven't seen you like this since . . . I can't remember when."

Opening another beer, I turn to him and sit down at the kitchen table. He grabs a beer for himself and sits down across from me.

"Are Suzanne and Emma here?" Before I go off, I want to make sure that we're alone.

"No, they went to visit her parents. I was working," he responds, motioning toward his home office.

"Good."

"Cole, what's up? Is there a problem with your dad?"

I close my eyes and let out a huge sigh. I don't want to worry him, but I need to unload all this shit. "No, it's nothing like that. Thankfully." He looks relieved.

"That's good, I'm glad. But what on earth has gotten your panties in such a bunch?"

Biting the inside of my cheek, I take another long sip of beer. "It's Rose. I've slept with her."

"And that's bad because?"

"You don't understand, Dan. It happened like ten years ago! And she didn't tell me!"

"Oh."

"Yeah, 'oh.' Can you believe it? I took her to a back room after one of my bar gigs at NYU."

"Okay. And?"

"And. *And.* And, what? I never saw her again until I hired Gruesome, but she looked so different in her work clothes, I never put it together. We've been working together for the past five fucking years and she's kept it to herself this whole damned time!"

"I get that. But what's the big deal?"

"*What's the big deal?!*" I shout and finish off my beer. "I thought we were starting something, you know—real—and I just figured this out. She never told me!" I push my chair back and stalk over to the fridge for another beer. "What kind of relationship is that?"

"I think I'm getting the picture."

"Just what's that supposed to mean, asshole?"

"At the risk of making you even madder, I believe that you're falling for Rose and you feel betrayed."

"Damn straight, I feel betrayed! Wouldn't you?"

"Well, since I wouldn't forget someone after sleeping with them, I don't think I would be in this particular situation."

"Screw you."

"Seems to me that's what got you into this predicament in the first place," Dan says with a smirk.

"I don't need this shit. I'm leaving."

I go to stand, but Dan puts his hand on my arm. "Cole, stay. I want to help, really I do. I'm trying to understand. Are you mad because you had sex with Rose and she didn't remind you of it when you hired her firm?"

"That's part of it," I admit as I return to my chair. Opening my new beer, I continue, "It's also that she's been playing this 'I can't sleep with a client' bullshit, which makes no sense considering we've already had sex. Plus, she keeps harping on about how important honesty is to her, but she kept this from me. That's a pretty big lie in my book."

"Well, it's a lie by omission."

"Yeah, and she changed her last name. For all I know, she did it to keep me in the dark. I'm sure she's been laughing at me behind my back with her girlfriends for all these years, just like Steffy did to me in high school."

As I pause to take another sip of my beer, Dan jumps in. "From my perspective, you have an easy solution to all of this."

"Really? What, 'cause I don't see it."

"Back away from her. Dump her lying ass and tell Greta you want a new account rep."

I stare at my friend. His words simply do not compute. "Dump her?"

"That's what I said. Problem solved." He snaps his fingers as emphasis.

The possibility of not seeing Rose again, of not hearing her laugh, of not listening to her newest ingenious publicity strategy, of not touching her, makes me physically ill.

"I can't do that," I whisper.

Dan leans in. "What was that?"

"I can't. There's no way I can dump her."

"Why not?

I pick up my beer and bring it to my lips, but then put it down without taking a sip. "She's different, Dan," I say. "At least that's what I thought. But it turns out she was just another random chick that I picked up."

"We're finally getting somewhere." He pauses. "You slept with her like ten years ago. Don't you think you both might have changed since then?"

When I don't say anything, he continues. "Cole, do you like her? Do you like the woman that you know her to be now?"

"Yes," I say, picking at the label on my bottle. "She's funny, cute, smart and very sweet."

"Does she ever bring up your past, how should I put this . . . indiscretions? If I'm right, she's had to listen to quite a few of the groupies you've dumped over the past five years."

My eyes fall to the floor. "No. She's only ever mentioned them to me in a professional context, and not since we . . . uhm, started this quasi-dating thing we're doing. Her only objection has been Gruesome's non-fraternization policy."

"So what I'm getting is that you like Rose. More than any other woman since that cheerleader in high school. Do you think Rose is using you as a placeholder like that girl did?"

My lips pull back and I shake my head. "No way."

He nods. "Okay." He brings his beer to his lips. After a moment, he continues, "So you think she broke your trust by not telling you that you had sex with her years ago."

"And by insisting on total honesty between us. I believe her exact words were 'if I ever get the whiff of a lie, I'm done.'"

"So you're being held to a higher standard than she holds herself to. Right?"

I mull over his last comment, feeling my anger draining away. "And I don't like people laughing at me behind my back." Even as the words leave my mouth, they sound stupid.

"Cole, think about it. Do you really believe that she's snickering with her girlfriends about how you don't remember having sex with her? If anything, she's probably deeply hurt by the fact that you didn't remember."

"Shit." I hang my head and run a hand through my hair.

"So, who are you truly mad at?"

I ponder his question for a full minute. "I've been a jerk," I admit. This sucks.

Dan nods his head. "Do you want to date her?"

For some reason, I find myself thinking about how she cried for me last night. No one outside of my family has ever expressed feelings like that for me. The chemistry between us is like nothing I've ever experienced, and I can't deny it's because there's so much more than a physical connection between us.

"Yes. I do." Fuck.

Dan's look of surprise mirrors my own. "Welcome to the wonderful world of relationships, my man." He brings his bottle to mine and taps the neck.

"You know how confused you're feeling right now? Well, multiply that by one hundred, because that's how you're going to feel from now on. You're in for a wild ride."

"That is, if Rose will have me," I say, feeling my stomach sink. "I said some pretty harsh things to her."

"I'm sure you did."

"And we'll have to work though these trust issues."

"Yes, you will."

"How do I do this? I've never had a girlfriend before."

"That's true. Well, what do you think about this?" Dan and I talk and strategize over the next hour while eating some heavy-duty sandwiches. I pray that Rose wants to try again with me.

On my way out, I give him a fist bump. "You missed your calling. You should've been a shrink. Give my love to Suzanne and Emma."

On my way home to lay my soul bare to Rose, I stop by a florist shop to pick up the three-dozen roses I'd ordered. Back at my house, I scramble out of my car, rubbing my sweaty palms on my jeans. Under my breath, I mutter, *"Please don't hate me for what I said earlier, Ro."*

Fortified with the flowers and Dan's advice, I take a deep breath and go in the front door. The house is still.

The patio is empty.

The guest room is empty.

My bedroom is empty.

The kitchen is empty.

"Rose!" I scream, racing throughout the house. She doesn't respond.

She's gone.

Fourteen

I RACE BACK INTO MY CAR AND drive to Rose's place in Venice. No lights are on inside her house, but she has to be there, right? I shudder thinking of her returning here after the robbery and break-in. It's not safe. *She has to be safe.*

I stay in my car for a long time, running through the strategy that Dan and I discussed earlier. Rehearsing. I need this second chance with Rose. Or am I already on my third chance?

Get a grip, Cole. It's time. Gulping down air, I grab the roses and walk toward the front steps, more anxious than pre-show jitters.

From off to my right, I hear, "Uh-oh, honey. What are you trying to make up for with all them roses?"

I quirk my lips and turn to see Rose's neighbor in her yard. Walking over to her, I say, "Nice to see you again, Grandma Gertie. I brought these for Rose. Do you know if she's home?"

Nodding, she replies, "I saw her walk in a little while ago. You must've done something real bad if you need that many flowers."

"Let's just say I'm hoping they'll get me out of the doghouse." I wink at the older woman and turn back toward Rose's house.

"Remember what I told you before, young man. You hurt her and you'll be answering to me!"

"Got it."

All too soon, I'm at Rose's front door. Trying to summon the courage to ring the bell, I hear Gertie follow up with, "Lordy, you must've done a doozie. Now ring that bell and ask her for forgiveness, Hot Stuff!"

Damn. If I linger any longer, Grandma Gertie will alert the whole neighborhood. I turn and give her a slight wave and a wan smile before returning my attention to the door. It's time.

I press the doorbell and wait. Nothing. I press it again and then follow up with a knock. She doesn't answer the door, but I swear I hear a noise inside. I repeat the process. From inside the house, she says, "Who is it?"

Well, that's good. She's being cautious following the break-in, as she should be. "It's me, Rose. I'd like to talk with you." I wait a beat. "Please."

"Cole?"

"Yes. Can we talk?"

"You've said enough."

"Rose, please give me five minutes. I'll leave you alone, forever if you wish, after that. I just want five minutes."

My breathing becomes shallower while I wait for her to respond.

Finally, she unlocks the deadbolt. Air fills my lungs.

The door opens slowly. *Think, Cole.* What the fuck was I going to say to her? My mind blanks, and I forget everything I discussed with Dan. Rose stands at the threshold, not stepping back to allow me to enter. She looks both defiant and deflated. Oh Christ, how can I make this better?

"Here," pops out of my mouth, and I thrust the bouquet at her face. She takes a startled step backward to avoid being hit with them. *Real smooth, Cole.* My palms are damp and I can't conjure up one word to say to her.

"You have four minutes, thirty seconds." She stands her ground, chin up, arms at her side. She doesn't take the roses.

Don't fuck this up again, don't fuck this up again, don't fuck this up again. I close my eyes to block out the sight of what my anger did to her, then slowly open them.

"Rose," I start. "I selected these for you. The light pink ones represent the past—I am so sorry that I let you slip away after our night in college. I was a complete fool. The yellow ones represent the present—I can't express how awful I feel for what I said to you earlier, and I promise to work to make it right, if you'll have me. The orange ones represent the future—the future I hope we'll have together, because I've relied on you for so long but only now am realizing how much I need you in my life."

Rose stands before me, head bowed toward the flowers. I'm still holding the bouquet in my sweaty hands. "Rose," I plead, shaking the flowers.

She looks up at me, but I can't read her expression. Her face is a mask. She finally reaches out and takes the flowers from me, careful not to touch my hands. Well, that's something, I guess.

She stands there in the doorway, holding the roses, for what seems like an eternity. Then she takes a deep breath and steps back, motioning for me to come inside.

I enter her place. The one I was helping her clean up only yesterday. After closing the front door, I sit down on the couch. Why is it so easy to write a three-minute song, yet so difficult to have an honest conversation with a woman who means this much to me?

She enters the kitchen and puts the flowers into vases. She places the yellow ones on the dining room table and brings the pink ones with her into the living room. The orange ones stay in the kitchen. That doesn't bode well. I swallow hard.

Taking a seat opposite me, Rose says, "Cole, I appreciate that you came by to make sure I'm okay, but I think it would be best if we kept our relationship strictly professional from now on."

Shit. I am not going to let her do this to us. I just found her—okay, again—and I know she feels something for me. She obviously did back at NYU, otherwise she wouldn't have slept with me all those years ago. And the way she responded to me this morning makes me even more convinced that she feels a connection. I need to unlock those feelings again before I lose my chance with her forever.

"I came over here because I realized what an ass I had been to you, and I wanted to make things right. I went back to my house, where I'd left you without a car, and found it empty. That killed me."

Rose sits there, looking at those damn roses. Since she's not telling me to shut up, I blunder forward. "I would like to understand why you didn't say anything to me about our night in college," I press. I wish I could touch her, hold her hand even, but while she's just across the coffee table from me, she might as well be on a solitary island.

"Cole, that was a lifetime ago. What would you have had me do? Blurt it out in Greta's office five years ago? I was relatively new to her company, and all her employees are made very aware of her strict non-fraternization policy. I figured you wouldn't remember me, and I was right. When you didn't recognize me, I breathed a sigh of relief that I wouldn't have to leave my dream job."

"I get that, Rose, I really do. We were both young and excited to be starting our careers. I am so sorry that I didn't recognize you." Now that Dan pointed out my stupidity to me, my heart literally hurts for how that must have wounded her. "But what about recently? When you knew my interest in you had become personal?"

"I didn't know what to do. You obviously had no recollection even after we kissed a few times, so I figured you'd never remember. I almost told you last night, but ..."

"Honesty isn't always easy."

"Yeah." Rose is still staring at the damn flowers. "Look, I meant what I said. We need to keep our relationship professional."

"I think that ship has sailed, Ro." Her lips rise slightly. I'm not sure if it's because of my choice of words or my use of her nickname. I choose to believe the latter. "May I ask what happened to Bloomer? It was the last name you gave me that night ..."

Rose's face falls and her mask seems to be fraying a bit around the edges. "Greta asked me to use a different last name when I started with her. She thought 'Rose Bloomer' was too cutesy. In order to be taken seriously as a female publicist, she said that I needed to be perceived as powerful in every way. So, I changed my professional name to Rose Morgan."

"I take it Greta VonStein is not her real name either?"

Rose shrugs. "I never asked, but I doubt it."

Needing to lighten up the mood and maybe get through her defenses, I say, "What do you think she's hiding? Maybe her real name is Ernestine Futterman?"

Rose laughs. I'm so happy to hear it, I join her. "Thanks, I needed that." She pauses. "Would you like a drink? I haven't been to the grocery store, though, so all I have is water. Or coffee or tea."

"Water would be great, thank you." Relief washes over me. If she's offering me a drink, I've survived the five-minute deadline. We still have a lot to discuss.

She sets down our water glasses and reclaims her chair across from me. At least I can see she has relaxed somewhat. My next question erases any goodwill I might have garnered. "Is Morgan your Mom's maiden name?"

"No," she responds. Her eyes turn stormy and dart back to those damn flowers.

What did I say? "May I ask how you chose Morgan?"

Rose is quiet for a bit, struggling to tell me whatever the story is behind the name. What could it be? Did she pick a name out of thin air? No, that wouldn't make her squirm like this. *Oh my God, what if she's married?* That can't be it. If she was ever married, she's not now. She's not the type to cheat.

"It's a long story, Cole."

"Ro, I would like to hear it if you're willing to share it with me." My fertile imagination is conjuring up all sorts of wild possibilities. I'm better off knowing the truth. She seems determined not to open up, so I decide to circle back to her last name later.

Sighing, I continue. "Listen, you told me last night that you wouldn't stand for any lies. I have to admit, that's one of the reasons why I went off earlier. I felt you had lied to me by not telling me about our night together. Or your real last name. I want us to have a chance, but that'll only happen if we're really honest with each other."

"I didn't see that as a lie. I'm sure there's plenty in your past that I don't know about."

"But this was directly about us."

"I didn't think it was my responsibility to fill in any blanks in your bad memory."

"Touché." We both take sips of our waters. This intense honesty shit certainly takes a toll.

Rose puts her glass down on the coffee table with a definitive clink. "I chose Morgan because I was engaged to Chris Morgan before I moved to Los Angeles."

Quietly, I place my glass alongside hers and look at her face. The mask has disappeared, and her eyes are full of sorrow. "What happened? Didn't he want to move to California?" I want to hold her, but I don't dare. Not yet. What man who was lucky enough to get this woman to say *yes* wouldn't have moved heaven and earth to keep her happy?

"Well, no, he didn't. But that's not why we didn't get married."

She collects her thoughts in silence, her fingers playing with her blue beaded earrings, then lets out a long sigh and starts speaking. "I met Chris when we were both sophomores at NYU, and we began dating right away. Senior year we lived together off campus in an apartment. We got engaged over winter break, and everything was great." Rose offers a sad smile while rubbing the ring finger on her left hand.

"Chris was an accounting major, and got several offers at big firms in New York City. I, of course, wanted to become a publicist. Most of the jobs I applied for were in New York, but I also sent in an application to Greta, never thinking she would grant me an interview. Well, she did. And, as you know, she offered me this job." She takes another sip of water.

"Chris and I had a series of fights about this. He didn't want to move out here at all. I gladly would have stayed on the East Coast, but I hadn't gotten any job offers out there. After one particularly bad fight, he said, 'I need some air,' and stormed out of the apartment. A few minutes later, I heard tires squealing and a big crash. I ran outside to see that a car had hit Chris. He died in the ambulance on the way to the hospital."

"Oh my God, Rose."

Those were the very same words I said to her earlier today before peeling out of my driveway. I can't even imagine how gutted that must have made her feel. No longer able to stay away, I rush over to her. Landing on my knees by her chair, I put my arms around her waist and hold her. She's quietly sobbing, and I'm only slightly surprised that my cheeks are wet, too.

"That was nearly seven and a half years ago. I've made a good life for myself out here. My job's been my lifeline." She continues to rub her empty finger.

A sudden realization hits me like a wrecking ball. I kiss her finger. "They stole your engagement ring, didn't they?"

Rose sniffs. "It was a starter ring, as Chris liked to call it. He promised to get me a bigger ring once we were both settled in our careers."

"You wouldn't have wanted to trade up, would you?"

She smiles wistfully at me. "No," she murmurs.

I make a mental note to check in with the police about this particular piece of jewelry. Hopefully the fuckers who stole the ring will pawn it, giving me the chance to buy it back for her.

Suddenly, it makes sense to me. Rose's single-minded focus on her career, her eighty-hour work weeks. Maybe even the way she dresses and wears her hair. They're all the result of losing her fiancé in such a horrible way. She's essentially been hiding in plain sight. Existing but not fully living. Needing to be in control of her life because of this horrible thing that was so out of her control. Gruesome's just a convenient excuse.

Still on my knees, I hold her tightly around her thighs. I need her to know she's not alone anymore. That it's okay for her to come out of her shell. Losing my mother was the hardest thing that ever happened to me. I can't imagine what her loss felt like. I'm grieving for the young woman who was so devastated. For the woman who hasn't really been living for over seven years.

But there's something else, too. Before I knew about Rose's past, I wanted to help her unleash a little. Now that feeling is so much more powerful. I want to help her laugh and enjoy life. I want to be the one who helps usher Rose *Bloomer* back into the world.

Her hand slips to the back of my neck, stroking my hair. I wonder if she's been with any men since moving to LA. Something tells me that she has not. A sense of pride surges through me because, despite all my failings, she's clearly thinking about letting me re-enter her life.

Sitting back on my heels, I rest my hands on her knees and look up at her. I give her a watery smile, and she returns it with one of her own. "You are a beautiful woman, Rose. Inside and out. I want to help you show the world how amazing you are."

She blinks, slowly. "I'm not that type of woman. I like to be in the background."

With her innate spirit getting ready to soar, she won't remain a wallflower for much longer. "I beg to differ, but there's no rush. I'm honored to share this journey with you." I reach up and cup her cheek, watching as she swallows. Wrapping my hand around the back of her head, I pull her toward me. Right before our lips touch, I whisper, "I'm not going anywhere, if you'll have me."

The kiss is soft and gentle. Memorizing her with my lips, I kiss her mouth, nose, chin, and eyelids. My hands similarly try to imprint her body, from her neck to her shoulders and down her back. She has to understand I'm serious about having a relationship with her.

And she tells me without words that she wants me in her life, too. Her hands roam up and down my arms and tousle my hair. She kisses her way from my lips to my ear, lightly sucking on my lobe. Hope sparks in my chest.

The kiss ends and we hold each other for a while. We're helping each other through the bad times, just like Aunt Doreen said at Mom's funeral. I pull back and look into her eyes. "You look tired," I say.

"It's been another long day." She is the mistress of understatement.

"Yes, it sure has, but we both need to eat. Why don't we order dinner in?"

"That sounds good. Chinese?"

Soon, we're stuffed on eggrolls, sweet and sour shrimp, orange chicken and lo mein. Rose is trying to hide her yawns as she puts the last carton into the refrigerator. Calmness envelops us after this morning's storm.

"Ro, it's late. We're both exhausted. Can I crash here and drive you to Greta's in the morning?" I pray I'm not pushing my luck, but I need to be with her. Even if that means sleeping on the sofa.

"You don't have to do that. I can make it to the office."

"I know you're capable of using public transportation, but I'm offering you a more comfortable ride. I'd like to stay here, on the couch, to make sure you're safe tonight. I can drive you in the morning, no problem, before going back to my house to change for the gym. You should have your car back by tomorrow afternoon, right?"

"Yes, that's what the police said. Cole, I don't want to put you out. You have a comfortable bed at home . . ."

"I want to be where you are." I say, cutting her off. I reach over to the orange roses and pluck one from its vase. Handing it to her, I lower my voice and say, "Please?"

Rose looks up at me and a single tear escapes her eye. I swipe the drop away with my thumb and lean in to kiss its trail. Stepping back, I guide her toward her bedroom. She places the orange rose on her nightstand, grabs something from her dresser and disappears into the bathroom.

I sag, recognizing she's allowing me to stay. Today has been emotionally charged, to say the least. I'm so sad for what Rose has had to live through, but proud of the strong woman she has become as a result.

Rose returns to the bedroom in her nightshirt, looking like she may pass out on her feet.

Turning down the quilt, I pat the bed. "I'll tuck you in and head out to the sofa."

"No."

No, what? Don't tuck her in, don't sleep on the sofa, or don't stay at her place? "What do you want?" I ask. *Please don't kick my sorry ass out.*

She walks over to me and takes my hand. "Please stay with me. Could you hold me tonight?"

"I would love to," I reply honestly. "Thank you, my sweet Rose."

After I strip down to my boxer-briefs, we both climb into bed. I wrap my arms around her. Soon her breathing evens out in slumber.

I lie awake for a long time, mulling over everything she shared with me today, marveling at her trust in me. I also keep probing my memory for any shreds of our one night together, but all I come up with is her birthmark. Which I hope to become reacquainted with soon. Selfishly, I look forward to reigniting her passion. Before my thoughts can wander any farther down that path, I follow Rose into sleep.

Fifteen

I'M ROUSED FROM A DEEP SLEEP BY Rose's squirming under my hand. More specifically, Rose's plump boob being pushed into my palm. And that's not all. My leg is intertwined with hers. I'm spooning her, holding her nightshirt-covered boob in my hand, and my cock is already at attention.

I jerk fully awake, my eyes flying open, and look over at the beautiful woman lying next to me. Her back is to my front, so I can't tell if she's awake yet or unconsciously responding to my nearness.

My eyes dart to the clock. It's almost six, so I figure we have about thirty minutes before she'll have to get up to get ready for work. I'm going to need hours to celebrate our second first time. But, I can use these precious few minutes to make her morning unforgettable. I've never before thought of a woman's pleasure to the exclusion of my own, but that's what she does to me.

I begin by kneading her boob under my palm. Plump and relax, plump and relax. Once again, I marvel at how perfectly it fills up my hand. Moving my ministrations to her nipple, I lightly stroke it with my thumb. My forefinger joins in on that action, rolling her nipple as it forms a tight bud.

Rose moans and arches her back, which puts her ass in direct contact with my cock. I tighten my leg over hers to keep her in place, ignoring my body's pleas.

Leaning up and over her, I kiss her neck. Her protestations about kissing before brushing our teeth in the morning pop into my head. When was that? Only yesterday? So much has happened since then that it feels like eons ago.

I continue my assault by moving my lips down to her shoulder and my hand down toward her waist. Her sharp intake of breath alerts me to the fact that she has joined me in the land of the conscious. I hope she's enjoying the sexual haze that surrounds her. "Pleasant dreams?" I murmur.

"Um huh."

"This morning is for you, Ro."

In response, she moans. I smile against her body and continue with my exploration, turning her onto her back. Her whole body is primed and ready for me, but this morning is all about her. Of course, my traitorous cock begs me to reconsider.

I reach down and grab the hem of her nightshirt, lifting it up and over her head. Her curves are even more delicious than Fantasy Rose's. Taking one nipple in my mouth and the other in my hand, I settle my body between her legs. My underwear helps keep my throbbing cock outside of her pussy. She, however, didn't sleep with any. Thank fuck I wasn't aware of that last night or I wouldn't have slept a wink.

"Gorgeous."

While I suckle, she moans softly, arching her back again. Oh yeah. Still strumming her nipples with both of my hands, I kiss my way down her body. I pay special attention to her bellybutton, which makes her squirm. From my current location at her stomach I smell her arousal, which turns me on even more. Finally, I can't hold back any longer. I bring my mouth to her lower lips while keeping my hands on her nipples.

"Cole. Oh, mmmm."

She smells amazing. My tongue runs over her wet folds, lapping up her juices, which already have started to flow. "So sweet, Rose."

The fact that she's this turned on fuels my desire to make her experience mind-blowing. I want her to crave my body as much as I crave hers.

I circle around her pussy, skimming over her clit but not giving it any direct stimulation just yet. My tongue makes its way to her entrance and dips in, earning another moan and back arch. I slowly work my way to her clit, plucking her nipples all the while. When I glance up, her eyes are closed and she's biting her bottom lip. Her hands are fisted in the quilt. How I love making this woman writhe.

Finally, I seize upon her clit and give it the attention it's demanding. I also plunge one finger into her warmth, searching for the rough patch. Damn, she's tight around my finger. Her lower body undulates with my rhythm. Her nipple strains under my other hand. Slowly, I insert a second digit into her, thrusting my fingers in and out in a rhythm dictated by my cock. I keep up my assault until I feel her body tense.

Pulling back inches from her clit, I demand, "Come for me, Rose."

Returning to circle that nubbin with my tongue, I press her G spot and flick her nipple to give her a short burst of pain. She clenches around my fingers and spasms beautifully, emitting a low groan of pleasure. I don't stop my onslaught until her orgasm subsides. Fuck, I want to plunge into her so badly.

Instead, I climb up her body and cup her face in my hands. Her eyes look dazed. The knowledge that I was the one who put that look on her face is better than any standing ovation. Careful not to rest on top of her for fear that my cock would ignore my direct order to stay away from her pussy, I slide my body to her side.

Rose's arms encircle my neck and she plants light kisses on my pecs. "Cole, that was the best wake-up call ever."

I chuckle against her hair, ignoring my lower body's desperate entreaties, and stroke her perspiration-covered back.

BEEP! BEEP! BEEP! The alarm clock goes off, startling us both and effectively ending her afterglow. I give her a swift kiss on the lips. "You'd better get ready for work. I'll drive you over and then hit the gym. Okay?"

"Yeah. But what about you?" She says, looking directly at my straining underwear.

"Don't worry, sweetheart. You'll take care of him later. I'm really looking forward to our second first time." I pull her in for another, longer kiss, give her a hug and then smack her on the ass. "Now, it's time for you to get up."

She giggles and gets out of bed, but she stops at the doorway, turns and races back to me. Leaning down, she kisses my cock through my boxer-briefs and says, "Looking forward to it!" She gives me a cheeky wink and leaves the bedroom.

Thank fuck we made it through yesterday.

A few hours and one wishing-it-was-hers-and-not-my-own hand job later, I'm sitting in the studio getting ready to record my third album. All in all, I'm pretty pleased with myself. It's barely noon, and I've already worked out with my trainer in an effort to neutralize my recent dinners, ordered an alarm system to be installed at Rose's house this afternoon and contacted the police about Rose's stolen engagement ring. It doesn't hurt that I pretty much feel like the King of the World after the way Rose responded to me in bed earlier.

Jon, my A&R rep, pops his head into the studio. "Ready to go, Cole?"

"Yeah. It's been a long time." After my second album dropped, I went on an extended tour to promote it. Then Mom passed away, and it took me a while to be ready to work again.

As soon as I step into the live room, the concept of time seems to vanish. Drums, bass and lead guitar already have been recorded by studio musicians. I spend a few hours laying down the piano tracks for "No One to Hold" and a couple of other songs on the album.

Damn, I miss Mom. I would love to talk with her about this song . . . and about Rose. I'm pretty sure she'd be excited that we're getting together. At least I think we're getting together.

A little while later, I'm in the control room listening to the playback. The door opens and my manager Russell walks into the room. "Hey, Cole. Good to see you back in the studio. How'd it feel?"

"Amazing."

Russell quirks a smile at my enthusiasm. He understands. Music is in my blood. "Great, man. Glad that you're back in here."

"Me too," I reply.

"I stopped by to let you know I lined up most of the same group of musicians from your previous two tours for the world tour. They're stoked. I did have to replace the lead guitarist, though. His girlfriend's pregnant and he wants to stay home with her. I was able to book Zed, so I thought you'd be good with him."

I nod. "I understand. Zed's good, and I'm sure he'll get along with everyone. Thanks."

The musicians I tour with are a good bunch, and Zed will certainly add some new punch. It'll be fun going on tour with them. And Rose. As my publicist, I'm going to insist that she travel with me. I glance at my watch—it's already well into the afternoon—and shoot her a quick text checking on her car while Russell listens to what's been recorded so far.

"Well, I'll let you get back to it."

Hours pass quickly. More recording, listening, making small adjustments. The album is coming together. I'm pumped to be recording again.

When I leave the control room, Jon and Russell are high fiving in the hallway, which must be a good sign. Russell says, "You've got another winner there, Cole."

"Thanks. From your mouth."

The sound engineer joins us in the hall. "What are you up to tonight, Cole? Want to go out and celebrate? And by celebrate I mean drink too much, dance a little and pick up the hottest chicks in the place?" The producer and recording engineer give each other fist bumps before turning back to look at me.

I smile at them. Before, I would have jumped at the offer. Hell, I would have been the one who suggested it. But now I only want to spend time with Rose. Get to know her from the inside out. My lips twitch at that thought.

I address the sound engineer. "As tempting as that sounds, Sam, I can't tonight. You go for the both of us."

"What's up? You've never turned down a good time before."

"Got plans, man." He snorts and turns away, muttering about looking for another wingman.

Russell's sharp eyes bore into mine. "Plans as in a date?"

I want to keep my relationship with Rose to myself. Of course, my brother and Dad know, as do Dan, Suzanne, Jessie and Amanda, but that's more than enough people who are clued in. I don't want her to lose her job because of me.

"Just getting together with Dan and his family. You know, I'm the godfather." I puff up with pride.

Russell slaps me on the back. "Well, have a good time. See you back here tomorrow."

After seeing Russell out of the studio and making sure everything is ready for tomorrow's session, I grab my cell. A text is waiting for me from Rose: *Car won't be ready until tomorrow. ☹ I'll catch the bus. Chat later.* The text was sent well over an hour ago. Where did the time go?

I dial Rose's number and listen as it rings. And rings. And rings. I send her a text: *Where are you? I'll pick you up now.*

While I'm waiting for her to reply, I check my other messages. Nothing from the police, but her alarm system has been installed, thanks to her landlord's cooperation. Good. My new message alert appears, indicating that Rose has responded. *On bus now. Be home soon. Hope you had a good day.*

Well, this sucks. But if I can't drive her to her house, I certainly can meet her there. And bring dinner. I grab my keys.

"Hiya, Hot Stuff!"

"Hello, Grandma Gertie," I call over my shoulder.

"Guess them flowers did the trick."

I turn and give Rose's neighbor a huge smile. Lifting up the dinner bag, I nod and reply, "Now it's time for dinner."

"Nice dimple you've got there. Well, you two enjoy!"

I'm still smiling as I ring the bell. Rose answers almost immediately.

"Cole. I wasn't expecting you."

"Well, I was in the neighborhood and thought we could enjoy dinner." I peer into the house and tease, "Unless you're hiding some other guy?"

She giggles, "I just shooed him out the back door." She gestures toward the back of her house, then shakes her head and says, "Come in."

Stealing a quick kiss, I go directly to her kitchen and we begin taking out the dinner containers. My stomach loudly tells us that it's been way too long since I ate.

After we've finished, Rose mentions the alarm system. "I can only imagine that the new alarm system is your handiwork. I sincerely doubt my landlord would have been so kind. Thank you."

"If you insist on staying here, I want to know you're protected."

"It was very kind. And it will make my advertisement that much more enticing."

Confused, I ask, "What advertisement?"

She's looking down, which I learned early on from working with her is never a good sign. It's one of her tells—indicating she thinks I'm not going to like what she has to say.

"Tommy sent me a text saying that he's moving out immediately. Not that I blame him." She shakes her head. "He doesn't think one of his exes wrote that on my windshield, either."

The thought of Rose spending any amount of time in this neighborhood alone, even with my new state-of-the-art alarm system, spikes my blood pressure. My need to protect her is shocking in its intensity. "Move in with me."

Rose gives a half-hearted laugh. "Cole. Really. No."

"No? Why not? It's the perfect solution. I won't even charge you rent."

"No."

"Stop being stubborn, woman. This area isn't safe."

In a transparent effort to calm me down, she grabs both of my hands. "Listen, Cole. We're just starting to date, or whatever we want to call what we're doing. Besides, single women live here and they're fine. This is my home. I can stand on my own two feet."

Ignoring the first part of her objection, I bring her hands behind her back and step forward to remove any space between us. Without any effort, I lift her up, bringing her eyes level to mine. "But it's so much more fun if someone sweeps you off them, isn't it Ro?"

Her pupils dilate. I press my luck. "Say yes."

"I'm not a charity case."

"I know you're not. You're—" I can't complete my sentence. Exactly what is she to me? Lover? Not yet. My girlfriend? Not yet either. But she soon will be both.

While my thoughts have been running rampant, Rose wriggles in my arms. "Put me down, Cole."

I manage to keep her off the floor. "Only if you agree to move in with me."

"I don't need you, or any man, to take care of me. Put me down."

Ignoring her request, I continue, "You're stuck with me. You've already been dealing with me professionally for years. We are going to explore this new side of our relationship. And you're going to move in to my house."

"You're a pompous ass."

"Maybe." I grin at her. "But you like me."

"Put me down," she says again, but with decidedly less heat.

I comply. Once her feet are on the ground, I cup her cheek in my right hand. "I need to know that you're safe. You make me want to protect you, and I've never felt this way before."

"I haven't lived with a man, romantically, since Chris. I can't do this."

A rueful smile tugs at my lips. "Looks like this is unchartered territory for both of us. How will we know where this might lead if we don't give it a try?"

All this emotional honesty is exhausting. My need to kiss the woman in my arms is overwhelming. "Fair warning, I'm going to kiss you. And when I do, you're going to forget all the reasons why we shouldn't do this. You're going to believe in me, in us. For my part, I'm going to experience what it feels like to be completely connected with someone for the first time. Consider it the first kiss of the rest of our lives."

I dip my head toward hers, stroking her cheek with my thumb, and hear her inhale. Her eyes close. For a split second, I watch the pulse at the base of her neck escalate out of control, matching my own rhythm.

My lips softly brush against hers. Soon, I deepen the kiss, asking and receiving permission for my tongue to enter her mouth. To dance with hers. Releasing her wrists, I crush her soft body against my hardening one. Her arms snake around my neck.

I plant light kisses on her eyes and the tip of her nose, reveling in the feel of her. We are caught up in each other, lost in a place where time doesn't matter. This is Rose and me, and it's exactly where we belong.

Rose's nails drift up and down my back, making me shudder against her. My mouth returns to hers in a frenzy, which is more than matched by her passion. I sense her trust in me developing as I send my assurances through my lips.

I could carry her off to her bedroom right now and fuck her senseless, but I know she's not quite ready for that. I don't want just her body either, although I'm sure it will give me untold pleasure. No, I need more than that.

Rose moans softly when I break our kiss. We're still wrapped in each other's arms with no space between us. She looks up at me. Her ice blue eyes are filled with wonder, and it brings me untold pride that I put that look there. "You make me almost believe, Cole."

"I'll take that for now. Someday soon, you'll believe 100%. Right now, I'll believe 200%, for both of us."

She gives me a heartrending smile that almost brings me to my knees. "I'll try."

"That's all I ask. Now, will you pack your bags?"

"How about this? I'm not saying that I'm going to move in with you, but

I'll pack for a few days and we can reassess once things are sorted out here, okay?"

Grinning, I say, "I'll take this indefinite trial period as a first step."

Sixteen

THE REST OF THE WEEK PASSES IN A BLUR. I've been recording *Moving Forward Slowly* every day, and my whole team is happy with the progress. I've been in the zone in the studio. It feels so damn good to get back to making music.

But music isn't the only thing that feels damn good. Each evening, I get to come home to Rose. Each night, I get to sleep with her in my arms. All the guys at the studio have been making wisecracks, fishing for intel about why I'm so happy all the time. I haven't shared with any of them.

It's finally Friday. Given our schedules this week, I decided to wait until tonight for our second first time. Rose gets up too damned early to get to Gruesome's office, and I've been working too late at the studio.

The phone interrupts my thoughts. "Hey Dan. What's up?"

He starts right in. "Rose, that's what's up! We haven't talked since Sunday afternoon. All I got was that text that you were working things out with her, and then you fell off the planet."

I have to laugh. "Dan, man, sometimes you're worse than a teenage girl.

You need to get out of that house more—too much estrogen."

"You're an asshole, Cole. Tell me this: should I keep scouting out dates for you?"

This is the moment of truth. "No. Rose and I are . . . well, I'm not sure what we are, but we're trying to figure it out. I'm not interested in seeing anyone else."

"So, what's the deal?"

"She's moved in with me for an indefinite trial period."

"Excuse me? A what?"

"She's not ready to admit that she's moved in with me. I'm just happy I got her out of the shithole she was living in. Well, it wasn't that bad, but her place was broken into, for fuck's sake. Rose is fiercely independent, so it's hard for her to lean on people. She's had it rough."

"How so?"

Dan's my best friend, but this information is Rose's to share. I don't have the right to tell her secrets, even to him. "Let's say she worked really hard for everything."

"I'm glad she has you now, buddy. Am I assuming correctly that you are after more than just sex with her?"

"Yeah. Sex, I can get anywhere. With Rose, I want so much more."

"Oh boy." He makes the sound of a whip cracking.

"Don't worry, Dan, I'm following your example."

"Touché."

"Listen, I'd better get going. I have a few more things to do at the studio and then I'm meeting Rose at home." I leave off the part about my plans for tonight. "Give Suzanne and Emma my love."

"Will do. Let's try to get together this weekend."

"Sounds good. Text me. Bye."

I put in a few more hours on the album and then stop at a couple stores before heading home. I'm all set for Operation Rose.

It's no surprise I've beaten Rose home. My Rose works extraordinarily long hours, but even though she's usually so tired by 10 p.m. that she's nearly comatose, she loves her job.

Rose got her car back on Tuesday, which made her extremely happy and me much less so. For one, that car is a breakdown waiting to happen. Two, its return effectively eliminated my role as her chauffeur, which I loved despite having to leave at such an ungodly hour. Three, the cops still don't have any leads about who wrote the warning to her across the back window, which makes me uneasy. Fourth, and most importantly, it gives her the independence to leave at any time, which scares the shit out of me.

Shaking my head to clear my thoughts, I put dinner in the oven to stay warm and make my way to my bedroom. While Rose and I have been sharing this room all week, we've done little beyond sleeping. I haven't wanted to rush our second first time together. That fact alone makes me a little nervous. I haven't given sex a second thought since high school. It's been so easy for me to find a willing body whenever, wherever I wanted. But with Rose, everything's so different.

I begin by setting up the bathroom with candles. I take pink, yellow and orange roses and scatter their petals across the bed and floor. The lighting is perfectly dimmed, and the playlists created especially for tonight are set to broadcast over the speakers.

After doing a final check to ensure everything is to my liking, I go to the family room to wait for her to get home. I pick up the book she gave me, but it's too hard to concentrate. Needing a distraction, I set about putting a bottle of champagne on ice and selecting two glasses. I'm about to sit down and try to read more of the book when I hear her car pull up.

Our evening can finally get started.

Before she reaches the door, I open it. I suck in my breath; Rose is unbelievably gorgeous. Even with her hair in a ponytail, wearing glasses, blazer and skirt, I've never seen anyone so beautiful. *How did I miss her for years?*

"Welcome home, Ro," I whisper, removing her laptop case from her fingers. "You're a sight for sore eyes. Come here." I open my arms and she walks right into them.

After several moments pass, I pull back to look into her blue eyes and ask, "Want some champagne?"

"What are we celebrating?"

"Us."

"Oh."

I set about opening the chilled bottle. The cork pops with a loud flourish, causing her to giggle. "I love your giggle. Never stop."

"You make it easy to laugh. Thanks," she says, accepting the flute.

I pour a second glass and return to her side. "Come on, let's sit poolside. It's a beautiful night. Besides, I love seeing you blush in the moonlight."

On cue, Rose starts to blush, which is adorable.

Taking her hand, I lead us through the kitchen to the French doors and over to one of the wicker sofas positioned on the patio, poolside. I swipe at my phone, and jazz music fills the evening air. She sits down next to me, taking off her shoes. Frowning at the distance between us, I pull her onto my lap.

"Much better. Now, let me make a toast." She turns her face toward me with a look of anticipation in her eyes.

"Rose, tonight is about us. You and me. This week has been better than I ever imagined it could be. It's been wonderful sharing my home with you, waking up with you in my arms each morning. Tonight's our time to celebrate."

I bring my glass to hers and we clink them. I stop before taking a drink. "No, wait. I want to do this right."

Entwining my arm with hers, we sip our champagne from the other's flutes, laughing at the awkwardness of the gesture. Yet it feels so right. Enjoying the simple pleasure of being together out in the evening air, we finish our champagne.

After pouring each one of us a second glass, I dip a strawberry into mine. "Open," I command, and she instantly obeys.

I circle her lips with the strawberry before putting just the tip into her mouth. When she goes to bite it, I pull back, resting it on her plump bottom lip. Slowly, I push the berry back into her mouth, deeper this time, but I return it to her lip when she tries to close her teeth around it again. Her mouth forms a sensuous smile as her eyes turn a smoky blue.

Holding the fruit in front of her, I ask, "Do you want the strawberry?"

"Only if you want me to."

"Oh, I have every intention of letting you enjoy it. Suck," I order, inserting the berry deeper into her mouth. Her cheeks hollow as she does as instructed. She's staring at me with half-closed eyes while she fellates the strawberry. My cock expands at the sheer sensuality of the act.

"Now, tell me how it tastes."

Rose takes a bite of the berry and some of its juices dribble down her chin. "It's delicious, Cole. Unlike anything I've ever tasted before. Sweet yet tangy at the same time."

Her words do me in. I'm unable to contain my groan as I pull her into my embrace, my tongue flicking at the dripping strawberry juices, finally kissing her like my survival depends upon it which, I'm guessing, it does. Even lost in my own vortex of desire, I recognize that she's returning my kisses with an equal passion.

I want to be inside her this instant, but I have to wait before ushering her upstairs to the bedroom I've prepared for us. Anticipation is something that I've never felt any need to experience in the past, but I intend on putting it to the test tonight. I've forgotten our first time, so I'm determined to make this once twice as memorable.

With that single thought in mind, I pull back from Rose's swollen lips. Gently, I pull her hair free of the ponytail holder, running my fingers against her scalp. She moans and pushes her head back into my hands.

"I want you, Ro." She looks at me with eyes filled with desire. It takes all my strength to utter my next words. "Let's go eat. I have dinner in the oven for us."

"But I thought we would go upstairs." The fact that she's blushing while she essentially admits that she wants to have sex with me is delectable.

"We'll make it up there soon. We have all night. We both need to eat to get our strength up."

"Well, I guess you do have a point. I wouldn't want you conking out on me."

An amused sound escapes my lips. "Sweetheart, there's not a chance in hell of that happening. I'm concerned about your strength, not mine."

Smiling wickedly, she reaches forward and cups my cheek. "Can I have one more strawberry for the road?"

"Miss Bloomer, your wish is my command."

If I thought feeding her that first berry was difficult, this second one nearly unmans me. As I hold it for her, her tongue darts out and she licks it all over before taking a big bite. "You're a minx. Now, to the kitchen, woman. It's your turn to feed me."

We make our way toward the kitchen slowly, stopping every few steps to kiss, caress, stroke and tease each other's bodies. The scent of her arousal is heavy in the air. My cock is at full mast. By the time we reach the kitchen, I'm doing my damnedest to stop myself from laying her out across the table. Instead, I throw myself onto a chair, almost needing to sit on my hands to stop from touching her. The worst part is that she knows exactly what she's doing to me.

"Dinner's in the oven. Serve me."

"When did you get this bossy, Cole?"

"When a beautiful, barefoot woman entered my lair." In response, she giggles, which causes my cock to jump in her direction.

"Yes, Master," she quips as she sets about placing the hot dish onto the granite countertop and gathering the plates and utensils. I should help her, but if I get up now, I might lose the rest of my tenuous restraint.

From across the table, she spreads a placemat in front of me. In turn, I grab her wrists and look deeply into her eyes. Passion simmers beneath the surface of her gaze, and I intend to make it erupt before the main course is finished.

Anticipation.

Leaning forward, I look into her eyes, willing her lips to part. They do, prompting me to give her a smirk. We hold this position for a few moments while she stares at my lips, lightly panting.

I whisper, "Dinner."

Frustration flares from her eyes. She pivots and walks toward the counter, swaying slightly as if drunk. I offer her a light swat on her beautiful ass as she passes, which earns me a sassy look from over her shoulder. This woman challenges me at every turn, and I'm loving it.

While Rose is dishing up our meals, I rearrange the placemats so that they are side-by-side. I also move her chair next to mine, although I have little intention of letting her sit on it when I have a perfectly serviceable lap. Completing the atmosphere, I switch to my "foreplay" playlist via my phone. Luther Vandross starts to croon. Perfect.

Rose approaches the table with our plates. Realizing how I've rearranged the seating, she stops abruptly. I look up at her unapologetically. Accepting my unspoken challenge, she puts the dishes on the table according to my new seating chart. She approaches her chair and straightens her skirt before sitting down. I make a big production of placing her napkin on her lap and pouring us glasses of Pinot Grigio to go with our dinner of salmon with pasta and truffle oil.

"This looks delicious, Cole."

"It's one of my favorites, and not only because it's a pure aphrodisiac," I reply, placing my hand on her knee.

She smirks at me. "Not taking any chances tonight, huh?"

Running my hand under her skirt and up her thigh, I pitch my voice lower and say, "It's all about taking chances, Ro."

Her fork stills en route to her mouth, and she lets out a small gasp. For my part, I continue my exploration, toying with her panties. They need to come off. "Eat."

I enjoy a few forkfuls of the delicious dinner while my left hand plucks at the waistband of her panties.

"I can't eat while you're doing that to me," she objects.

"Then take them off." Seems like a reasonable solution to me. "Let me help you. Open your legs." Her compliance will show me that she trusts me. It's the moment of truth.

After a few seconds, Rose's legs open slightly. Not wasting any time, I turn her whole body toward mine, grab her panties on both sides and tug sharply, rending them in half. "I'll get you another pair." The look on her face is priceless.

"In fact, I don't think you need that chair either." I pluck her up and put her where I've wanted her all along, right on my lap. Her legs are on either side of mine; her back is resting against my chest. "Now we can eat."

I shovel in some of the delicious pasta. Of course, I finish my plate before she's even halfway done with hers. "Are you enjoying the dinner, Ro?"

"It's really good. Oh!" That last exclamation resulted from my fingers invading her sleek pussy. The tinkle of a utensil hitting the tile joins the dulcet tones of Sade.

"Tsk, tsk. You dropped your fork on the floor. Lucky for you, I don't seem to be using mine at the moment. But that means I'm going to have to feed you." It puts a wicked smile on my face when she arches up against me, lightly thrusting her hips.

"Okay," she responds with a small sigh.

"Good girl. Now open wide." Her upper lips part in anticipation of the pasta while I open her lower lips with my fingers, running my thumb over her clit. Her mouth closes and she leans back into me. "Rose, we're not leaving this table until you eat all of your dinner."

"I don't want food."

"What do you want?" I murmur, kissing her neck.

"You know," she sighs again.

"Yes, I do. And you'll have me. After dinner. Eat." Feeling how wet she is for me is killing me, but I need to know that she's as out of her mind for me as I am for her. She's not quite there yet.

She makes a frustrated noise, but obediently opens her mouth. I reward her with a few more bites of the salmon, moving my hand to her inner thigh. "Good?"

"Very."

I bring another bite to her lips, stroking her clit with my other hand. It's heady to have her at my mercy, but my straining erection is getting difficult to contain. "Just one more bite."

"Thank God. I can't stand much more of this torture."

"Good torture or bad torture?"

"The best."

"Right answer. Now finish your dinner."

She eats the last bite of pasta. I drop the fork, causing it to clatter on the plate. Rose jumps slightly, and I take advantage by kneading her boob through her blouse and plunging a finger into her opening.

"You're playing me like one of your instruments."

"Hmmm, do you like to be strummed like my guitar?" I pretend to play the intro to "Prowling."

"Oh, God." She pants. "Please."

"Please, what? Oh, I know. You want dessert."

"No," she groans. We're almost there. Maybe *she* is going to ravish *me*. Despite my body's insistence on fucking her senseless right now, I'm enjoying seducing her. It's a novelty.

"Yes, my dear, sweet Rose. There's a chocolate lava cake in the microwave and ice cream in the freezer. Now go get them for us." Despite my own body's protest, I stand her up and gently push her toward the appliance. Her unsteady footsteps bring a huge smile to my face.

"You're a menace."

"It'll be worth the wait, I promise."

She returns to the table with both the cake and ice cream. Instead of assuming the same position, she sits on my lap facing me this time. To complete my torture, she hikes up her skirt so that she's bare-assed on my thighs, with her legs dangling on either side of mine. "I think it's time for me to serve you," she murmurs, nuzzling my ear.

My cock is nearly bursting out of my pants, but I remember my buzzword. Anticipation. I may have anticipated us both out of a long first round.

She brings a spoon filled with the delicious dessert to my lips. "Open wide."

On a growl, I do, and she rewards me with a bite of cake and ice cream. It tastes good, but not as good as I know she does. It's time for me to regain control of this scenario.

Leisurely, I lean in and give her a kiss that promises everything. My fingers lower from her cheek to her boob and down to her slick pussy. I dip inside and then bring my finger to my mouth. "I prefer my dessert without a spoon."

She gasps and thrusts her hips on my cock, looking at me with eyes filled with passion.

"Cole."

"Yes."

I crush her trembling body to mine and kiss her like a starving man. Her kisses are no less passionate. I stand up and carry her upstairs to the bedroom. Yet another silent thanks goes out to my trainer. When I open the door, she takes a sharp inhale. The room does look romantic, if I do say so myself.

"You like?"

"It's perfect. Now, make love to me."

I place her on her feet and pull out my phone, changing the playlist to pure sex music, starting with Marvin Gaye. Then I make quick work of removing the remainder of her clothing. Her trembling fingers join mine in tearing the clothes off my body. At last, we're both naked.

"You are so beautiful, Ro." I run my finger across her collarbone. "Are you sure you want to do this? Because once I touch you again, that's it. I'm not letting you go. I'm going to make you scream my name all night. And when we wake up, I'm going to do it all over again. You're going to be all mine. Tell me you want this."

"I want this. I want you to make me feel again. Please."

Who am I to refuse such a pretty request?

Ruthlessly ignoring my own body's demands, I set about getting Rose even more aroused. I bring her to the edge of the bed and sit her down, getting on my knees between her thighs. "Your scent has been driving me out of my mind all night. Let me show you what you do to me."

I lean in and lick her clit, relishing her body's response. Although she stays quiet, her body bows toward me. I insert two fingers into her opening, feeling her spiral toward her climax. Within minutes, she's coming hard, clenching around my fingers.

I need to hear her say my name. To acknowledge who gave her that orgasm.

"Did you like that?"

"Oh God."

"I want you to scream my name when I make you come again. Every time. Got it?"

She looks down and bites her bottom lip. "I'm pretty quiet during, well, you know."

"I need to hear you. I need to know that I'm pleasing you." *Rose's pleasure is paramount.*

"If I promise you I'll try, will you join me on the bed?" she asks, scooting backward.

Smiling, I crawl next to her. "You are so special to me. Thank you for this second chance." I have no idea how I performed with her before, but I hope I wasn't so drunk that I was totally selfish. "Now, come here."

She turns to me and I suckle at her nipple while exploring her delicious curves with my hands. My need to be inside of her is driving me to be rough, but she doesn't seem to mind at all. She reaches down and strokes my cock, coating her fingers with my pre-cum.

"I need to be inside of you now," I growl.

"Yes."

I reach over to my night stand for a condom, and rip the packet open with my teeth. I roll it quickly over my straining cock. "I wanted our second first time to be sweet, but it's not going to be," I pant. "I can't hold back."

"Please."

I'm not sure what she's asking me for, but I'm beyond rational thought. I line up my cock with her opening and wrap her legs around my body. With a deep kiss, I inch into her tight, wet body.

"You feel amazing, Ro. Are you okay?" I know it's been a while for her. Years. It makes me proud that she chose me.

"You feel so good, Cole. You're so big."

I like the sound of that. I push forward until I'm seated all the way inside her. "So good," I murmur.

I still and wait for her to signal that she's gotten used to my cock. God, don't take long.

"Cole."

Yes! "Yes."

I begin to pump into her slick pussy, kissing her lips all the while. Moving my head downward, I suckle her nipples. My cock wants to explode, but it's more important that Rose is with me, so I reach between us and flick her clit. I'm rewarded with a long, quiet moan. She's almost there again.

As I desperately pound into her, her hips rise to meet my every thrust. Sweat is covering both our bodies. I look deep into her eyes. "Who is going to make you come, Rose?" I demand.

She groans in response.

"Say it. Tell me."

She remains silent. In response, I take a deep breath and stop my hips from moving. I want her to understand that this is important. She looks into my eyes and whispers, "You are."

"That's right. Now, scream my name." I pump into her tight pussy again, circling my hips and feel her shattering beneath me.

"Cole!"

If I had the muscle control, I would smile, but her scream has unleashed my own climax deep within her body. I shout her name as I release into her, milking every last bit of pleasure for both of us.

Once our bodies are no longer shuddering, I turn to her and brush a stray tendril of hair off her damp forehead. After a long pause, which I need to regain control over my mental faculties, I whisper into her ear, "You're amazing, my beautiful Rose. I love how you screamed my name."

"Cole, it's never been like this for me. Ever."

"Me either. And we're only getting started."

Seventeen

I WAKE BEFORE ROSE AND WATCH HER sleeping peacefully. Memories of our night together replay in my mind. Exploring her delicious body and beginning to learn what turns her on. Getting reacquainted with her flower birthmark. Mostly, however, I hear echoes of her screaming my name as she came. I'm a lucky man, and I'm determined to do everything possible not to fuck this up. Again.

Rose sighs in her sleep and turns onto her back. She pushes the sheet to her waist, exposing her glorious boobs to my ever eager gaze. An uncontrollable desire to suck on her nipple leads me to do just that. My fingers tease and reawaken her tiny bud, causing her back to arch off the bed. Sleepy ice blue eyes greet mine.

"Hello there," I offer before latching onto her nipple.

"Mmm, Cole. Good morning to you," she replies while reaching for my cock.

I grin at her. "It will be, Ro."

And it is.

SOMETIME LATER, WE'RE BACK in the kitchen, enjoying my signature omelets.

"Do you have anything on your to-do list today? Other than me, of course." I wink at her and am rewarded by her blush. I will never tire of that blush.

"I need to stop by my place and pick up my mail. Plus, I haven't talked with my mother in a bit, so I want to call her. I also need to check the web to see if there are any hits on you, Brandan or Jessie that I need to address."

"Is that all?" I ask with a chuckle.

Smiling, she bumps me with her shoulder. "It won't take that long."

"Good, because I need to hear you scream again."

"I thought you just did."

"That was ages ago, babe. I need constant reassurance."

"I'll see what I can do."

"You do that." I stand and start collecting our plates. "Why don't you go get on your computer while I clean up in here? Feel free to work in my office."

She gracefully rises from the table and gives me a lingering kiss. "Hopefully there won't be too much to deal with."

My eyes follow her every movement as she leaves the kitchen. Out of the blue, a song filters from my brain and I scramble to find my notebook to write it down. Oddly, it's come to me fully-formed, lyrics and music together. Seems like I have a new muse, and her name is Rose. Scrambling to capture the words and music, I make my way to my music room and begin to play the new tune on my piano. It's a song about forbidden love.

I'm lost in composing my new song, oblivious to the time. My stomach lets out a loud grumble, and I check the clock. It's nearly 3 p.m. No wonder I'm hungry. Why hasn't Rose sought me out? Well, I'm going to find her to rectify the situation.

My first stop is my office, but she's not in there. I check the living room, pool and even our bedroom. Still no sign of her. Her car's still in the driveway, so I know she has to be here somewhere. But where? On a whim, I go to the guestroom she stayed in the night her place was robbed. Bingo! She's on the bed with papers surrounding her.

"What's up?"

She looks up at me with a distracted look on her face. "Nothing."

"That was convincing. Let's try again: What's wrong?"

She sighs. "Something popped on Brandan. I just got the green light from Greta to act on it."

"What did The Ass do now?"

"He's not a bad guy, Cole. I meant what I said the other day."

"Right. Well, I bet Gruesome was happy she didn't have to lift a manicured fingernail." I move some papers so I can join her on the bed.

"Cole, she's trained me over the past seven years. Brandan's her client. As are you, I might point out."

"Yeah, but you're the brains behind her operation."

"You give me too much credit. No, she lands all the clients, and if I'm good at my job, it's because she's taught me what to do. I always run my strategies by her before executing them."

"Does she ever give you any feedback about your strategies? Or compliments, for that matter?" My need for her to get the recognition she deserves is foreign to me, yet I don't question it.

"She's been good to me."

Snorting, I reply, "Fine, let's drop it. What did he do?"

"Seems like he had a run-in with a paparazzi."

That's not something I can pin on his bad behavior. Sometimes the paparazzi are so pushy and rude in their quest to snap a photo. It doesn't matter to them if it's a good or bad shot, all that matters is whether they can sell it.

It's my turn to sigh. "What happened?"

"The photographer made snide comments about his DUI. But what really set him off was what the guy said about his sister."

"Ouch. That hurts."

"Not as much as the paparazzi's nose. Brandan broke it."

"I don't blame him." Sucks having to side with someone Jessie doesn't like. "So, what's your plan?"

"His sister got a video of the paparazzi's venomous verbal attack on Brandan. I plan on releasing the footage to the Hollywood gossip website. Let those guys and the web-o-sphere defend Brandan. As for the broken nose, he'll have to pay hospital bills, of course, but not before that photographer offers a public apology."

She moves some papers to her other side, and continues, "I need to get Brandan some positive publicity, though. I know we were talking about getting you back together with Jessie, but now I'm thinking of making her stand by him."

Jessie will *not* be happy about this development. Over the past week, Rose has been working behind the scenes to get my name linked with Jessie's again.

"I'm going to ask Jessie and Brandan if they're available to go out to a club tonight. They'll be out together and you can show up and cause a little scene. Jessie can stay with Brandan and send you packing. It will show the world that she supports him."

"What if I'm busy tonight? I hope I have a date." I remove her hand from her earring and bite her lobe.

Giggling, Rose replies, "You'll have to schedule it for a different evening."

"But I'm thinking that I'm going to be busy all night. My girlfriend has expectations."

There. I said it. I called her my girlfriend. I hold my breath to see her reaction.

Rose sucks in her breath and her eyes widen, but she doesn't contradict me. "You'll have to tell her to keep calm and learn patience."

I lean over and give her a possessive kiss. "Mine."

Rose gives me a preoccupied smile, which I detest. When I kiss my woman, I want her to lose every thought in her head. I bend down and claim her lips again. Lifting my head again, I notice that her eyes are dreamy. Much better.

"Send the texts now, and let's go eat lunch."

She offers me an adorably embarrassed smile, and it seems to take her a while to collect her thoughts. *Good.*

Standing beside her, I grin and wait patiently while she digs her cell phone out from under some papers. As soon as she sends off texts to Jessie and Brandan, she takes my hand. I pull her to her feet and maneuver her arms behind her back while pressing her fully against my body. I love how perfectly she fits me.

After a scorching kiss, we walk back to the kitchen hand-in-hand, and are greeted by the remnants of our breakfast and a sink full of pots and dishes. *Shit.* I was so involved with writing my new song that I never finished cleaning up. "Let's go out."

Rose raises an eyebrow at me, but doesn't comment on the mess. "How about we pick something up and eat at my place?"

"Afraid to be seen in public with me, Ro? Not to mention you're trying to pawn me off on an actress. You might be giving me a complex," I tease.

She laughs and responds, "I think your ego can handle it."

"You know how fragile we creative types can be."

With a smile, she offers, "How about we compromise? We can go out for pizza near my place and swing by there. I have to get my mail and Greta is sending a courier there with some of Brandan's paperwork from last night."

"Ever the negotiator, huh? How about I'll see you one pizza joint of my choosing and drive us to your place, then raise you a slow, hard fuck on a surface of your choosing over there." This is not meant to be a question.

"Well, since you put it ever so nicely, you're on." Her stomach rumbles in approval, which, like a yawn, causes mine to chime in loudly. We both fall into fits of laughter.

Ten minutes later we're seated in my favorite New York-style pizza place in California. The teen waitress starts throwing flirty looks my way while doing her damnedest to shoot Rose the evil eye behind my back.

"Don't look now, but I believe our waitress has the hots for you."

"Really? I didn't notice. Since I'm here with my publicist"—I stress the word *publicist*—"maybe I should see what she has to offer? After all, I'm about to be publicly dismissed by my starlet ex-girlfriend."

She glances at the waitress. "Well, if you're lucky, she might not be jailbait. I'll leave you to it."

The young waitress approaches our table. Ignoring my date, she flashes me a brilliant smile, which earns her one in return from me. I'm sure my dimple is getting into the action. Rose kicks me under the table, which only makes my smile broader.

After several moments of grinning at me, the waitress finally realizes that she hasn't taken our order. Clearing her throat, she addresses me. "Cole Manchester. I'm a huge fan! I've heard you come in here, but never when it's my shift. What can I do you for?"

I glance at Rose, who looks incredulous. I'm so used to this type of behavior that it barely registers anymore. I check her nametag and begin, "We're starving, Deanna. We've been working all day. Can you please bring us a pepperoni pizza and two bottled waters?"

"Sure thing, Mr. Manchester. I'll get this for you right away. Let me know if there's something else I can do for you. Anything." With that, she licks her lips and walks toward the kitchen, never once checking in with Rose. Oh boy. Cautiously, I glance at Rose.

"You seriously deal with this all the time?"

I shrug. What can I say? Since Rose is now my girlfriend, she's going to get a first-hand glimpse at this type of behavior. This was pretty tame, actually. Thank fuck she didn't ask me to sign her tits.

"This place is usually pretty good since I'm sort of a regular. I don't get harassed too much when I come in here."

"Good to know," she says dryly.

"Why, Miss Bloomer, are you jealous?"

"Of course not!" She looks affronted, but I know it's just a façade. "It's just so weird. For me, that is. I deal with publicity all the time, but usually from behind the scenes." She tips her head toward the waitress. "Does that sort of thing bother you?"

"They're my fans. They're the reason I'm able to make a living playing music and writing songs. The day they stop acting like this will be the beginning of the end of my career. In that sense, I'm grateful for their stares, stutters and innuendos. I hope you'll get used to it, too." I want to grab her hand, but I know we can't do that in public. Not yet, anyway.

"I know you're right. I did admire how you addressed her by name to make her feel special. Honestly, I've always respected how you take time out for your fans. And what you did for that boy Josh, setting him up with violin lessons all those years ago, really changed his life."

"When I met him and his mother at the meet-and-greet in Phoenix, I knew I had to help them out. He reminded me of me, so taken by music, and I was happy to sponsor his lessons. I just wish I could do more."

"You've already done so much." Rose's eyes drift toward the stand where all the restaurant's workers are gathered. "In any event, our waitress can go tell all her friends that *the* Cole Manchester knows her name." She adds teasingly, "All her high school friends, that is."

Our conversation is interrupted by Deanna returning with our food. We both devour the pizza.

"This is really good, Cole. Not quite New York City pizza, but good. Much better than the place near my rental. Thanks." With a giggle, she adds, "You know, I would kiss you, but don't want to keel over dead from Deanna's bad juju."

"Yeah, I think I'd be pulling pins out of a doll for weeks if you did," I reply with a smirk.

Depositing some bills from my wallet on the table, I wave good-bye to our teen waitress as we exit. "Now I'm ready to go christen your place."

About thirty minutes later, I put my car in park and rush around to open Rose's car door. As I close it, I hear, "There you are, girlie! I've missed you around here. And still with Mr. Hot Stuff, I see."

We both turn and give Grandma Gertie a big smile. I blow her a kiss.

"Looks like you two have worked things out. Well, good for you! Remember to treat her right and we're all good."

I give her a big thumbs up, while whispering "Is she always that protective, Ro?"

She nods. "She's amazing despite all the hardships she's had to endure. I'll tell you her story sometime." Rose collects her mail from the mailbox and we go to her front door, where I grab the package from Gruesome. Rose opens the door and turns off the alarm.

We walk into the living room and Rose immediately opens the packet, filled with photos, what looks like a police report and hospital forms. Sighing, she looks up at me. "This will probably take me some time to digest, Cole. I need to speak with Brandan, too."

I give her a kiss on the forehead. "No worries, doll. I'll get my guitar out of my car and work on my new song. I think I'll take over your bedroom."

When I come back inside a few minutes later, Rose is hunched over the documents at the dining room table. Deciding not to interrupt her concentration, I make a beeline for her bedroom, guitar case in hand. I open it and pull out my favorite guitar as well as a small bag that I had picked up yesterday. I'm excited to use my new gift on Rose. Placing the bag on the side table, I resume working on my new song.

Sometime later, I put my guitar back in its case. The song is nearly finished. I need to talk with Russell and Jon about adding it to my album. Not right now, though. Now it's time to play. I take the vibrator out of the bag and bring it to the small bathroom across the hall to prepare it for Rose. Grinning, I wash it and put in new batteries. Then I return to the bedroom and place it on the side table beside the lube.

Feeling predatory, I stalk out to the living room, finding Rose on the phone. I make a big show of removing my shirt and throwing it over my shoulder. Her eyes light up and she acknowledges me with a smile. She says, "I will, Mom."

I take a seat next to her on the sofa and begin to nibble on her throat. My hands knead her boobs through her clothes.

Frowning, I whisper, "You're overdressed." I try to pull up the bottom of her shirt, but she swats my hands and gives me a dirty look. Is that a challenge? Game on.

"I've put an ad on Craigslist for a new roommate," she says into the phone.

Moving my hands to her calves, I run them up her legs. I'm less than pleased to hear this news – especially since I'm the second person to hear it – so I lean over and nip her free ear to express my displeasure.

"I'll keep you posted, Mom. Well, I better go. I have to deal with this mess with Brandan. Love you!" She disconnects the call.

"How's your mom?"

"She's good."

"Does she know about us?"

She looks down and shakes her head.

What did I expect? We've only just begun to date, but I can't hide my disappointment. "You'll tell her soon, yes?" I reach out and raise her chin with my fingers so that I can look into her eyes. "Promise me."

"I'll let her know when the time is right, Cole."

What the hell does that mean? Not letting her chin go, I ask "Any idea when that might be?"

"It's complicated."

"Why? Because you're my publicist?"

"That too. I'm nervous how my mother will react given her history with my father. And . . . Please, let's drop it for now, okay?" She kisses my fingers, then continues, "I finished tying up all the loose ends in the paparazzi situation and confirmed this evening's plans with Brandan and Jessie. We're meeting them at The Ice Lounge at 10:30 tonight. They're getting there at ten, and will text me when they're settled."

"Fine, we'll put your mother on hold. I know we can't go public right now because of Gruesome, but I'm not happy about being your dirty little secret."

Rose leans in and gives me a kiss, which I know is meant to soothe my ruffled emotions. I'm still prickly. "Let me go through my mail, and then I'm free until the club tonight."

She can't be embarrassed to tell her mom that she's dating me, can she? Rose has been responsible for all the publicity surrounding my public image for years, so at least she knows the truth about my so-called relationships with many of the women I've been publicly linked to. Maybe she needs to explain that all to her mother. And what could she have meant by that comment about her father? What else don't I know about her? This sucks.

"Oh my God! Not again!"

I rouse from my funk to look at my girlfriend, who is shaking. "What, Ro?" I'm immediately on high alert.

She extends a letter toward me in a trembling hand. I take it and stare in disbelief. Written in red lipstick, the note reads, "I SAID TO STAY AWAY YOU SLUT! HE'S MINE!"

"Fuck!" Who the hell sent this to my girlfriend?

Resolutely, she picks up her cell and places a call. "Hello, Detective Mahoney, this is Rose Mor-Bloomer." Seeking comfort, she leans against my body now that I've settled in next to her. I encircle my arms around her, all thoughts of my sulk erased.

"I'm so sorry to bother you on a Saturday, but I just opened a piece of mail that you should be aware of." She reads the message to the cop. "Yes, I'm at my place. See you soon." Ending the call, she drops both her cell and the letter, and embraces me tightly.

"I'm here, Ro. You've got me." I place a light kiss on her cheek. I pull back and offer her what I hope is a reassuring look. Her eyes reflect so many emotions: fear, annoyance and trust. The trust, I know, is for me. Fat lot of good it has done for her so far, but I intend to rectify that situation immediately.

"I'm going to hire a private investigator to look into this. Maybe he can find out something that the cops overlooked."

"Cole, I appreciate that, but—" Before she can utter another word, I put my finger across her lips.

"This isn't up for debate. I should have done this a week ago." While we wait for the detective to arrive, we make a copy of the letter and envelope it came in to show whoever we hire.

"Please, come in." I usher Detective Mahoney into the living room. "Can I offer you a drink? I think all we have is water, though. We've been spending all our time at my house."

Why am I compelled to explain our whereabouts to him? I frown at the obvious answer—I'm staking my claim. These emotions are still so new to me.

His response brings me back to the matter at hand. "No thanks, Mr. Manchester. Nice to see you again, although not under these circumstances."

He turns to Rose. "Miss Bloomer, may I see the letter, please?"

Before he takes it from Rose, he puts on gloves and inserts it into a baggie marked "Evidence."

"I'll have forensics dust for fingerprints, and we'll look into the manufacturer of the lipstick. May I have the envelope, too?" He puts that into a separate evidence bag.

"We brought in your roommate's ex-girlfriends and they all had alibis that checked out in regards to your car. I don't think this has anything to do with Mr. Stone."

Confused, we look at each other and then at the officer. Rose says what we're both thinking. "What do you mean, Detective Mahoney? Who could be responsible for this, if not one of Tommy's exes?"

He clears his throat and looks at us. I'm standing protectively behind Rose, my hands on her shoulders. "Well, we need to finish our investigation of your past, Rose, but I doubt we'll find anything. This feels like a female stalker to me. Not to get personal, but are you two dating?"

I nod.

"My theory is that the stalker is yours, Mr. Manchester."

Well, hell.

Eighteen

Once Detective Mahoney leaves, I give Rose a reassuring hug. The detective's theory is tearing me apart. I want to be the person who protects her, not the one responsible for her needing protection.

"Let me reach out to Dan and Russell for some private investigators' names, Ro. Why don't you go pack up more of your things? We'll get out of here." I brace myself for her refusal.

"Sounds good. Thank you." She goes into her bedroom, leaving me staring at her with my mouth open.

Shaking my head, I reach for my cell and pull up Dan's number. Before I can press "send," Rose shouts, "Cole!"

I race into the bedroom. "What?" I'm frantically surveying the room for signs of trouble when my gaze lands on Rose, who is holding the vibrator in front of her. "Oh." I smirk. "You found your present. I was planning on giving it to you later."

Rose's icy blue eyes become a shade darker, but she doesn't say anything. I approach her with slow, cautious steps. "Hey, it's okay. We'll bring it back to my place."

She clears her throat. "I think it could be fun using it with you. I've never done that before."

"My brave Ro. Believe me, I'll blow your mind." I lean toward her and capture her lips. Despite the letter, she responds beautifully to me. But I'm anxious to get us out of here and back to the safety of my house.

"Pack it."

I physically turn her toward her closet and swat her ass. Not waiting for her reaction, I return to the living room and place my calls to Dan and Russell, running my finger over the one framed photo left on the bookcase. It's of Rose and an older version of her, presumably her mother.

Rose rolls her suitcase into the room, stopping next to me. "Got everything you need?"

"Yes. Including your new present," she smirks.

"Why, are you smirking at me, Miss Bloomer?"

"Looks like it, Mr. Manchester." I'm grateful she's able to be so lighthearted with me despite the dark turn our day took. I smile at her and together we return to my house.

"Are you ready?"

"Almost. I ran this by Jessie and Brandan already, so now I need your attention."

"I love it when you get all bossy." I say, nibbling on her neck.

"Stop it," she says, pushing back against me.

"C'mon, Ro, wouldn't you rather neck?"

"Neck?!" She starts giggling uncontrollably.

Giving her an exaggerated sigh, I say, "Fine." She goes over the details she spent the day crafting.

"Impressive. If I were wearing a hat, I'd be tipping it to you right now, sweetheart."

Tracing my dimple, she asks, "Any questions?"

"Yes. Once I'm done rehabilitating Brandan's reputation, at the expense of mine, I might add, what's next for me? I don't want to squander our time with more publicity appearances."

Rose counters, "Why don't you think of it as an adventure? Look how Jessie and Amanda handle it. They find it humorous."

"Actually, that's not a bad suggestion. Maybe I'll talk with Amanda about that tonight. Or we can get together with them tomorrow?"

No sooner do those words escape my mouth than I remember Dan's invitation. "Wait, we can't tomorrow. Unless you have other plans, Dan invited us over for a BBQ. I want to introduce you to his wife, Suzanne, and my adorable goddaughter, Emma."

A smile lights up her entire face. "I'd love that. I remember seeing Dan with you in college."

I run my knuckles down her cheek. "Done."

Rose looks down.

Uh-oh. "What?"

"It's just that this is moving so fast. Maybe we shouldn't go to your best friend's house."

"It will only be them and us, and they won't talk with the press. It's safe, I promise."

"Thanks for including me." I can tell she wants to say something more, but this evening's drama is fast approaching, and she's the puppet master.

"I'm proud to take you." I check my reflection in the mirror. "Am I ready for my close-up?"

She smiles, and smooths my shirt. "Perfect."

"Then, let's go hit The Ice Lounge. The sooner this is over with, the sooner I can get you naked and under me. Again."

Nineteen

"**W**HY CAN'T WE AT LEAST WALK IN together?" I'm whining and I know it.

"Stop it, Cole. You know why. Drop me off before you get in the valet line. I'll see you inside."

A long line of people extends around the side of the club. This could pose a bigger problem than Rose realizes. "Um, sweetheart, look at the line. If you want to get in before I leave, you may want to rethink your strategy." I drive past the building.

Rose sighs. "I've got it covered. I'll see you inside."

I quirk my eyebrow at her, and she looks confident. And slightly annoyed. At me. "What?"

"You're not the only one who can get doors to open for them in this town, Cole."

Shit, I've riled her independent streak without even trying. "I didn't mean anything by that. Of course you have connections. I wasn't thinking."

"Don't underestimate me."

"Believe me, I don't." I park the car in a strip mall parking lot a block away from The Ice Lounge. This is our last alone time before Operation Save The Ass a.k.a. Brandan, and I don't want to go in there on bad terms with Rose. The night is going to be awful enough.

Turning to face her, I say, "Look, Ro, I don't want to go in there with us fighting." No use beating around the bush.

Her face softens. "Sorry I was short with you. I'm anxious. I hope everything goes according to plan."

This I can easily handle. "Give me a kiss and I'll reassure you."

Rose gives me a half-hearted smile as she leans forward with lips puckered. I capture her lips, my tongue seeking and gaining an invitation into her mouth. She comes alive under my gentle persuasion. My cock starts to respond in kind, and I pull back. It won't do for me to walk into the club with a woody. I suck in a breath when I look into Rose's eyes, relishing the happiness I see there.

Clearing my suddenly dry throat, I ask, "All better?"

"Yes." She leans in and gives me another, tender kiss, as if reassuring me that everything will be fine. Wasn't I supposed to be the one offering her reassurance? "Are you ready, Cole?"

I glance down toward my cock. Rose's eyes follow mine and a delightful smirk crosses her kiss-swollen lips. "I promise to take care of that for you. Later."

"You better, since you're responsible for it," I retort.

I put the car back into drive and get into the long valet parking line. "See you in there," I say as she discreetly exits the car and melts into the crowd.

As I hand my keys to the valet, my name erupts from the crowd. Showtime. I plaster a smile on my face. Cell phone cameras start snapping from all directions. "Cole! Cole! Can I get a picture with you?" Knowing how important this night is for Rose, I walk into the outskirts of the line and pose for some photos while fending off groping hands. The paparazzi are having a feeding frenzy too, but I ignore their pleas for photos and pretend not to hear their comments about Jessie and Brandan being inside. *If not for the paps, I would be balls deep in Rose right this very second.*

A few minutes later, I walk toward the main entrance, nodding at the nameless bouncers standing guard. They drop the rope and let me pass.

Once inside, I'm greeted by a couple of Barbie Dolls who offer me a logoed parka and gloves. They eagerly help me put them on my body, but from the lascivious looks they're casting in my direction, I bet they would rather be taking all my clothing *off*.

"Thanks, ladies." I offer them a smile, and am rewarded with giggles. The brunette, by far the more aggressive of the pair, adds, "Find me later and I'll be sure to get your motor revved up."

Choosing not to respond to her suggestion, I enter the main club area. I haven't been here in months, but it's exactly as I remember. The bars, furniture, everything is made of ice. The lighting makes the most of the venue, sending different colors and patterns reflecting off the ice. The chilly temperature seeps into my consciousness, snapping me out of my reverie.

I walk straight toward the back bar situated adjacent to the VIP section, where Rose has arranged for Jessie and me to meet. On my approach, I see a bundled up Rose deep in conversation with Brandan. At least she got in without a problem. Like we're connected, she lifts her head in my direction and I give her a barely noticeable nod, which she returns. All set. Catching the bartender's eye, I order a beer and check my watch: 10:30. Time to set the plan into motion.

Taking a sip from my bottle, I survey the VIP section. Several women give me "come hither" looks, which I politely ignore. I sign a woman's cocktail napkin and give her a kiss on the cheek, causing her to swoon.

Jessie and Brandan are now seated at the same table, a few chairs apart. All set. I need to give the impression that I'm on a mission to get Jessie back, so I stalk determinedly over to her. I hear a buzz erupt. Feel the pricks of many pairs of eyes following my progress.

I stop in front of my friend, and Jessie places her hand on my arm. She asks, "Can we talk?"

Making a show of being romantically interested in Jessie, I lean down and give her what I hope appears to be a possessive kiss on the lips. They're the wrong lips. I brace for what's coming next.

Slap!

Damn, that woman didn't sugar coat it. Putting my hand to my cheek, which has to be bright red, I step back. The crowd has fallen silent; everyone in the VIP section is openly staring at us. They pull out cell phones to capture this lover's quarrel, manufactured by my girlfriend. The irony.

Moving my jaw back and forth, I say in a low roar, "Jessie, you can't want to be with him." I nod toward Brandan. "I don't believe it."

"Cole, I've moved on. And, yes, I'm with Brandan." Jessie's voice is low, but loud enough to be overheard by the onlookers. She looks at Brandan with what appears to be true devotion. She's good.

"But we belong together. I know that now." My volume is increasing. I reach out and grab at her shoulders. She shrugs me away.

"Don't make this any harder than it has to be," she says, shaking her head.

Brandan approaches us with a shit-eating grin on his face. I smell the alcohol on his breath as he places a possessive arm around Jessie. Looking directly at me, he pulls her to him and plants a kiss on her lips.

"You can't be serious, Jessie!" I shout.

Breaking away from him, she gives me a sad look and says, "We're over, Cole. I'm happy with Brandan, happier than I've ever been in my life."

She pauses dramatically, but not overly so, allowing her words to sink in for our audience. "Just go away. Find someone else to take to your backroom."

I'm impressed with her reference to the title of my first album, but I can't show it. "Low blow, Jessie. Well, don't you worry, I'll find plenty of willing women to join me. And when you're done with him, don't even think about crawling back to me. We're through."

Feigning disgust, I slam back the rest of my beer and leave the empty bottle on Jessie's icy table. "Have a nice life."

Storming away, I join a group of about ten women who all seem more than happy to ease my pain. I make a big show of ordering tequila shots for everyone. It gives me no small amount of pleasure to know the bill is going on Brandan's tab.

Once we all have shots in hand, plus salt and limes, I get the group's attention and say, "Here's to a night that's off the charts, ladies! Lick it, slam it, suck it!"

A chorus of giggles erupts, and the ladies chant each instruction before acting it out. Damn, tequila does go down easy. I order another round and a bottle of beer. Two shots for me will be enough.

After the second round is delivered, one brazen chick approaches me. "Body shot?" she offers.

Fuck. I can't refuse her, but I have no desire to drink tequila from her bellybutton. I give what I hope looks like a wolfish grin rather than a sick grimace, and answer, "Gladly, darlin'." I don't dare glance in Rose's direction.

She quickly opens her parka, lays down across an ice table, lifts her top up to her lacy black bra. At least it's too cold for her to take it all the way off. Trying not to think too much about what's about to happen, I whisper, "Lick it."

Dutifully, I turn her head and push her bleach-blonde hair to the side, licking her neck and sprinkling salt onto it. I position myself between her open legs, drape myself over her and take a long swipe of the salt with my tongue. She shudders. The circle of women around us are all hooting and hollering their encouragement. Cell phones are capturing every second of the fiasco.

Ignoring them all, I murmur, "Slam it."

I take my shot and pour it directly into her bellybutton. Wanting to get this over with as quickly as possible, I immediately bend down, grab her around the waist, and tilt her hips. I bring my lips to her navel and coax the liquid down my throat. Not even the burning of the tequila can erase my guilt for doing this. *Please don't see me now, Rose.*

"Suck it," I mutter, much to the delight of the girls around me, especially the blonde chick on the table.

I crawl up her body, supporting my weight with my arms, and watch her position the lime in her mouth. I just have to get that lime into my mouth and I can get off her. Smirking down at her, I mentally curse Brandan for the hundredth time tonight and promise the bartenders an overly generous tip on his behalf.

As I position my mouth above the lime, the circle around us chants, "Suck it! Suck it!"

I extend my lips to grab the lime. Of course, Blondie won't let me off so easily. She pushes her mouth to mine, encircling both her arms around my neck and her legs around my waist and pulses into me. Really?

Gaining possession of the lime, I retreat up and away from her, disentangling her body from mine. I hold up the lime as if it were a trophy and the group erupts in applause. Blondie is smiling rapturously up at me. Just how many of those shots has she already had?

Offering her a hand, I graciously help her smooth down her shirt and refasten the parka. The old me wouldn't have bothered—I would have been looking for an alcove where I could explore what she is so freely offering. The new me, however, returns her to her friends, grabs my beer and makes a deliberate show of looking for Jessie to gauge how much more of this I have to endure before escaping. I'm terrified of what I'll see on Rose's face.

Jessie is sitting on Brandan's lap, staring at me with what appears to be venom in her eyes. Brandan's arm is around her, and he's nibbling at her ear. *Please leave soon*, my eyes beg her. She blinks slowly, and though she turns into his arms and continues their intimate show, I believe she got the message.

Before returning to the group of ladies, I quickly scan the crowd. Rose is talking with Amanda now. This must be so difficult for Amanda too, seeing Jessie all cozy with Brandan. Rose won't look at me. I *knew* this was a bad idea. I take another long drag on my beer.

Sighing, I turn back to the bar and order another beer to replace the one that seems to have magically emptied itself. I've had enough tequila shots, that's for sure. Blondie sidles up to me with a giggle and clinks her glass to me.

"I can help you forget all about that one," she propositions me, nodding in Jessie's direction. It's amazing how easily people are led to believe a completely fabricated narrative.

"Darlin', what's your name?"

Smiling up at me, she replies, "Skye."

"Skye, that's very sweet, but I'm no good for you right now." Not to mention not interested. "My heart's over there." Well, that's true, just not in the way she thinks.

"It's not your heart I'm after, Cole."

Well, that's direct. I shake my head, "Thanks, Skye, but I'm afraid not." With girls like this, there's no choice but to be blunt. I kiss her on the cheek, gladly accept my beer from the bartender and join another group of women. I notice Jessie and Brandan are making the rounds at their table, obviously saying their goodbyes. *Thank God.* Once they leave, I only have to stay here for another thirty minutes before I can make my escape.

This new group of ladies seems more interested in harmless flirting than Skye's group did. Thankful for the reprieve, I chat them up for a while. Around midnight, Jessie and Brandan finally gather their things and say their goodbyes. I make a big show of watching Jessie. The girls around me try their damnedest to comfort me, so I guess it's convincing enough.

A few minutes pass and I'm cajoled onto the dance floor. I'm on my fifth—or is it sixth?—beer. Feeling elated that I'll soon be able to leave this night behind me, I want to do a celebratory dance. Rose will be under me soon.

My friend Ozzy Martinez's latest song starts playing, and we all start gyrating to the beat. It's a good rhythm. I need to shoot him a text congratulating him.

Another blonde woman is getting a bit too handsy with me, so I politely try to move away. She must have been taking lessons from Skye, though— she mimics my actions and somehow gets even closer to me.

I turn my back to her, hopefully in a playful move, and she grabs my hips and grinds against me. She slips one hand into my pocket. *Ugh.* In response, I place my hands on top of her wrists, pull her hands away from me and turn to face her. Taking both her wrists in my right hand, I lift them above her head. Now what are you going to do with her, Einstein? She's obviously expecting a kiss, but she's out of luck because she's not Rose. All the alcohol raging through my system is making it difficult to coordinate my movements. At least this woman appears buzzed, too.

"What's your name, darlin'?" When in doubt, stall.

Licking her lips, she replies, "Whatever you want it to be, Cole." The name "Rose" pops into my head and almost straight out of my mouth. Thankfully, I stop that train before it wrecks. A vision of an angry Rose, naked and begging me to let her come, pops into my head, making me smile. The girl in my arms apparently thinks the smile is for her and tries to wriggle her arms free, but I keep them raised.

"I'll call you Starr." Why not? That's better than Skye Squared, I suppose. She looks at me with adoration. Clasping her by one hand, I twirl her away from my body and then let her hand go. She turns to face me again on unsteady legs, but luckily another woman has stepped in between us.

Whew, close call. I need another beer. Turning and leaving the dance floor, I make my way to the bar. Before I even reach it, the bartender is handing me another beer. I check my watch and know that my escape is minutes away.

A few guys stand by the other end of the bar. I've done enough cavorting with the ladies and don't want to spend the rest of my night fending off unwanted advances. So, I walk over to them instead. "Hey."

The guys nod at me and extend their bottles toward me. We all take sips.

"Looks like she went with that other guy. Tough break, dude," one of the guys says.

"Yeah. This whole night sucks."

Another chimes in, "Why don't you take your pick of one of those chicks over there to help you forget her?" They all snicker. At least the charade seems to be working. Everyone believes Jessie chose Brandan over me.

"Not interested, you know? But I'm sure you guys could lift their spirits."

The third guy responds, "We may not be Cole Manchester, but we can show them a good time."

I give him a smile, my first real smile since walking into The Ice Lounge, and say. "Listen, I'm so done in here. Let me introduce you to that group," I point to Skye's circle. "Just promise me that you'll give me cover while I leave."

"You got it, thanks. Hey, you're pretty cool."

"Appreciate it." We walk over to Skye's group and I introduce my new friends. As arranged, they provide a good diversion and I make my escape.

As I walk rapidly toward the exit, two different greeters step forward to strip the parka and gloves from my hands. "We hope you had a good night, Mr. Manchester." Assuming they are well aware of what went on inside, I don't bother to answer.

I purposefully weave toward the valet. I have to endure only a couple of minutes more. One last scene for the paps. Fishing out the ticket for my car from my pocket, I hand it to the valet. The bouncer reaches over and takes the ticket.

"We're sorry, Mr. Manchester, but we can't let you drive out of here in your condition."

"What the hell, man! This has been a shitty night and now you won't let me leave?"

Calmly, he repeats, "You're in no condition to drive. But Ms. VonStein has provided a limo to take you wherever you want to go." He points to a sleek black limousine with dark tinted windows.

Grumbling and thrashing, I'm half led, half pushed toward the vehicle. At least the paps are getting their shots.

"How does it feel to be left behind?"

"Why did Jessie Anderson choose Brandan Rogers over you?"

"Is Brandan a better man than you?"

"Is Jessie pregnant? Is the baby yours or Brandan's?"

The paparazzi are ruthless. Throwing one last growl for the cameras, I let the bouncers thrust me into the limo and slam the door behind me.

My eyes take in the privacy screen separating me from the driver, then find the car's only other occupant. "Oh God, Ro, that sucked. Please say you're not mad at me."

"Of course I'm not mad." She pauses. "Maybe a little jealous, even though that makes no sense." She shakes her head. "Come here and let's both forget the past couple of hours."

She opens her arms in welcome, and I hungrily fall into her embrace. Ravenously, I kiss her, taking time to worship her eyes and nose and ears with my lips as my hands explore her body. My tongue plunges into her mouth. I remove her top and bra in record time, even with all that alcohol in my system. Her jeans and panties follow in quick succession, while she opens my belt and pushes my jeans and underwear down my legs. She dips her hand into my jeans' pocket, pulls out a condom and rolls it onto my rock hard cock.

My index finger enters her pussy. Knowing she's wet just for me crumbles whatever restraint I had left. "I can't wait, Ro," I utter, thrusting into her.

She takes me all the way, moaning softly. Our eyes lock. This is where I should have been all night. I thrust into her warmth, eliciting a shudder from her body as I bring my hand down between us and begin stroking her clit.

"Come for me." I can't hold back much longer. My hips are moving faster than a drum roll, pounding into her body. I latch onto her nipple and give her little bites.

"Ahhhh, Cole!" She starts to climax under me, so I let myself go with a roar.

Once our breathing returns to normal, Rose giggles. "When I promised to take care of that for you, I didn't quite think it would happen this way."

Could I love this woman anymore? Wait, what? Thankfully, I didn't say that out loud. I need to slow way down. It's the alcohol talking. Yeah, that's it.

"That was perfect," I say. Slowly, I pull my cock out of her delicious body, tie off the condom and help her get dressed before fixing my own jeans.

With a start, I realize we're driving down the freeway. My eyes shoot to the front of the vehicle. "Thanks for raising the privacy screen, Ro. I doubt I could have stopped even if there'd been an earthquake, but I don't want any other man to see your hot little body. For my eyes only, baby."

She smiles broadly. "Sounds good to me."

Twenty

M Y CELL CHIRPS. WHO THE HELL would call me at whatever ungodly hour it is on a Sunday morning? I ignore it and turn to wrap my arms around Rose, pulling her back into my front.

Our Sunday morning snugglefest is interrupted once again by my cell phone. Can't people just leave us alone? Rose murmurs in her sleep, and wiggles her bottom against me. My cell finally stops.

I reach around and caress Rose's luscious boob, bringing my lips to her neck. We're both exhausted from last night, but I need to maintain my connection with her. She's quickly becoming as necessary as air.

My phone chirps for a third time. Seriously? "They're not going to stop until you answer, Cole. I'm not going anywhere."

"Ever practical, Ro." I grumble.

When I finally pick up my phone, Jayson's picture takes up the full screen. "This better be good, bro," I say, answering the call.

"What the hell were you up to last night, Cole? You're all over the media. Dad's worried."

As Jayson is prattling on, Lady Gaga's "Telephone" bursts from Rose's phone. Gruesome is checking in with her, too. At least she won't be surprised by the drama that unfolded at the club. Rose answers her phone and gets out of bed, putting on my discarded shirt from last night.

Sighing, I focus my attention on Jayson. "There's nothing to worry about. I texted you and dad yesterday to let you know what was going to happen. You know how this goes."

"Yeah, I do. It's not my first rodeo. But they're calling it The Slap Heard Round The Ice Lounge. There are a bunch of reports that say you got trashed and macked out on countless women. There's even a video of you licking some half naked woman!" His voice is getting higher by the word.

"Whoa there, cowboy." I hold my hand up, even though he can't see me. "This was all planned. Well, mainly. It's fine."

"They're also saying that Brandan rubbed your nose in it and acted smug. They're calling him arrogant. It's Team Brandan versus Team Cole, with your team winning."

"Shit."

"Guess that wasn't planned, huh?"

"No. Brandan was supposed to get a boost from this. Rose needs to rehabilitate his image after the DUI and whole punching the photographer in the nose incident."

"She's got more work to do, then."

"Fuck. She's on the phone with Gruesome right now. I hope she's not getting chewed out."

"So, you and Rose are rockin' it?"

Despite my dismay at hearing the plan has backfired, I have to chuckle. "We're, uh, dating."

"Cole, you've never dated a woman in your entire life."

"Well, I'm dating Rose now," I growl.

"Oooohhhh. Rose and Cole sitting in a tree, K-I-S-S-I-N-G."

"Shut up, Jayson. What are you, like twelve?"

"Hey, did you see the photos of our little baby that I texted you? T-Rex is the best in her obedience class."

God, if he's starting in on that Shih Tzu, I'm never going to get off the phone. I better take control fast. "So, you and Carl are good?"

"Yuppers."

"Great." I mean that. "And Dad. How's he holding up?"

"He's doing all right. Carl and I go over for dinner every Tuesday, and there are Sunday afternoon dinners at Aunt Doreen's, of course."

"That's good. I'll give him a call today." After I meet with potential private investigators, but there's no need to worry the family with that. "Listen, I better go find Rose and figure out what's going on. Thanks for the heads up, even if I was still sleeping."

"What's family for?" With that, I disconnect the call.

I check my missed calls, and see that both Dad and Aunt Doreen have left messages. I dial my father.

"Hi, Dad."

"Cole, what the hell were you up to last night?" Patiently, I explain the events at The Ice Lounge to him. He seems to get it. "So, you and Rose are dating?"

"Yes, she's great. I've never felt like this about anyone before."

"Glad to hear it. Rose is very special. Your mom always used to rave about her."

I collapse back into the pillows. "I know."

"Do you have any idea when you might come back out to Jersey?"

"Well, right now I'm recording my album. When that's done, we have to do prep for the tour and record the first video for Mom's song." I kick the comforter off my legs. "I think I mentioned this before, but we'd like to include pictures of Mom in the video. I'm planning on coming home sometime in the next couple of weeks to sort through photographs."

"That sounds good, Cole. I'll get the photo albums out. Will you bring Rose?"

"I'll ask her."

"It would be good to see her again. I'll prepare the guest room for her."

"Dad, we're adults." I'm thirty-two and Rose is twenty-nine. Seriously?

"So? You're not even engaged. She'll stay in the guest room. Mom would expect it."

How can I argue that? "I'll let you know, okay? Oh, and before I forget, Aunt Doreen called me this morning, too. Can you explain what happened last night to her for me? I need to take care of a couple of things here." Namely, interview PIs and give Ro another screaming orgasm or five before heading over to Dan's.

"Oh no. I'm not doing your dirty work," he responds. I actually hear him laughing at me. It's good to hear him laugh, so I can't even be mad.

"Fine. I'll text her," I grumble.

"She'll appreciate it." We finish up our conversation and say our goodbyes. Once I disconnect the call, I immediately shoot a text over to Aunt Doreen.

Now that I'm finally off the phone, I get out of bed and put on my jeans from last night, going commando. From the pocket, I pull out a piece of paper. There's a phone number on it scribbled in red lipstick. The chick on the dance floor must have stuck it in my pocket last night. Shaking my head, I toss the paper into the garbage and make my way to the spare bedroom suite, which I've dubbed Rose's Command Center. She's still on the phone with Gruesome, notebook out and pen tapping. I give her a thumbs up and thumbs down sign, which she returns with a thumbs up. Well, that's something.

Nodding, I leave her to her boss and wander down to the kitchen to start the Keurig. Figuring that Rose needs the coffee even more than I do, I select a dark roast, extra bold for her and set it to brew while putting two slices of bread into the toaster. I dig out a breakfast tray, and arrange it with a jar of Nutella, a banana and a plate and knife for the toast. Once all of the gadgets have done their work, I complete the tray with sugar and cream, and bring it up to her. She offers me a grateful look and immediately reaches for the jar.

After kissing her cheek, I return to the kitchen all proud of myself. I can take care of my woman.

My eyes land on the mess from yesterday's breakfast omelets. Not even this can dampen my spirits. I busy myself with cleaning up while more coffee brews, although I do take breaks to place calls to the two private investigators recommended by Russell and Dan. They'll come over later this morning to talk in person. I also text Dan to thank him for the recommendations and confirm that Rose and I will be joining them for their BBQ later.

As I'm putting the last dishes into the dishwasher, Rose enters the kitchen. "Everything okay, Ro?" I can't read her expression.

"Well, there's a bit of unexpected fallout, but I think we can play it off without too many problems. I told Greta that you went home alone." I give her a wolfish smirk.

I walk up behind Rose and my arms encircle her waist. "That's not entirely true, sweetheart. I happen to have a thing for one particular publicist." She giggles. "Can you take a break? Or do you have to deal with Team Cole?"

She turns in my arms. "What do you have in mind?" Her eyes widen, and she gives me a broad smile. "I think I can spare an hour."

"You might want to make that two."

Twenty-One

"**S**O THE COPS THINK THAT YOU HAVE a stalker?" Dan asks.

I nod. "Tommy's ex-girlfriends' alibis all checked out. It's just that we've been so careful out in public. If I have a stalker, she must be watching us pretty closely if she's figured out Rose and I are together."

Dan's eyebrows go up. "She?"

I shrug. "The cops think it's a woman."

"Did you have a chance to interview any of the PI's I sent you? It sounds like you need someone to get to the bottom of this, pronto." He presses the spatula down on the tops of the steaks.

"Yes. You and Russell sent me some of the same names. Ro and I interviewed two before coming over here, and we hired Nolan Kates. We gave him copies of the latest letter and a photo of Rose's car window. He's going to hire bodyguards for us for twenty-four-hour surveillance, starting tomorrow. We've also got him looking into the break-in at her place, which seems to be unrelated to the stalker."

Dan shakes his head. "Man, this sucks. There's no telling how a stalker might escalate things once she realizes you're serious with Rose."

"I have to make sure she's safe. Rose is my number one priority."

Dan flips the steaks. "I take it things are going well?"

I glance over to the patio where Rose and Suzanne are chatting while watching Emma in her baby swing. Pitching my voice lower, I reply, "Great, Dan. I mean, really fucking great."

He smiles at me. "I'm happy for you, buddy. She seems like a nice woman. Level headed, just what you need."

"She can't be too level headed if she's with me, huh?"

Dan barks out a laugh, causing Emma to giggle in her swing. "I'd say that you have it bad."

"I know that we've only been together for a short time, but we've known each other for years." I pass him BBQ sauce and a brush, which he slathers on the steaks.

I continue, "She's the last thing on my mind when I fall asleep and the first thing I reach for when I wake up. I think about her constantly while I'm recording, and I even wrote her a song."

Dan glances at me. "You did? Have you played it for her yet?"

"No. It literally came to me as a fully-formed song yesterday, lyrics and music together."

His eyebrows raise. "That's a first for you, isn't it?"

"Pretty much." Silence hangs between us, commemorating the momentous occasion.

I clear my throat. "Maybe I'll play it after dinner."

Another silence.

Barely above a whisper, I utter the words that have been rolling around my head recently. "I think she's the one for me, Dan."

Dan gives me a mocking look. "I could've told you that last Sunday when you were so mad at her."

"You're a douche, you know that?"

"The fun is only beginning. I am *so* looking forward to the fall of the mighty Cole Manchester."

Grabbing the platter filled with steaks, sausages and corn on the cob, Dan leaves me standing at the grill trying to compose myself. After a moment or two, I follow him to the table. Once there, I kiss my beautiful goddaughter on the forehead, causing her to squeal in delight. Next, I kiss Suzanne on the cheek and say, "Thanks for having us over."

Finally, I pull Rose up to a standing position and dip her dramatically, kissing her on the lips. She's flushed and giggling as I return her to her chair.

I walk over to Dan, who is desperately shaking his head. "No way, buddy, don't even think about it!" I put my hands on his cheeks and pretend I'm about to kiss him on the lips, but I turn his head at the last moment and give him a loud raspberry instead. Emma mimics the sound and we all laugh.

Settling down, we enjoy the wine, delicious food, beautiful weather and excellent company. This is one of life's perfect moments. Dan and Suzanne include Rose in the conversation, asking about her work and family, and Emma smiles at all of us. She seems to have taken a particular shine to my girlfriend.

Grinning, I say, "I have a surprise for you all. I wrote a new song for the album yesterday. I want to play it for you guys first."

Dan looks at me with approval. I often play my new songs for him, and in the past he's offered some great suggestions that ended up making the final cut. Suzanne claps in excitement, causing Emma to clap as well. Rose looks surprised and excited.

"Let me get my guitar."

When I return to the backyard, the table has been cleared, so I grab my chair and strum my guitar. I put my notebook on the table.

"Dan's been through this before, but I need to warn you that the song isn't in final form yet. Feel free to give me your feedback at the end. Right now, I'm calling it 'Taboo.'"

While I'm setting up, Suzanne shoots a warm smile at Rose, whose blush makes me smile. Before I start, I sneak one last kiss with my girl, whispering, "I hope you like it, Ro. It's about us."

Taking a breath, I begin:

I see you there
Where you've always been
Only now, now, I really see you
Were you always there?
Will you always be here?

I need to know you
I need to feel you
It doesn't matter that it's taboo
'Cause everything's so right
When we're together
Were you always there?
Will you always be here?

People only see what they want
Illusion, fantasy is everything
Hiding in plain sight
I want to scream your name
Now that I've found you

Were you always there?
Will you always be here?
I know I will

I play the last chord and open my eyes. Rose is staring at me with tears streaming down her face. Suzanne has her hand over her mouth, and Dan is looking at me with approval. For her part, Emma is kicking her feet and banging her little fists on her swing.

No one says anything. I've never felt so vulnerable, even with "No One to Hold." I place my guitar back into its case. The noise brings everyone to life all at once.

Dan starts, "Cole, that was amazing. Honestly, your best."

Suzanne vigorously nods her head in agreement. "It's beautiful. I'm so honored you shared it with us first."

I'm happy to hear their praise, but Rose hasn't said anything yet. It's her opinion that matters most, especially for this song. "Did you like it, Ro?"

Her eyes meet mine. Deep emotion swims in their watery depths, but there's an undercurrent of what looks like fear. Oh God.

"Cole, that song is . . ." A couple of seconds tick by, and she starts again, "The song is so . . ." Closing her eyes, she sucks in her breath and tries again. "It's beyond words. Spellbinding. Haunting."

Haunting? That's not the emotion I was going for. I quirk an eyebrow at Dan, who shrugs. Suzanne makes a big show of getting Emma out of her swing, then brings her around the table for goodnight kisses. Tactfully, Dan offers to help her put the baby down, leaving Rose and me alone together.

"Did you hate it, Ro? Tell me. I'll never play it again." I pull our chairs around so we're facing each other, knees almost touching but not quite.

Swiping an errant tear from her eyes, she looks at me. "Hate it? Are you kidding? It stole my breath away. It's beyond anything anyone has ever done for me."

She wraps her arms around my neck as she speaks, which makes it easy for me to lift her onto my lap. I bury my face in her neck and hold her. She's trembling.

"I take it she likes it?" Dan's voice floats from somewhere near the grill.

I smile up into Rose's face and then we both look over at Dan. He's holding Suzanne's hand. I know in this moment that we'll overcome whatever obstacles are thrown in our path.

Twenty-Two

I TAKE ROSE'S HAND AND LEAD HER to the pool. Even though the sun set
hours ago, the lighting provides an inviting ambiance that complements
the warm night air. She was pretty quiet on the ride back from Dan and
Suzanne's. I bend down and take off her sandals before removing my own
shoes and guiding us both to the edge of the pool.

When both of our feet are in the water, I ask, "What's on your mind,
Ro?"

Blue eyes look directly at me. They're not revealing any of her emotions,
which is concerning because I can usually read her pretty well. "I feel a little
overwhelmed, to be honest."

"What do you mean?" *Make me understand so I can fix whatever's bothering
you.* Once again, the depth of my feelings—of our connection—catches me
off guard.

"I could lose my job because we're together, yet I can't stay away from
you. Mom thinks all wealthy men are untrustworthy, and she always tells me
the guys out here are playboys. I know, for a fact, about your previous, umm,

liaisons. Plus, I seem to have acquired the wrath of your stalker. All of this is telling my head to run and never look back." She tucks some loose hair behind her ear. "But my heart won't let me."

"I'm scared too."

In response to her incredulous look, I admit, "I am. Mom was worried that I was getting too involved with the rock and roll lifestyle. She told me that more than once over the years, but I never gave it much thought until I lost her. But with you, I'm starting to understand what she was trying to drum into my thick skull. Life is better with a partner to share it. You've helped teach me that, too."

"Have you been pining for your high school sweetheart, the cheerleader, all this time?"

Rose has a good memory. "No way." My lips curl downward in disgust. "When she used me like that, I just decided that love wasn't worth pursuing. That is, until I found you. Again."

She gives me a small smile. I'm curious about one thing. "Why'd you choose me that night in college?"

She blushes and looks down. Clearing her throat, she says, "You were a senior and I was a freshman. Everyone on campus knew you—your talent was undeniable. When you noticed me that night, well, I jumped at the chance."

"And I was too dumb back then to realize how amazing you are." She smiles at me, and I pull her to me for a kiss.

Against her lips, I breathe, "Teach me how to love you."

"You're doing a pretty good job of sweeping me off my feet," she admits.

"I want to make love to you." I kiss her hand. "Will you let me?"

In response, she nods her head and leans toward me for another kiss. "You're so beautiful," I say just before our lips meet. It's a different kiss. There's passion, certainly, but it's tinged with something else, too. Something more.

We sit with our feet dangling in the pool, connected by our lips and tongues for a long while. Then I place my right hand on her cheek and pull back, smiling. She returns my smile with a dazzling one of her own.

"Yes. Please, Cole. Make love to me."

It's hard to breathe when I hear her use those words. Despite the many sexual encounters I've had, I'm not sure I've ever made love. But that's exactly what I want to do with this woman. I nod. "Let's go upstairs."

I help Rose to her feet and then kiss her with all the emotion raging in my body. She responds passionately, which feeds my need for her. Impatient, I sweep her into my arms and carry her up the stairs to our room.

After I shuck my clothes, I stand before her naked, silently offering her all of me. Her eyes roam my body, stopping to look deeply into my eyes. She takes the proffered condom and rolls it onto my throbbing shaft, then shimmies out of her own clothing.

I step forward and pull her into my embrace, running my hands up and down her back. While I'm kissing her neck, I walk her backward, stopping when her legs touch the bed. Taking her mouth in an adoring kiss, I guide her down onto the middle of the bed and settle between her thighs. I push the tip of my hard length into her wet pussy, because I need to be surrounded by her, but then immediately pull back. Not yet.

I roll us so that she's on top, straddling me. Her luscious, perky boobs stare at me, so I obligingly knead them, causing her back to arch and a moan to escape her lips. It's her turn to grind against me, which is driving me insane. "Cole," she pants.

I quirk my eyebrow up at her and thrust my hips. "I'm right here, sweetheart."

"Oh God." She circles her sex against my throbbing cock, but I don't enter her. I need more than a physical connection right now.

Suddenly, I sit up so that we are face-to-face. Wrapping my arms around her back, I bring her flush against me. Her boobs are pressed against my chest, her legs cupping my hips, her fingernails scraping my back. She kisses my jawline.

"Ro, look at me."

She pulls back a fraction and our eyes meet. We silently share our emotions, neither of us ready to put words to them. Bringing my hands to her hips, I position my straining cock at her wet opening and ease my way in, never breaking eye contact. I move my hands to the back of her head and pull her forward the last few inches to seal our joining with a kiss. Our tongues mimic the powerful roll of our hips.

Our bodies continue to dance as we kiss and caress each other. Our breathing becomes more erratic. We are both covered in sweat. This is not just sex. I trail my lips from her lips to her neck and lave her nipples before pulling back to seek the reassurance of looking into her eyes. Greeted by smoldering blue irises, I'm nearing my breaking point.

"Ready?"

"Yes, Cole!"

Her internal muscles squeeze around my cock as her orgasm overwhelms her, and within seconds, I'm coming deep inside her body. We both hold on to each other as the shudders overtake us.

"Thank you for teaching me how to make love to you," I whisper into her ear.

Twenty-Three

ONDAY MORNING ARRIVES TOO SOON. Rose is wrapped in my arms, exactly where she belongs. I wish we didn't have to get up, especially since the first thing on our schedule is a meeting with our new bodyguards. One will go with Ro to work while the other will shadow me. I must ensure hers knows the importance of discretion, as Gruesome can't be privy to his existence. But the most important consideration is that my Rose has to be safe.

Sighing, I stare into the clock's glowing numbers. I can't delay any longer. I quickly kiss her lips and whisper, "Time to stop dreaming about me."

She groans and turns her head. I fucking love that she is not a morning person. Of course, I'm starting to fucking love *everything* about this woman.

I pull back the blankets and caress her boobs. "Up, Ro."

In response, she arches her back. Another few minutes of this, and I won't be able to leave the bed. Unfortunately, we don't have the luxury of time.

Reluctantly, I remove the blankets from both of our naked bodies and sit up. "Unless we want to give our new bodyguards more than an eyeful, I suggest we both get up now."

She struggles to an upright position. Grumbling, she says, "Why did they have to come over so early?"

I chuckle. "Sweetie, they have to go with us to our offices. You know this."

"Yeah, but it sounded like a better idea yesterday afternoon."

I ruffle her hair. "I have to know that you're safe."

She sighs and looks up at me with sleepy eyes. "I hate that you're right."

I smile broadly. "You're adorable in the morning. Let's go."

She sits up and traces my dimple with her tongue.

Grabbing her hand, I haul her to the bathroom. I never thought that I would be so content to share such mundane tasks as brushing my teeth and flossing with another person. But I am. I check the mirror and see myself grinning like the village idiot.

"What?"

"Nothing. I'm just happy."

She shakes her head. "You're crazy."

"Maybe. Crazy about you, definitely. Now, do you want to get into the shower first, or shall I? We don't have a lot of time."

She starts the water. "I'll be quick."

Within moments, the scent of her floral-scented shampoo fills the air. Screw it. After she rinses her hair, I join her under the spray of warm water.

"Here, let me," I say, taking the washcloth from her hands. Smiling at her stunned expression, I squirt the body wash onto the cloth. I lather up her back, taking care as I skim down her gorgeous ass. "Spread your legs."

She does, and I soap each limb, using sensual circular motions, earning a little moan from her.

"Turn around." Focusing on my task, I wash her slender neck and boobs and shoulders and arms.

"What have I missed?" I tease, earning a small moan from Rose. "Oh, I know." Having Rose in my shower is so much better than I even imagined the first night she stayed here.

Gently, I push her back against the tiles and drop to my knees, guiding one of her legs over my shoulder. Immediately, I set about cleaning her sweet pussy with my tongue. Her hands travel to my shoulders, flexing as I lick and suck her clit. I slide my index finger into her warmth, quickly joining it with my middle finger. I curl them inward while maintaining my rhythm at her clit. Within seconds, she's exploding for me.

I stand and hold her up while she regains her balance.

"My turn."

She picks up the body wash from the shelf. Circling around me, she washes my back and ass, giving me little bites on my butt. I'm entranced by this new assertive, sexy side of Rose. She comes around to my front, washing my upper body, taking special care with my six-pack. Then it's her turn to drop to her knees. She washes my legs before taking my shaft into her hands.

"You don't have to do this."

"Quiet down, Cole. Enjoy."

Bossy too? "You're fucking hot."

She licks my cock from root to tip, causing me to close my eyes and lean my head back. I groan as she circles the head with her tongue before opening her mouth and sliding it in. Deep. Opening my eyes, I watch her suck me. This has to be one of the most erotic moments of my life.

"Ro, stop. I'm going to come."

She pulls back from my cock long enough to say, "That's the idea."

Right away, she takes me back into her mouth, reaching around to grab my ass and pull me forward. I widen my stance and give her one last warning before erupting deep down her throat. "God," I manage.

She giggles and stands up, wrapping her arms around my neck. "I think we're both clean now."

Twenty minutes later, we're dressed and in the kitchen eating breakfast. The doorbell rings, announcing our bodyguards. "I'll show them into the living room. Finish your cereal," I say, grabbing my coffee mug. She nods. After stooping to give her a quick kiss, I walk to the front door.

"Gentlemen, please follow me."

The two hulking men say their hellos and follow me into the living room. Wills, the blond hulk, introduces himself and his partner, Roberto. "Mr. Manchester, our goal is to protect you and Miss Morgan. We don't want to interfere with your lives any more than necessary. Shawn, who is outside in his car, is going to watch your house and Jake is already at Miss Morgan's. They will trade off with Miles and Mike in twelve hour shifts."

Before Rose gets here, I need to set a few ground rules. "Thank you Wills. I'm sure that Mr. Kates has briefed you about my apparent stalker, and the danger she poses to Miss Morgan."

They both nod.

"On a more personal note, I want to stress that no one is to know that Rose and I are a couple. Wills, are you going to be accompanying Rose to work today?"

"No, Sir. Roberto is assigned to Miss Morgan."

I turn my attention to the dark-haired, dark-eyed Latin hulk. "Roberto, keep your distance from Rose while she is at work. We don't want any questions raised about your presence from either her boss or other colleagues."

"Understood."

"If Rose needs to leave her office building for any reason, she has agreed to contact you to let you know. You'll either drive her or follow the car that she's riding in. Discreetly, of course."

"Yes, Sir."

All three of us turn as Rose walks into the living room, tightening her ponytail. I scrutinize the hulks' reactions. Luckily for them, they remain professional. Since Roberto will be taking care of her when I'm not around, it's paramount that I'm assured he won't try to take advantage.

She stops next to me, and I perform the introductions. I actually feel a twinge of jealousy as she extends her hand to each of the hulks. Those hands that were stroking my cock in the shower minutes ago. And those fingers—

"Right, Cole?"

Shit. "Sorry, Rose, what were you saying?"

She gives me a quizzical look. "I said that we're taking separate cars to work, so Roberto will follow me."

"Yes. Okay. Do you have any meetings scheduled outside your office today?"

"No. I've been trying to schedule appointments with potential roommates during lunchtime, but none today."

That response makes me frown. I want her to stay here, but I won't be discussing this in front of Hulk 1 and Hulk 2. "Good."

It's her turn to frown at me. I guess she's not sure if my "good" was in response to her not leaving her building today, or not meeting with any roommate candidates.

"Do you have all your things?"

"I just need to run upstairs to grab my computer and notes. I'll be right back and then we can go, Roberto."

"I'm ready whenever you are, Miss Morgan."

"Please call me Rose." With that, she heads off toward her Command Center.

"Excuse me, gentlemen. I'll be right back."

As pathetic as it sounds, I can't stand the thought of being away from her any longer than is needed. I can hear the whip all the way from Dan's house now.

"Got everything?" I ask from the doorway.

"Yes."

"Good. Now come here and soothe my ego."

Giving me a puzzled look, she stops right in front of me, briefcase slung over her shoulder. "Why does your ego need stroking?"

"I said soothe, not stroke," I say with a smirk. "Why are you still looking for a roommate? I want you to be safe. Here. With me." I had promised myself this would wait until later, but the words just spilled out.

"I never agreed to move in here permanently."

"Just indefinitely."

"Your words, not mine. Look, I need to get going. Someone made me take an inordinately long time in the shower this morning." She grins up at me.

"We'll discuss this later. As for the shower, it seems to me that someone needed to go tit for tat."

"Or lick for suck," she giggles.

I pull her into my arms and give her a heated kiss. Stepping back, I swat her on her ass and say, "Don't get overly friendly with Roberto. You're mine." *Wow. Did that just come out of my mouth?*

"I like the sound of that."

Hand in hand, we return to the living room. I give Rose one last kiss before she and the Latin Hulk head out the door.

I turn to Wills. "Ready to hit the gym? I have a ten a.m. appointment with my trainer. You can work out with me if you'd like."

He smiles and agrees to work out with me. I look forward to showing him that I'm not some soft rock star just because I have highlights in my hair and the world's whitest teeth, thanks to Gruesome.

After a grueling workout, Wills and I hit the sauna to soothe our aching muscles. I swear my personal trainer made today's workout worse than usual as a sort of rite of passage for the blond hulk.

"That's some workout he put you through. How often do you train?"

"Three times a week."

Blond hulk nods his head, and we lapse into a comfortable silence. My mind goes over all the things I need to get done today. I'm going to the studio to continue recording my album. I also want to go over "Taboo" with Russell and Jon.

In addition to work, I'll check in with Nolan Kates to see if he's turned up anything. He's been on the case for only a few hours, but the sooner it's solved, the sooner our lives will return to normal. Whatever normal means.

"I'm going to hit the shower and then go to the studio. I'll have lunch brought in for us there. Sound good?"

"Yes, Mr. Manchester."

Geez, I guess I didn't tell him to call me Cole. "This Mr. Manchester business needs to stop, Wills. Call me Cole."

Blond hulk gives me a smile. "Sure thing, Boss."

I shake my head as we leave the sauna. "No offense, Wills, but I hope not to be needing your services for too long."

"I understand. I hope not, too."

Under an hour later, we arrive at Platinum Records. Although I invite Wills into the studio, he opts to stay outside in the hall. I seriously doubt anyone is after me. I tend to agree with Kates that my stalker is more likely to harass Rose than to threaten me. I leave him outside the door and get to work.

A couple of hours later, Wills enters the studio with our lunch order—sandwiches, sodas and chips. "My man!" exclaims Sam, from his sound engineering station. Soon, we're all devouring food like we've never eaten before in our lives. One of the perks of working with all men.

My cell beeps, and a text from Rose pops up. *Missing you. xx*

I reply: *Tonight you're mine.*

Her response is nearly immediate: *Again?*

Chuckling, I return: *You'll beg for more.*

Sam notices me texting and says, "Yo, Cole, what you got going on? Who's the lucky model now?"

"No one you'd know, asswipe," I respond with a smile. I catch Wills's eye and a look of understanding passes between us. My secret is safe with him.

Sam changes tack and addresses Wills. "Cole's tighter than a minister's daughter. Give me some intel, man."

"Sorry. No can do. I'm just his hired muscle."

"And since when do you have a bodyguard, Cole? What's up with that?"

I don't want news of my stalker to get out. "He makes me look cool."

"Whatever, dude."

My phone rings. It's Kates. Answering, I leave the room for a more private setting. After a few niceties, I ask, "Any updates?"

"Not yet, Cole. We agree with the police and are investigating the break-in and the stalker incidents as crimes committed by separate individuals. I wanted to ask you about the jewelry that was stolen."

"Only one piece of value was taken. Rose's prior diamond engagement ring. All the other pieces were costume. I think Rose gave information and a photo to Detective Mahoney at the LAPD as well as her insurance company. I'll make sure you get a copy."

"That's perfect. I've already put feelers out to pawn shops in the area. If anything new is brought in, I'll be notified."

"Good."

"How are Wills and Roberto working out?"

"I hate that we need them, but they seem fine."

"Better to have other sets of eyes looking out for you."

I sigh. "Let's hope you can get to the bottom of all this sooner rather than later. Thanks for the update." We end our call and I reach out to Rose in her office.

"Rose Morgan."

"So formal."

"Hello, Cole, how may I help you?"

Gruesome must be nearby. "Now that's a loaded question, sweetheart. You're going to have to ask me that again when we're both naked. Which should be in just a couple of hours."

"That sounds interesting."

"I love how you scream my name when you come."

"Really?" she squeaks.

Chuckling, I take pity on her. "Kates needs a copy of the insurance information you prepared."

"I understand." I hear her talking, presumably with Gruesome, although I'm not sure because the sound is muffled. She must have put her hand over the speaker. "Cole, Greta wants me to thank you for your part at The Ice Lounge on Saturday night. You helped Brandan out, and she wants me to let you know that we owe you one. Greta promises to fix you up with any *model* or *starlet* of your choosing."

"Anyone?" I say, ignoring the two categories she's provided.

"Yes. Greta believes you should be seen around town with arm candy to deflect the whole Jessie and Brandan triangle."

"Oh does she?"

"She would like to set something up for this Friday night. Who would you like to be fixed up with?"

I'm positive Gruesome is hovering over Rose's desk, eavesdropping. Dropping my voice, I respond, "You."

"You don't have anyone in mind? I can make a few suggestions."

This conversation is making me nauseous. And the fact that Rose is the one arranging the whole charade only makes it more surreal. "I'm not sure I can do this."

"Greta thinks that the best thing for your image is to be seen in public with someone. As you may know, there's a Team Brandan and a Team Cole, and we need to manage this situation."

I sigh. "Do I really have to do this?"

"Yes. Why don't you think about it and send me the names of some ladies of interest? I'll work on a list from my end also."

"Fine. This sucks."

"Thanks for calling, Cole."

After hanging up, I text Rose: *I only want to go out with you.*

She replies: *It'll just be a few hours.*

Shaking my head, I realize that I'm grumbling about being forced to spend time with some gorgeous chick. Rose truly has taken up residence in my heart.

Twenty-Four

"THAT WAS DELICIOUS," ROSE SAYS, placing her fork down on her now-empty dessert plate.

"Yeah, not too bad, huh?"

"It's nice having a personal chef."

"It doesn't suck," I say truthfully. "I do enjoy cooking, but having Lana preparing meals makes life much easier during the week when I'm in town."

"After work, I usually only have the energy to make a bowl of cereal. Sometimes, if I'm being industrious, I make popcorn. When I'm really lucky, Grandma Gertie stops by with some of her fabulous cooking."

"Well, stick with me baby, and I'll treat you right."

I mentally pat myself on the back for not saying anything about her being overworked by Gruesome, or living so far away that she wastes time commuting, or even anything about her finances. I don't want to get her Rose hackles up.

"Well, it certainly is nice to have a home-cooked meal that I didn't have to actually cook. And no pots or pans to clean up. Thank you."

"Thank me with a kiss."

She stands up and walks over to my chair, places her hands on my shoulders and gives me a sweet kiss on my lips. Unable to resist, I plant my hand at the back of her head and crush her lips back to mine. Our tongues begin their familiar dance, and she wraps her arms around my neck.

By the time we pull apart, we're both panting. God, how I want to get lost in this woman. "You're very welcome."

She looks bewildered for a second. A teasing glint enters her smoky blue eyes. "I wonder how you would thank me if I cooked you a meal."

My mind races with the possibilities. "How about Saturday? You can feed me, and then find out what a proper 'Cole thank you' looks like." I gauge her reaction. "And feels like." She turns pink, causing me to chuckle.

I stand up and give her a playful swat on the ass. Then we clean up together, working in sync, like we've been a couple for months instead of a matter of days. While she's loading the dishwasher, I pour us some Cabernet. "Let's go poolside."

Walking hand in hand, we wander to the chaise lounges. I sit and pull her onto my lap. "This is where you belong," I whisper into her ear, enjoying her shudder in response.

"You're spoiling me."

"You deserve all this and much, much more, babe."

"Penny for your thoughts?"

"Oh, they're not worth that much. So, tell me about your day."

Rose sighs. "You first."

"Okay. Well, I played 'Taboo' for Russell and Jon, and they both like the song. We've added it to *Moving Forward Slowly*. Recording is going smoothly, but I hope to be done with my part of the album by the end of the week. Then comes all the mixing and post-production stuff, and I'll have to start working with the team on prepping for the concert tour and videos."

While I've been talking, Rose has been driving me crazy by rubbing slow circles on my thigh. I place my hand on top of hers to stop the torture. "Your turn. How did Roberto work out?"

"He was fine. I didn't leave the building, so he didn't have much to do today. He did accompany me to my house when I went to get my mail. Jake introduced himself and he seems nice, too."

"Good. I'm glad he was unobtrusive. Your house is going to be covered 24/7 until the stalker is caught."

"I wish they weren't needed."

Time to change the subject. I clear my throat, "Does Gruesome really want me to go out on a publicity date on Friday night?"

Rose looks down. She's as unhappy about the situation as I am. "She wants you out in public with a new woman pronto."

"Did you tell her about the stalker?"

"No. Until it's confirmed that you actually have one, I don't want to bring it up. Besides, you hired the PI and all those bodyguards, so whoever your date is, she will be safe."

"Hey, you know I don't want to do this, right? I want to go out in public with *you*. You're my girlfriend. I want to show you off."

I earn a small smile from Rose.

"Thanks, Cole. But you know what we have to do." She shifts her hips but remains on my lap. "Is there anyone you'd like to be want to be seen with?" Rose pauses, and leans over and gives me a sweet kiss. "Other than me?"

What a weird conversation to be having with my girlfriend.

"Honestly, I've been trying to come up with some names all afternoon, but I'm drawing a blank. I adore Jessie, but she's out of the running, obviously. How did you pick out dates for me in the past?"

I'm truly curious about this, more so considering how uncomfortable Rose looks. "I, uh, well, I . . ." she stammers.

I pull her in for a kiss. "Now, I'm intrigued. Tell me," I murmur in her ear, running my hands over her boobs.

With a look of determination, she starts again. "I would compile a list of models and actresses who were currently unattached in public. Then I'd pull their photos and stats, and decide which ones would look best beside you. If

I didn't know the woman, I would ask around about her personality, intellect and conversation skills. I'd also determine which ones were already working with Greta, which ones were with friends of hers in the industry and which ones she might want to represent. I'd make my selections from that list."

My eyebrows rise. "You actually did some digging on their personalities?" She nods her head in the affirmative.

"So how come you set me up with so many empty-headed bimbos who couldn't string two words together?"

Rose studiously looks down at the cement, each one of her fingers flicking her thumb sequentially. I swear she's sporting a cheeky grin on her face. "You set me up with the bimbos on purpose?"

"Not all of them were, ah, intellectually challenged." A blush steals across her face.

"You went out of your way to hook me up with women who you knew would bore me within minutes. Like that awful Mimi Barker." Gotta hand it to her. She's good. "So, that's how you exacted some revenge on me for forgetting our night at NYU."

"I didn't look at it that way."

"Really? And just how *did* you look at it?"

"I was only doing my job."

"To the letter, huh?" I smile at her; I can't help myself. "Remind me never to get on your bad side again, babe."

Rose is grinning broadly at me. "You're not mad at me, are you?"

"Mad? No." Highly amused is more like it, but I don't want Rose to know that yet. "However, this does seem like a punishable offense."

"Punishable?" she squeaks.

"Oh yes, baby. You've punished me with some crazy-ass dates over the years. Seems only fair that I get to repay the favor." While I'm speaking, I tighten my hold around her waist to ensure that she can't escape.

"I was just doing my job, Cole," she repeats, half-heartedly struggling in my arms.

"Consider this part of my job as your boyfriend. You need to curb your wayward ways, my dear."

Quickly, I turn her so that she's facedown over my lap and her ass is right where I want it to be.

Rose struggles in earnest now, but my left hand on her back keeps her in place. Using my right hand, I caress her bottom. "I wasn't doing it to be mean, Cole!" Rose exclaims.

"No? Not even a little bit?" I ask her, caressing her ass. I've never spanked anyone before, but this seems like a good time to start.

"I was doing my job," she mutters softly.

"What was that? I didn't quite hear you." As I'm talking, I slowly lift up her skirt, leaving it bunched around her waist.

"Job! I was doing my job!"

I raise my hand and bring it down on her panty-covered ass. Not too hard, barely more than a swat. "Was it nice of you to fix me up with so many vapid women?"

"How was I to know, Cole? You never complained."

Her response stops my hand mid-air. She's right, I never spoke up, mainly because the women were so hot and all I wanted to do was screw them. But that was in the beginning. After a while, I got bored with all the empty conversations. Jessie made me realize that.

Smack—a bit harder this time. Rose squirms.

"I didn't complain because I didn't know I could put in requests." I take hold of her panties and give a quick tug, tearing them to reveal her gorgeous ass. She sucks in her breath as I stroke each cheek, skin on skin.

"I wasn't a mind reader. I thought everything was fine."

"You were enjoying it, though, weren't you? Imagining me out with someone as vacuous as Mimi Barker." She's one of the reality star "celebrities" that's just famous for being famous. A real social media whore. She even ordered menu items solely based on price, even if she hated the food. When I told Dan of the dates, he immediately nicknamed her MooMoo. So appropriate. I give Rose two quick smacks on both cheeks. They turn a light shade of pink.

Rose moans. "Cole. Okay ... maybe ... yes!"

I smirk, knowing that she can't see me. So, she *did* punish me for not remembering our night together. This woman is diabolical. And perfect.

Two more spanks and I let my fingers enter her pussy. Wet.

"Seems like you're turned on by spanking. I'll have to remember that for the future," I whisper in her ear, relishing her moan.

"Stand up." Rose obeys without hesitation. Her skirt falls to her legs and the material that was her panties flutters to the ground. I stand and crush her body to mine.

"Cole," she pleads.

"Upstairs, baby." I bring her lips to mine for a passionate kiss, and we go up to my bedroom. "Take off your clothes and stand at the end of the bed."

Minutes later, she's done exactly as I commanded, which makes me smile. She has no clue that her punishment hasn't ended yet.

"Turn around and place your hands on the bed."

"But you're still dressed."

"I see that. Don't worry your pretty little head about me. If I were you, I'd be more concerned about the punishment still to come."

Her sharp intake of breath confirms that she thought the spanking was her full punishment. She turns to face me and says, "I'm sorry." Her posture belies the sentiment.

"No you're not." I chuckle. "But don't worry, you will be. Now, turn back around."

She stays facing me, her hands finding her hips. "I'm not some puppet you can order around, Mr. Manchester!"

"No. You're my girlfriend who needs to be taught a lesson about payback." I try, but fail, to control the smile that overtakes my face. "Now. Turn. Around."

She returns my smile with a wicked gleam in her eyes. *She understands this encounter will bring her pleasure. Eventually.*

Her naked body is fucking perfect, but I refuse to be distracted. I quirk my brow, yet she doesn't move. "I was doing my job," she repeats.

"I got that, Ro. Thanks for Jessie, by the way. She was the one bright spot in all those fake dates. Now, turn." I reach out and forcibly turn her body, placing her hands on the bed so that she's slightly bent over. "Don't move."

I go to the nightstand and pull out the new vibrator, lube and condoms. Rose is going to scream my name louder than ever before.

Walking up behind her, still fully dressed, I wave the vibrator in front of her face. "I believe you're acquainted with this?"

She shudders in response. Even though her pussy is dripping, I lube up the toy, turn it on and rub it around her folds. I avoid her clit for now.

"You're so beautiful," I whisper in her ear.

She moans when I nip her earlobe but maintains her position. Trailing kisses down her spine, I continue to work the vibrator, finally giving attention to her clit.

"Oh!" Rose screams while thrusting toward the vibrator. I continue my assault, measuring her body's responses until she's about to fall apart.

"You're not allowed to come, Rose. Do you understand?" She'll thank me for this later. All this teasing will lead to an explosive result.

"What?"

Smiling while kissing her neck, I repeat, "Do *not* come."

"Cole!"

"Trust me."

I remove the vibrator from her pussy, giving her time to recover. As soon as her breathing approaches normal, I resume my ministrations on her body. *Fuck!* I want to rip off my clothes and bury my straining cock balls deep into her, but not yet.

When her breathing speeds up, I pull the vibe away from her again. She groans in disappointment. "Frustrating, isn't it babe?"

"Please, Cole. I'm sorry! It was the only revenge I could get."

"Thanks for admitting that. You may,"—I pause for dramatic effect, knowing full well that she expects me to let her climax—"take off my clothes."

Heaving a loud sigh, she turns and makes quick work of my belt. While she's lowering my zipper, I admire her boobs and glistening pussy. Inserting two fingers into her tight hole, I flick my thumb over her clit, causing her to pause in pulling my jeans and underwear down my legs and whimper my name.

"That's right. You can't come until I say so."

"I want to," she grumbles.

Knowing the payoff will be worth it—for both of us—I reply, "Not yet." I step out of my jeans and remove my shirt. Carefully, I insert the vibrator where my fingers just were. "Now suck my cock."

Rose gives me a pleading look, but she drops to her knees and starts giving me a blow job while holding the vibrator with her hand in her pussy. I almost come at the erotic sight. All too soon, it's time to end this game.

"Up, Ro." She stands and I hand her the condom packet, looking from it to my painfully erect cock. Obediently, she rolls the condom on me.

"Remove the vibrator." Looking embarrassed, she completes the task. I swear she's so turned on that a breeze would set her off like a rocket. Well, I'm going to give her a hell of a lot more than a little breeze.

"Lie down on your back." When she follows my instruction, I thrust into her wet body and place her legs on my shoulders, feet by my ears. I reach down and flick her nipple, eliciting a long groan from her.

Her body climbs again, searching for her orgasm. Writhing, she pleads, "Cole!"

I'm not going to be able to hold back much longer, so I reach between her thighs and tap her clit while thrusting deep. "Okay, now."

Rose lets out a series of incoherent screams, punctuated by "Cole!" Her orgasm seems to go on forever, which pushes me over the edge. I pump into her with a primal shout and then collapse next to her on the bed. Pushing her sweaty hair from her face, I look into her satiated, languid eyes.

"That was amazing, Cole." She strokes my cheek and gives me a tender kiss. "Even?"

"Even? I think we're just getting started."

Twenty-Five

H OW ABOUT THE ACTRESS CASSIE JOHNSTON? It's Wednesday and I'm eating lunch in the studio while texting with Rose. We're still trying to figure out a good publicity romance for me. Like I have nixed all of Rose's other suggestions, this one is a non-starter, considering she was my fuck buddy when I first moved to LA.

Shaking my head, I reply: *No way.* She doesn't need to know why.

C'mon, I need to get this set up today.

Not Cassie. Actually, I don't have anything against Cassie. We had some banging times, but that was a lifetime ago and I don't want to stir that pot again.

How about a model? Good for your Q Score.

This sucks. I hate that I can't go out in public with my girlfriend because of Gruesome's edict and a fucking alphabet rating of a Q Score. Not to mention my stalker. Picturing Rose torturing her earring while she's solving this problem, I respond: *Which one?*

Emilie Dubois.

Don't know her?

Rose texts me a link with Emilie's photo and information. She's a twenty-four-year-old French model who's the face of a couple of well-known brands. *Fine. She'll do. But she's not you.* ☹

Let me see if she's available.

"What's got you looking so glum, Cole?" Russell asks me.

"Rose is setting me up with a model for publicity so that it looks like I'm over Jessie."

"Messed up business, huh?"

"Yeah."

"Who is she thinking of fixing you up with this time?"

"Emilie Dubois."

Russell's eyebrows nearly reach his forehead and he gives a low whistle. "She's a hot piece of ass, my friend. You're one lucky dude."

As if. "Don't let your wife hear you talking like that."

"I ain't dead. Besides, the wife knows that I'd never cheat on her."

Come to think about it, I've never known him to cheat on his wife, which is rather unusual for this town. *Good for him.* "Do you know Emilie?"

"Not personally. But she's a piece of eye candy, that's for sure. Good choice, especially since you're going on a world tour for this album. Brings in the international crowd."

That thought brings me up short. Gotta give props to Rose for this suggestion. "Should be interesting. If Rose can arrange it, I'm going to meet her on Friday night. Need to diffuse the whole Jessie and Brandan thing."

"Your life doesn't suck."

I smile at my manager, wishing I could share the whole truth with him. Though I told him about the stalker situation, I'm honoring Rose's need to keep our relationship a secret. A ping indicates that I've received another text.

Emilie's a go. I don't respond. There's nothing more for me to say.

A few hours later, I arrive home. Wills leaves, and I wave to the Night Watchman, a.k.a. Miles, the guard who has the night shift watching my house. Rose should be home soon, so I busy myself with preparing dinner. Well, I pull the containers marked "Wednesday" out from the fridge, review their preparation instructions, and preheat the oven.

I'm pouring two glasses of Pinot Noir when the garage door opens. Putting down the glasses, I rush over and help her bring in her laptop and bags.

"How was your day, sweetheart?" Putting her stuff down on the kitchen table, I lean over and give her a kiss.

"It was busy," she answers quietly.

Her tone gives me pause, and I give her a thorough once-over. "You look beat. Are you feeling all right?"

"Just a bit tired. Someone kept me up late last night," she says with a smirk. I grin back at her.

"Let's eat," I suggest. "Should restore your strength."

While we're eating our steaks, Rose gives me the run down about her day and her ideas about Emilie Dubois. "So, you're going out to dinner on Friday, then on to a club."

Taking a bite of the suddenly sandpaper-like steak, I nod in understanding. Not in agreement.

Rose continues, "How's the album coming along?"

"Instrumentals are all laid down. I'm still working on the vocals. When I'm done, hopefully on Friday, it will need to be mixed and mastered. Label's excited with the new material."

"How about making Friday a celebration of your return to the studio? Can you invite the people working on the album to go out with you? It'll be too weird for you to go out with Emilie alone right away. Better for you to hook up in a group setting. That way it can look like you two casually met and hit it off."

"Will you be there?"

She shakes her head. "No."

"Why not?"

Rose sighs. "Cole, when have I ever been at one of these parties?"

It's my turn to sigh. "You should. Gruesome always puts in an appearance."

"She loves to be out and seen. It's her company, and she's your rep."

"You're my account rep."

"Well, it's her company. She'll meet up with you at the club."

I put my silverware down. "There's no way around this?"

"No. Listen, it looks like Brandan and Jessie are the paparazzi's top-choice couple right now, and you'll provide a good diversion for them. The paps still aren't happy with him after he broke that one guy's nose. Now that he and Jessie are supposedly back together, we want the media hoopla to die down for them. I'm hoping that Brandan can get his life back on track."

"He's not exactly my number one concern," I mutter. At least Jessie told me that he's been treating her better. "Russell was impressed that you chose Emilie for me, seeing as she's French and I'm about to go on a world tour."

Rose's cheeks flush with the praise. "She is a big deal in France. The media loves her there. I figured, if you approved of her, she'd give you good press."

A thought occurs to me. "Just how long is this romance with Emilie going to last, Ro?" A few fake dates here in LA is one thing; having her with me on tour is entirely different.

"I'm thinking through at least the European leg of your tour." *Through March—eight months?* Seeing my scowl, she quickly adds, "She's a popular international model, Cole. She has shoots already lined up for most of the next few months."

"Okay. So long as I don't have to tour with her. Well, I don't care if she comes along, but you're the one I'm going to be touring with, Ro. Got that? I want to explore Europe with *you*, not some French clothes hanger."

"Cole! You haven't even met her." She looks away from me, prompting me to reach out and turn her face back toward mine. We silently stare at each other for a long moment. She looks worried, nervous even.

I break the silence. "You have my heart, Rose Bloomer. I'm proud that you're my girlfriend. I'm excited to tour Europe and Australia for the first time, but mostly because you're going to be at my side. You challenge me, and I like that. Your mind scares me sometimes, but that's good, too. And I find you so much sexier than any model or actress I've ever met. No one's going to change my feelings for you."

During my little speech, her blue eyes have gone from nervous to stormy. They're shining with something approaching love, but neither one of us is ready to go there yet.

She clears her throat. "You know it's not 100% that I can go with you on tour."

"Having Gruesome with me on Friday will give me a good chance to discuss that topic with her."

"Are you for real? Maybe you should pinch me. I keep waiting for the other shoe to drop."

"This is as real as it gets. How about instead of pinching you, I bite your butt to prove it?"

In response, she giggles and runs away from the table, hands protecting her ass. She turns at the threshold and says, "I'm going to run a bath to finish unwinding from today."

The next second, she's gone. And the imp didn't even invite me to join her. We'll just see about that.

Twenty-Six

"**G**OOD JOB, COLE," THE PRODUCER ANNOUNCES when I finish the vocals for the last track, "Taboo." Everyone in the studio starts clapping and high fiving.

"Way to go, man," the sound engineer says as he gives me a fist bump. "The tracks sound friggin' awesome and I haven't even done my magic yet."

"Thanks, Sam." I'm pumped to be finished with my third album. It's not like the album is ready to be released tomorrow, but the vocals, overdubs and instrumentals are done on my end.

"Party tonight!" This from Jon, which earns a chorus of "fuck yeah" from across the room. No matter how happy I am with the work we've done, I can't get pumped about tonight. I'd much rather be having an up close and personal celebration with Rose, but that's going to have to wait one more day.

"Look at that shit-eating grin on Cole's face. Now that your work is all done, pretty boy, you're gonna play."

"Something like that, Sam. But by your logic, you shouldn't come out with us because you still have work to do on the album."

Sam flips me the bird and replies, "No way am I missing out on one of your parties. They're legendary. I'm looking forward to hooking up with a hot piece of ass tonight."

I can't believe that my life has changed so much since my last album. Last time, I was first in line to celebrate. I can't even remember which—or how many—women I fucked to commemorate the occasion. I can only shake my head. An imp has stolen my heart, changing everything for me.

"Cole, Greta has arranged for us to have dinner at The Ivy," Jon says. "It'll be you, me, Russell and his wife and a few others from Platinum."

"Sounds good."

"We'll meet up with the rest of the crew at Ultra Nightclub after dinner." I nod, remembering to keep a smile plastered on my face. Jon continues, "I have some work to do before dinner. See you at The Ivy at nine. Oh, I almost forgot, Greta's sending a limo to pick you up so you can get hammered and not worry about having to drive."

"How thoughtful. Looking forward to it. Thanks." He claps me on the back and leaves the room.

Russell comes up to me next. "See you at The Ivy," he says, shaking my hand. But before walking off, he takes a good look at me. "Hey, are you all right, man? You don't seem your usual self."

Trying to make my smile seem more genuine, I say, "Just tired. I'm pumped about finishing the album, though. Think I'll run home and take care of a few things before dinner."

"I'll walk out with you."

Russell and I wave to the rest of the crew before we step out into the hallway. Wills lets us pass and follows at a reasonable distance. "How's Nolan Kates working out?"

"Everything's good." At the front of the building, we part ways.

Wills and I drive back to my house, where we both crash in anticipation of the long night ahead. Around seven, Rose settles in beside me. She starts kissing my shoulder and neck while her hands roam lower and finally settle around my fully alert cock. She strokes me, running her finger over my lower head, wiping off my pre-cum. Her mouth finds mine and our tongues begin the dance that our bodies demand to mimic. Soon, she's rolling a condom onto me and crawling on top of my body and easing her drenched pussy down onto me. My hands are plucking her nipples, which makes her squirm. I trace her flower birthmark lovingly, and thrust up into her tight body. Her head lolls back and she lets out a moan that has me grabbing her hips. Our movement becomes more erratic. We both shatter.

Sometime later, my little imp is lying across my body, languidly drawing circles on my chest. I check the clock and know I can't delay showering and getting ready for tonight any longer. Not wanting to make this any more difficult than it has to be, I give Rose a lingering kiss and slip into the bathroom. I hate leaving her naked, in my bed, all alone. But we both know that tonight is part of my job description.

"Cole, the limo's out front," Rose lets me know. I come to stand before her, dressed in black slacks and a white button-down shirt that I've left untucked, per Rose's instructions. She's wearing one of my T-shirts, which falls nearly to her knees. Inhaling her scent, I give her a kiss that tries to convey all my emotions for her, plus my sorrow about her not being with me tonight.

"This is the first night we're spending apart in weeks. I'll make it up to you tomorrow."

"I'm making dinner for you tomorrow, remember?"

"How could I forget? You're going to be in my kitchen, barefoot and cooking," I tease, earning a shy smile from her.

"Have a good time tonight. Enjoy the party. You've worked so hard. You deserve this."

"The real celebration will be tomorrow. I don't know what time I'll be back tonight, but it probably won't be until really early in the morning. I'll try not to wake you."

"I was thinking of spending the night at my rental," she says while looking down.

Does my girl need some reassurance? I reach out and raise her chin with my hand. "Stay here, Ro. I need to know that you'll be here when I get home.

That thought is the only thing that will keep me sane tonight. Don't leave."

Rose looks at me with her gorgeous ice blue eyes, which seem bigger somehow. Whispering, she acquiesces, "I'll be here. Wake me up, okay?"

Tracing her cheekbone with my finger, I agree and give her another kiss. "I'll see you later."

All too soon, Wills and I are walking into The Ivy. Of course, paparazzi snapped away when I got out of the limo. The Ivy is notorious for pushy paps, which I'm sure is why it was selected for dinner tonight. Wills walks over to the bar and I'm escorted to my table.

"There he is," Russell says, shaking my hand.

I turn and give his wife a smile before kissing her on the cheek. "Good to see you again, Wendy." The last time I saw her was at Mom's funeral, but I don't want to dwell on that.

"I understand congratulations are in order. Russell tells me this is your best album so far."

"From his mouth. I hope the fans like it."

"I'm sure they will," chimes in Jon. "You remember Tyler Slate?" He gestures to the man beside him, whom I do indeed recognize.

"Of course, how could I forget the man who discovered me in New York City? It's great to see you again."

I'm sincere. Tyler and I have run into each other a few times over the years, and it's always nice to sit down and have dinner with him. I'm introduced to the remaining Platinum people and do my damnedest to remain focused on the present rather than on the woman waiting in my bed.

Remembering what Rose told me to do, I make sure to look around the dining room until my eyes land on Emilie. Thanks to Google, I have seen enough images of her to easily spot her. Every so often, I force my eyes to return to the model. Sometimes I even catch her looking back at me. Seems like everything is right on track.

"Someone catch your eye, Cole?" Tyler asks.

I point my chin toward Emilie. "Who's that?" At least I don't choke.

Wendy places her hand on top of Russell's and leans in. Whispering, she says, "She's that French supermodel, Emilie Dubois. You know her Russell. She's on the cover of every magazine."

Jon joins our conversation. "What's all the whispering about?"

"Wendy was just giving me the run down about that chick over there," I nod toward Emilie. "But we didn't get to the good part yet. Is she dating anyone?"

"Not that I'm aware of. If memory serves, she was linked to some Spanish soccer player, but I don't think they're still together."

I file that tidbit away to ask Emilie about it if and when we become friends. Was it a real relationship? "Seems like she might be lonely, then."

"Cole, you're not going to—" Wendy starts to say, but I'm already up and moving before she finishes. I know that was rude, and I'll apologize later, but time is running out. I need to make sure I publicly invite her to come with us to Ultra. Her and her friends are finishing up their coffees.

"Hi, ladies," I inject myself into Emilie's table. Three pairs of eyes greet me. Or, more accurately, three pairs of eyes run up and down my body before ending up at my eyes. They all giggle.

Emilie replies, "*Bonsoir.*"

Great. I thought she spoke English. I don't know French.

Leaning down, I murmur in Emilie's ear. "You look lovely. Are you ready to come to Ultra with me tonight and begin our fake romance?" Might as well be truthful. Fascinating concept, that. Thanks, Rose.

She smiles up at me. She is striking. Turning to her girlfriends, she relays the invitation and I see the ladies nod in agreement. "*Oui.* We would love to join you at the club," Emilie says with a thick, but understandable, accent. Thank fuck.

I stand. "Great. Come join us at our table when you're finished here, and we'll go over together." More head nods and smiles.

Returning to our table, I remember to grin. No wonder actors get paid so damn much. It's exhausting.

"Looks like we added three more to our list for Ultra," I declare.

"Just like that?" Wendy asks.

"Just. Like. That." I snap my fingers to illustrate my point. I lean over to her and say, "Sorry I was rude back there. I was swept up in Emilie, you know?"

Wendy gives me a big smile. "You're forgiven."

Emilie and her two friends join us while we're finishing our desserts. Once our bill is paid, our larger group heads off to Ultra. Of course, Emilie agrees to ride in the limo with me. Her friends take their car.

Flash bulbs explode, documenting every millisecond of Emilie and me leaving The Ivy together. The paparazzi are in a feeding frenzy over our budding fake romance, trying to get the money shot of us. They scream:

"Were you cheating on Jessie with Emilie?"

"Does Rinaldo know about Cole?"

Ignoring them, I usher her into the limo. Once we make it inside, Wills closes the door and joins the driver up front. The cacophony is silenced. Thankfully, the limo has tinted windows.

I sit facing Emilie. We're alone for the first time. Extending my hand, I force my lips upward and say, "Hi, I'm Cole Manchester. Nice to meet you."

Emilie gives me a blinding smile and shakes my hand. "Emilie Dubois."

"You have a great accent, Emilie."

"Thanks, *Monsieur*."

"Are you ready for all the craziness our fake romance is going to stir up?"

"Yes. It is good for both our careers, no?"

I'm impressed. For a young woman, she seems to have a good grasp of how the business works. "Yes, it is. So, tell me a little about yourself." I smile. "Other than that you're a model and French."

Emilie tells me about her childhood in Paris and her family. I ask her this Rinaldo, and she sighs heavily. "We met at a charity event when I was eighteen. He was playing football—soccer—in Barcelona and I was just starting to get into my modeling career, so we didn't have time to be together too much. But when we did, poof. Fireworks, you know?"

I smile and nod. Yes, I do know.

"We got together every chance we had, but it wasn't even every weekend.

More like once a month, if we were lucky. Everything became too difficult."

"So you ended things."

"*Oui.* It's been six months." She runs her fingers up and down her purse strap. "I still miss him, but I'm sure I'll see him again. In the meantime, there are plenty more men to meet." Giving me an expectant look, she places her hand on mine.

Gently, I remove my hand from her grasp. She's young and nursing a broken heart, even if she's putting up a good front. "I'm sorry, Emilie. I hope you see your Rinaldo soon, or that you meet someone else who sweeps you off your feet. Everyone deserves that sort of happiness." I lick my bottom lip. "I'm involved with a wonderful woman, but it took me years to find her."

"Is it Jessie Anderson? You two look great together."

Smiling, I say, "Thanks, but no. Jessie is a wonderful friend, though. I'll introduce you if I can." I look out the window and realize we're close to Ultra. "We're nearly at the club. Are you ready for the paparazzi?"

"Yes. I live my life in front of a camera." She says this without any negativity. I'm impressed.

"Now, I'm going to apologize upfront for any fooling around that we may have to do in there. If you feel uncomfortable, please let me know and I'll stop, okay?"

She smiles and places her hand on my arm. "Cole, what a gentleman you are. We do what we must do, *n'est-ce pas?*" A look of understanding passes between us.

Thinking back to my pre-Rose days, I realize Emilie shouldn't exit the limo in the same pristine condition as she entered it. Sighing, I say, "Emilie, I think you should muss up your hair. You know, make it look like we were fooling around back here."

Without hesitation, she replies, "*Oui.* You are right."

She flips her long blonde hair over her head and shakes it back into place, so that it looks like I had my hands in it. I run my fingers through my own hair, giving it the ever-popular "just fucked" look while she unbuttons one of the top buttons on her blouse. Not precisely how a passionate tryst would look, but it will pass. People see what they want to see.

The limo stops in front of the club, and Wills opens the door. I step out first, then turn around and hold out my hand. The paparazzi, tipped off by their fellow vultures and probably Rose, are eating this up. Emilie places her tiny hand in mine, and I assist her out of the limo. Tilting her face up toward mine, she offers me an adoring look. Flash bulbs nearly blind us both.

Hand-in-hand, I lead her into the nightclub while ignoring the questions being hurled at us from all sides. Emilie's a little nervous about all the hoopla, judging from the death grip she has on my hand. Gotta give her credit, though. No one would ever guess her inner turmoil.

Once my eyes adjust to the dim lighting, I lean toward her ear and tell her, "Don't worry, darlin', the worst is over. For now, anyway. What can I get you to drink?"

"I'll have a glass of champagne. *Merci*, Cole."

I walk her over to her girlfriends who have commandeered a couple of white sofas in an alcove facing the dance floor, and then leave to get our drinks. I join Russell at the nearest bar, which has mirrors behind it that perfectly frame the models.

"How's it going with Emilie?"

"She's a nice girl, Russell. She's somewhat overwhelmed and definitely heartbroken, but she's putting on a brave front."

"So, is she going to be treated to some Cole magic tonight?" He smiles, bumping my shoulder.

"This is just for publicity, Russell."

"Never stopped you before."

His reply brings me up short. He's right. Beautiful and unattached women were all fair game for me in the past. I'll let him believe what he wants, at least until Rose and I can come clean. Leading this double life sucks.

"We'll see what tonight brings," I respond as I take the beer and champagne from the bartender and return to Emilie.

I place her glass on what passes for a table, an LED cube that glows a different color every few seconds, and slide onto the sofa beside her. "Here you go, darlin.'"

"*Merci*, Cole."

The other models sitting around the sofa giggle and sip their drinks. Sam and a guy from Platinum have joined the little group, and they're doing their best to chat up Emilie's friends. I really should give her a kiss for our audience, but I'm not ready. At that exact second, I receive a text from Rose.

Hope you're canoodling with Emilie. Make it look real. I'm okay.

How did Rose know that I was struggling right now? Her words give me the reassurance I needed. *Thanks, babe. Can't wait to show you how much you mean to me.*

With Rose's text echoing in my brain, I take a deep breath and a long pull of my beer. Leaning over to Emilie, I place a chaste kiss on her cheek and run my hand up and down her arm.

We sit like this for a long while, sipping our drinks, chatting and taking in the atmosphere. The music is pounding. The dance floor is filled, a light show whipping dancers into a frenzy. Every so often, a smoke machine adds to the high-voltage energy. One-by-one, her girlfriends pair off with my crew, leaving us alone on the sofa.

"Do you think people are watching us, Cole?"

"I'm sure they are. That's why we have to keep up appearances." I catch the eye of a server and order us another round. Even if we aren't hooking up, there's no reason not to enjoy the night.

"Cole, how wonderful to see you!" Gruesome. Ugh. She's wearing a tight black dress and stilettos. Too bad her personality doesn't match her banging body.

I stand and give her a kiss on both cheeks. "Greta, have you met Emilie?"

Emilie rises gracefully from the sofa and extends her hand to Greta. "Madame VonStein, I have heard so many good things about you and your firm. A pleasure."

"The pleasure is all mine," Greta coos. "Well, from the looks of it, the pleasure is not *all* mine." She smirks and continues, "Cole, a word?"

I turn to Emilie and see her reaching for her purse. "You two stay here. I will run to the lavatory," she says in her accent.

As soon as Emilie leaves, Gruesome starts in on me. "How's it going, Cole? Emilie and you look perfect together. She's just what you need on your arm before your big world tour."

"It's going well, Greta. I think she could use a friend right about now."

"You go on being that friend," Gruesome says with a knowing look in her eyes. I get her message: *Don't mess things up because you're stuck with her for months.*

"We're cool."

"Good." Gruesome is almost purring, sliding her talons up and down my forearm. "You're a natural at this. Keep up the good work. I'll make sure to have Rose call you in the morning to fill you in on the public reaction to your new romance."

God, I hate the idea of Rose having to sift the Internet for all the gossip about my fake fling. At least this is a good segue for me to ask for what I want. "Speaking of Rose, I want her to come with me to manage the publicity for my world tour." I pause. "Since you're obviously needed here in LA."

"Let me see what I can do," she responds offhandedly. I've already lost most of her attention. She's scanning the room, searching for fresh meat. Whether the meat is for her business or her pleasure remains to be seen.

Emilie exits the ladies' room. "Greta, I see Emilie coming back. We'll keep doing what we're doing."

"Ramp it up. You've been stuck at PG all night." Gruesome nods at Emilie politely and waves at a familiar face in the crowd.

Emilie returns to her spot on our sofa while Gruesome schmoozes. Smoke and mirrors. At least we seem to be in the right place, given the décor.

"She is a very powerful lady. You are so lucky to have her on your team, Cole."

"Yes, Greta and her team are excellent at the publicity biz. She thinks we need to ramp it up." Might as well get it out there.

After a long pause, Emilie says, "You mean go dancing?"

Her response makes me chuckle. Her language challenges are adorable, although she seems to have done a pretty good job of mastering English. "Well, dancing can be part of it, Em, but she meant that we need to put on more of a show."

She frowns, puzzling through my statement. "Oh! She wants us to become lovers."

It's a struggle, but I manage to swallow my mouthful of beer rather than spit it out all over her. "Not quite that far, darlin', but she does want us to get a little cozier."

"That will be, how do you say? A cinch."

My eyebrow shoots up with her characterization, but I don't say anything. What's there to say? I glance at my watch. 1 a.m. I probably don't have to stay here more than another couple more hours, but I have to make a less PG move on her otherwise people may start to wonder.

Sending sincere "forgive me" vibes to Rose, I take Emilie by the shoulders and deliberately pull her toward me. She places her hand on my cheek, stroking it. The atmosphere around us shifts, and I sense that cell phone cameras are being pointed in our direction.

"I'm going to kiss you now, Emilie."

In response, she nods her head and I see her eyes drift shut. Reluctantly, I close the distance between our lips. Her hand on my cheek gives me an idea. I put both my hands on her cheeks, obscuring our audience's view of the lip-lock. After what I believe to be a long enough, yet chaste, kiss, I pull back. Our foreheads are touching, my hands still on her cheeks. I kiss her nose and smile as her eyes open; she smiles back.

"I'm sorry I'm not the man you want to be here with, Emilie."

"I am happy to be here with you, Cole. It is I who am sorry that I am the wrong woman."

"You're very sweet. Your Rinaldo was an idiot."

She stiffens in my arms. I pull her in for a tight hug, trying to impart the sense that everything will turn out okay.

I'm stroking her back in comfort when someone taps me on the shoulder. A backward glance reveals Russell and Wendy are standing behind us.

Disengaging from our embrace, I wrap my arm around Emilie's shoulder to mark my figurative territory. I invite them to join us on the sofa. The more the merrier, in my opinion. Wendy gushes over Emilie, which lifts her spirits nicely after my *faux pas* of mentioning Rinaldo.

"We're going to head out . . . well, when I manage to disengage my wife from your date," Russell announces. He leans over and continues, "She's been watching you two all night and is convinced you're a perfect pair."

I contain a snort and don't contradict him. We must be doing a good job of pretending to fall for each other.

Once they leave, I invite Emilie to the dance floor. Not surprisingly, she's a good dancer. We enjoy dancing to several of my friends' songs, and I feel myself actually start to relax. That's when Gruesome catches my eye from across the room. She makes an impossible to misinterpret gesture; she's demanding that I grope my date.

A slow song starts, so I pull Emilie tightly against my body, placing my hands on her ass. "Sorry, darlin'. I got a look from my publicist over there. She seems to think we're being too tame again."

Please let Rose be able to handle the photos that are going to be published after this evening. Hell, I hope I can handle them.

In response, Emilie wraps her arms around my neck. Given her heels and height, she's only an inch shorter than me. She tilts her head, obviously expecting a kiss. One that I have no option but to give her. I can't cover our faces this time, so this kiss has to look real.

I place my mouth over hers. One Mississippi, two Mississippi, three Mississippi. That has to be long enough. Well, maybe not. How long would I kiss Rose? Like fucking forever. I can't keep kissing Emilie like this, I just can't, so I move my lips down to her long neck while stroking her back. For her part, Emilie has her hands curled in my hair. Damn, I wish this girl were Rose. I pull back and offer her what I hope looks like a sexy smirk.

"Wanna get out of here?" I ask loud enough to be overheard.

Smiling, Emilie nods in agreement. I give her a real smile, deep enough that I'm sure my dimple is showing, because soon I'll be in Rose's arms.

I kiss her hand, and we say our goodbyes to our friends on the dance floor. From what I can tell, Sam is going to get lucky tonight with one of Emilie's friends, which bodes well for a productive Monday. I wink at him and he gives me the thumbs up sign.

We make a show of leaving together. The paparazzi take many more photos to document our departure. Soon we're safely ensconced in Gruesome's limo once again.

"Sorry for all the groping I had to do in there, Em."

"Do not be sorry. We were doing our jobs." She giggles. "Besides, it is not a hard job to kiss with such a handsome man."

I smile. "You're not too hard on the eyes either."

A short ride later, we arrive at the high-rise building where Emilie has an apartment. From the front of the limo, Wills says, "There are a few paparazzi out front. Do you know, Miss Dubois, if there is a back entrance?"

"I do not know, *Monsieur*. I only moved in a short time ago."

I don't want her to have to face the paps alone. But, if I walk her up to her apartment, I'll have to stay all night. After all, I have a reputation to live down to. Fuck.

"Have the driver circle the block while you call the building and ask, Wills." I need to get home.

Emilie tries to comfort me, but my panic rises to a crescendo as the minutes tick past. I can't spend the night apart from Rose. There has to be another way for Emilie to get into her damned apartment.

Finally, Wills says, "We've located another entrance."

Exhaling, I say, "Thank God. Let's go."

"There's a small problem. We're working it out."

I want to punch something, but that won't get me anywhere. Wills is a professional and he's working on it, so I cling to that thought.

"Did you have a good time tonight, Cole?"

She's trying to distract me. Sighing, I answer, "Yes, Em. You're a lovely date. Another time, I probably would have asked to join you upstairs."

She smiles at me. "I might have let you come up."

Her response wrings another real smile from me. This girl has a fun personality, which will make the next few months bearable. Considering the alternatives, I lucked out. *Thanks to my girlfriend.*

Wills clears his throat. "The night watchman in your building, Miss Dubois, has unlocked the delivery door in the back. We're going to transfer you to another car that one of my associates is bringing to a nearby parking lot. That car will drop you home. We can't have the limo drop you off because it's too conspicuous."

Geez. All this cloak and dagger crap just to get her home? Even with this solution, I can't chance being seen sneaking her into her apartment. My eyes land on Wills. "I'm sorry that I can't walk you to your door, Em. I'll have Wills go with you to make sure you get inside your apartment safely. I would do it, but—"

"I understand, Cole. Do not worry, I will be fine. You can keep your Wills with you."

"I'd feel better if he went with you." I raise my voice, "Wills, would you please accompany Emilie to her door."

"Sure thing. I'll get home in the decoy car. See you on Monday, Boss."

I stop Emilie's protest by placing my finger across her lips. "No arguments. Now, thank you for a fun evening. I'm sure our reps will be in touch to schedule our next outing."

I lean over and give her a peck on the cheek. To my surprise, I genuinely do like her. She's like a little sister I never had.

"Thank you, Cole. Until we meet again." Wills whisks her into a black Escalade with tinted windows.

My limo takes off in the opposite direction. I'm finally on my way home.

Twenty-Seven

THE CLOCK READS 4 A.M. WHEN I finally walk into my house. I need to be with Rose. As I place my keys into the bowl on the foyer table, I catch a whiff of perfume. It's Emilie's.

I refuse to go to our bed smelling of another woman, even if Rose set me up with her. Climbing the stairs, I veer away from the master bedroom with my girlfriend in it and enter Rose's Command Center. At least I can feel her presence in here.

After my shower, I wrap a towel around my waist and walk over to the sink. Taking a fresh toothbrush out of the cabinet, I brush my teeth to rid my mouth of any remnants of this evening. Finished, I look into the mirror and survey my reflection, making sure I'm scrubbed clean for Rose.

I pad down the hall and into my bedroom. After dropping the towel to the floor, I slip in alongside Rose and draw her warm body to mine. I frown, realizing that she's wearing a nightshirt. Placing my hand at the top of her thigh, I slowly move it upward, not encountering any panties. Better.

"Cole," Rose mumbles in her sleep.

She turns so that she's facing me and sighs. As much as I want to be inside her right now, she looks so peaceful that I don't want to wake her.

Kissing her forehead, I respond, "Shhh, sweetheart. It's early. Go back to sleep."

"Okay," is her garbled response, and she's instantly out again. I stroke her hair and revel in the sight of her sleeping form.

Even though it's late, I'm too wound up to fall asleep. As I stare at Rose, I find myself thinking of Mom and Dad, Dan and Suzanne, Jayson and Carl, Jessie and Amanda. All the couples I know and love.

With Emilie tonight, I felt nothing beyond brotherly vibes. Yes, she has a great sense of humor, cute personality and good business sense. As a person, I like her. But there was no rush when we kissed for the cameras. Yes, Emilie is a beautiful woman by anyone's standards, mine included, but I didn't have the urge to scratch an itch with her. And it was because of the woman lying in my arms right now. I'd rather let her sleep than wake her up in the hopes of satisfying my own body's desires. There's only one possible explanation.

I'm falling in love.

Instead of feeling panicked by this thought, I'm calm. Rose challenges me, makes me laugh, makes me want to protect her. God, she's been through so much in her life that I just want to put a permanent smile on her face. I want to take away the financial burdens she's been shouldering for herself and her mother. I want to make love with her—and only her. What else can this be, but love?

Inhaling Rose's floral scent, I cuddle her closer to my body and finally drift off.

"Wake up, sleepyhead," Rose nudges my shoulder.

When I turn my head, she's standing beside my bed with a breakfast tray in hand. "I thought you might like some nourishment," she says with a giggle. My cock instantly responds to that sweet sound.

"You're all the breakfast I need, Rose," I respond, grinning at her.

She places the tray on the side table and then sits down beside me. She's wearing my *favorite* apron and, if I'm not mistaken, nothing else. I stifle a groan.

As she's leaning over and shoveling scrambled eggs onto the fork, I make a show of plumping the pillows behind me. She brings the food to my mouth and instructs, "Open wide."

"You too," I say, reaching under her apron to part her lower lips. Closing my mouth around the fork, I begin to stroke her clit in a matching rhythm. We continue feeding each other until all of my eggs and bacon are gone and Rose's pussy is dripping wet for me. My cock is rock hard and demanding attention.

The fork clatters to the plate. Keeping my left hand inside of her pussy, I reach around and untie the apron from around her waist before tossing it over my shoulder. "Now it's time for dessert."

"Eek," she exclaims as I toss her, face first, onto her stomach. I grab one of my pillows and put it under her hips, raising her ass.

Leaning down, I lick her pussy from behind, fluttering my tongue against her clit. "Oh, Cole!"

"Not yet, baby. I want to come with you. In you."

"Yes!"

I grab a condom and roll it on in two seconds flat. I move behind her and grab her hair. Despite my body's urgent demands, I slowly ease into her.

"This is where I belong," I hiss as my cock disappears into her pussy.

"God. Yes, Cole. Right. There."

Watching my cock work her pussy is turning me on even more. After I wrap my hand around a mass of her brown hair, I pull back with a slight tug, which causes her head to jerk upward.

She turns her head, and our lips crash together. I'm pounding into her tight, wet pussy while kissing her senseless, my hand tight in her hair. I've never felt so out of control, so desperate to come.

"It's you, Ro. Just you."

She keeps pace with my frantic thrusts, moaning her encouragement. All too soon my balls tighten, signaling that I'm about to come.

"Now!" I order, and her pussy contracts around my cock.

"Oh, Cole!" she cries out. "Yes!" With one more thrust of my hips, I come in long spurts. A few minutes pass while our breathing calms. Then I turn us on our sides and take care of the spent condom.

"That was," she starts.

"Amazing." I finish.

"Yeah. Amazing." She nuzzles my neck while I run my hands up and down her body, paying particular attention to her ass.

She giggles. "You're a true ass man, aren't you?"

"What can I say? You found me out." She shimmies her ass in my hands.

"You better stay still, or else I'm going to have to make you scream again."

In response, Rose thrusts up against me once more, accompanied by another one of her delightful giggles.

"Game on," I murmur into her ear.

Later, after she's had three more orgasms to my two, I say, "I seem to remember your promising to cook me dinner." I'm staring at her reflection in the bathroom mirror. We've just come out of the shower, sated from the day's sexual escapades. At least for now.

Smiling, she responds, "I already prepped everything, so it won't take me too long. I even made red velvet cupcakes for dessert."

"I can't remember the last time I had red velvet. I think Mom made a red velvet cake for Jayson's birthday a couple of years ago." The memory makes me smile.

Picking up on my good mood, Rose says, "If you want to eat dinner while it's still dinner time, we better get down to the kitchen. Someone was asleep most of the day."

"But I was worth the wait, right, baby?"

"Always. Let me go grab my apron," she pauses and grins at me. "And I'll start cooking."

My eyes follow her as she sashays out of the bathroom in one of my button down shirts. She bends over to pick up the apron in the corner of the bedroom, giving me another glimpse of her perfectly round, bare bottom. After winking at me, she turns and leaves the room.

I'm as close to pure bliss as I've ever known. I want to bottle this feeling to protect us from the outside world forever.

I throw on a pair of jeans and a T-shirt, and join her in the kitchen. The oven is on, something is simmering in one large pot and she's working over another sauté pan on the cook top. The scent of fresh herbs makes my mouth water. She has my iPod on and is humming tunelessly, dancing through my kitchen. My chuckling makes her turn and stare at me with a dangerous glint in her eye.

"You're not making fun of my singing, are you, Mr. Manchester?"

Placing my hand over my heart, I shake my head. "Of course not. I'm laughing with you."

Her eyes narrow as she shakes a wooden spoon in my general direction. "I don't remember laughing."

A good offense is the best defense, so I ask, "What are you making? Looks complicated."

She smiles. "I'm making Chicken Milanese with coconut rice and a white bean soup. They're my mother's recipes."

"Smells wonderful."

"Take a seat. Salad's on the table."

"I could get used to this. I love seeing you in my kitchen. It appeals to the caveman in me."

"Well, plant your ass, Tarzan, 'cause soup's up."

Playing along, I grunt in response, which elicits a giggle from my Jane. "Told you I was laughing with you."

"Right." She gives me a stern look that almost makes me pull her down into my lap. "Now enjoy."

I bring a spoonful of the soup to my lips, praying that it's good. The bacon makes the beans pop. "Rose, this soup is delicious. Sit down and enjoy it with me."

Her face flushes pink at the compliment. Sliding into her seat at the dinette, she says, "Glad you like it."

The following course is just as delightful. So is dessert. I can't get over how much I love eating dinner together like any other normal couple. Patting my full stomach, I offer, "Compliments to the chef. Dinner was perfect."

"Thanks. It was fun cooking for you, but don't get too used to it," she quips. "I'm home later than you most nights."

The mention of her job raises the specter of last night. "Did everything play out the way you wanted it to in the press, Ro?"

Placing her napkin on the table, her lips form a smile that doesn't reach her eyes. "Yes, you and Emilie were the talk of all the tabloids."

"Hey," I reach for her hand. "We did what we had to do. Gruesome was there, at Ultra, giving us directions."

She nods. "I know. I spoke with Greta while you were sleeping. Everything's right on track."

"It was rough for me being out with Emilie last night. She's a nice girl, but she's not you. My heart was here with you all night. You know that, right?"

In response, she looks down and says, "Yeah."

"Hey," I say, grabbing her chin and forcing her face up to mine. "I'm telling you the truth. You can ask Emilie. I think she got sick and tired of hearing about you."

Wide-eyed, Rose asks, "You didn't tell her my name, did you?"

"Of course not. I just told her that I have someone very special in my life."

"Oh. Okay." Rose's voice turns to a whisper as she says, "The pictures of you two look great. You're a striking couple."

"Rose, stop it. You fixed us up for a purpose and we were both playing our parts. This situation is tough on all of us. Emilie's nursing a broken heart. I think the fact that I wasn't interested rubbed some salt into it, I'm afraid."

Rose's ice blue eyes meet mine, and I continue, "You know, I showered and brushed my teeth in your Command Center before getting into bed with you last night. I didn't want to bring my work into our bedroom."

"Really? Why didn't you wake me up?"

"I didn't want to disturb you. Besides, I enjoyed watching you sleep. You're so beautiful."

"You don't have to lay it on that thick."

"I'm telling you the truth. You are beyond beautiful to me. When I look at you, I don't just see your gorgeous body. I see straight to your wonderful and giving heart, scary-smart brain and wicked sense of humor." I touch her heart, head and mouth to emphasize my points and pull her in for a long, deep kiss. "Not to mention your great rack, perfect ass and tight pussy."

She swats at my hands as I try to emphasize these points. "Nice, Cole. Way to make a girl feel special."

"Oh, I want you to feel special, all right." I grin at her, and she smiles back. Her smile reaches her eyes now. "Are we good?"

"We're good, Cole. I needed that. After seeing the photos from last night and having to post on your social media sites today about Emilie, I felt a bit . . . off. Which I knew was ridiculous because I was the one who suggested her. But Mom said," she stops short with a quick intake of air.

I cock my brow. "What did your mother say?"

She stands and brings the dishes over to the dishwasher. "I called to confirm I had her recipes right. When she asked why I was cooking such an elaborate meal, I told her about you. About us."

My heart jolts. I'm no longer her dirty little secret. Grinning, I bring more plates over to the dishwasher, and kiss her cheek. "I can't wait to meet her."

"Yeah, well, don't be so quick."

"C'mon, I want to meet the woman who made you who you are."

She steps around me, and wipes down the counter. "Remember when I told you Mom doesn't trust men?" She scrubs at an invisible stain and continues, "Well, most men. Her best friend's son, him she adores." Under her breath, she mutters, "She's obsessed that he and I will get back together."

My mind ticks back and I remember that her mother and her first boyfriend's mother are best friends. That's ancient history. I place my hands over hers, stilling their path. "Once I meet your mom, I'm sure she'll understand I'm not most men. That I'm with you for the long haul."

Troubled blue eyes reach out to mine. I try to share her worry, but I've yet to meet a woman who I can't charm. With Rose as my incentive, I'm sure I'll win her over in no time.

"She's quite stubborn."

"Hmm. A Bloomer trait?" I tease.

She smiles and swats at me with the sponge, dripping water down my shirt. I look down my torso to the water stain that's rapidly expanding, and then back up at her face, which is now starting to flush.

"Seems like I'm already wet. Now it's your turn."

Twenty-Eight

"OKAY, EM, HAVE A SAFE FLIGHT. I'll see you when you get back from Rio." I kill the call.

Walking over to the patio, I join Rose by the pool. "Love your bikini, baby."

She smiles at me and asks, "Was that Emilie?"

"Yeah. She's on her way to Rio for a magazine shoot."

Rose nods. "She'll be back here in a couple of days, and then you're flying out to New York together."

"The paps will love that."

"Your media romance is going very well, Tarzan. This morning I saw a photo of you and Emilie that was supposedly taken a few days ago in Paris."

I snort. "As if. I've never been there. Even if I wanted to leave LA, the album's post-production schedule has been too crazy." The past few weeks have been intense, finishing up *Moving Forward Slowly*. Not to mention navigating life with my stalker, who seems fixated on Rose. She sent an ugly email to Rose's work address, which was promptly turned over to both our private investigator and Detective Mahoney. Thankfully, Gruesome didn't find out about it. I want this dealt with like yesterday.

I'm done thinking about my stalker and talking about my fake girlfriend, especially since my real one is sitting right next to me. My eyes zero in on Rose's bikini top and I move one cup to the side, exposing her boob.

With a pink face, she swats, half-heartedly, at my hand. "Cole."

"Rose," I counter, catching her nipple between my fingers and rolling it, enjoying its instant puckering. Leaning down, I lave it with my tongue, which elicits a little gasp.

"Tarzan, we have to get ready for the party."

"Mmmmm." I suck hard on her nipple, knowing it drives her crazy.

"Agh," she moans as her body arches in the chaise. "People will be here in an hour."

"Relax." My fingers move southward, pushing her bikini bottom to the side to stroke her wet folds. "You're so ready for me, Ro."

"We have to prepare," she says unconvincingly. "The party."

In response, I find her clit and begin the ministrations that soon bring her to the brink. Stopping suddenly, I tease, "I guess we should make sure that everything's ready for the party." I begin to pull my fingers away from her wet heat.

"No!" Rose grabs my hand to keep it between her thighs. "Finish what you started."

"Bossy." I kiss her neck. "I like it." I nip at her earlobe as I insert two fingers into her opening.

"God."

"No honey, it's just me. Cole."

I torment her with a rhythm that brings her to the precipice but doesn't allow her to fall over it. My cock strains against my bathing suit, demanding to join in the action. Pulling a condom packet out of my pocket with my free hand, I turn it over to Rose. "Please do the honors."

With glazed eyes, she takes the packet from me and rips it open with her teeth. I fucking love that I can make Rose, who thrives on control, so crazy.

She pulls my bathing suit down and rolls the condom over my throbbing cock. Not bothering to remove her bikini, I bring her astride me, move the material of her bottoms to the side and thrust into her hot pussy. I trace the flower birthmark at her hip with my fingers. She rides me fast, rubbing her clit against me, and we both shatter within minutes.

Following a short respite, Rose says softly, "You'd think some of this would have worn off by now."

Chuckling, I push her hair from her face. "What would have worn off?"

"The crazy monkey sex we always have."

"Monkey sex?" That makes me laugh so hard that she nearly falls off my lap. "If you haven't figured it out by now, you always turn me on."

"Yeah. But it's been over a month and our sex life only seems to be getting hotter."

"And that's a bad thing?"

"No. It's a great thing." She blushes. "It's just different."

"We're different, Ro. We're us. Don't overthink, keep enjoying."

Noise from inside the house draws our attention. Quickly, I right her bikini while she fixes the front of my bathing suit.

Wills leads the caterers onto the patio. "Just in the nick of time," I whisper in Rose's ear, causing her to smile. Hand in hand, we walk over and direct the set up.

Rose leaves to get changed for the party. I turn to Wills and ask, "Everything all set for tonight?"

"Yes. Roberto and I are at the front gate, and Shawn is watching from the street. We have everyone's photos, so we know who to let in. Of course, we did background checks on every one of the caterers. You're good to go."

We shake hands, and he disappears back into the house. I hate that some nut job stalker has forced me into living like this, but I refuse to take any chances where Rose is concerned.

Fifteen minutes later, all the preparations are well underway and I'm up in our room getting dressed. Rather, I'm changing into a different pair of trunks and throwing on a T-shirt. Rose has a sexy dress over a tankini, and her hair hangs loose around her shoulders.

"I appreciate that you only wear your bikinis for my private pleasure."

"Don't let your ego get too out of control. This was my only clean bathing suit."

I walk over and play with the strap of the bathing suit underneath her dress. Pitching my voice low, I say, "You're fucking hot, especially when you're dirty." Her shudder brings a smirk to my face. "You were made for my private pleasure, though. Don't forget that." I smack her on the ass as a reminder.

"Okay, Tarzan. Let's get downstairs and greet our guests."

We wander down the stairs and check to make sure that everything is in order. The party is a small gathering of our closest friends to celebrate my new album. I'm excited to share the cover art with my "inner circle," but, more importantly, this is the first party that Rose and I are hosting as a couple.

The doorbell rings and I open the door. Little Emma stands between her parents, holding their hands.

"Wow. And did you drive over here, Miss Emma?" Smiling, I bend down and scoop up my goddaughter.

"How are you doing, baby girl?" She gurgles in response.

"Hi, Suzanne," I lean over and give her a peck on the cheek. Shifting Emma slightly, I give Dan our patented man-hug.

I walk into the family room with Emma in my arms, moving toward the new toy I bought for her: a tiny, baby piano. Rose and Suzanne make for the bar area, and Dan joins me and Emma. "She's getting more gorgeous every time I see her, Dan. Thank God she takes after Suzanne."

"Thanks, man." He rolls his eyes. "She *is* the most beautiful baby, if I do say so myself." We both smile and listen as she plays. Rather, bangs the keys.

Dan faces me. "So, have you told her yet?"

Even though I haven't told him so, Dan's guessed that I'm in love with Rose. "No. I haven't found the right moment."

"You will. I'm happy for you. Rose is an amazing woman. She keeps you in line and on your toes. I like her." He leans in and lowers his voice. "Don't screw it up."

"Yeah, well I'll try not to."

Dan ruffles his daughter's hair, then fixes her pink bow. "How are things with Emilie? You're all over the gossip sites, you know. Rose is a fabulous publicist."

"Among her many other talents." I smirk. "Em's fine. She's in Rio now."

"Does that woman ever stay in one place? I get tired just hearing about her schedule."

Emma's babbling and pounding on the keys draws our attention for a moment. "Yeah, she's all over the globe. Which is great for her career and even better for me since I don't have to actually go out with her much in order to keep our names linked."

"How's it all working out on Rose's end?"

"Well, Ro's the one setting up all our dates, so at least she has some control over it. But seeing photos of us kissing and stuff kinda freaks her out. I wish Rose and I could go public, but with my stalker . . ." I pause and we look at each other, concern written on both our faces. Clearing my throat, I continue, "Plus, Gruesome would have a cow if she found out about us."

My gaze travels to Rose and Suzanne, who are sipping their drinks and chatting like old friends. Dan glances at them too, then says, "Your security for the party is good. Discreet."

"Thanks."

The doorbell interrupts our conversation. Leaving Dan to watch over his musical prodigy, I greet Jessie and Amanda. Rose comes up and gives them both hugs before ushering them into the house. I'm about to close the door when my friend Ozzy walks up the sidewalk.

"Manchester!"

"Martinez!"

I slap him on the back and he punches me on the shoulder, our typical greeting. I ask, "How's it hanging?"

"To the right, as usual." Smirking, he hands me a bottle of Cristal and enters the house.

"Thanks for this." I hold up the bottle. "I'm stoked you were able to make it. It's been way too long. How's the tour been?"

"Fucking rocking. Been all over the States and Canada. Some of those women up north are freaks." He elbows me in the ribs to make his point.

"Yeah, well those days are over for me, dude." I wave Rose over. "I want you to meet my girlfriend, Rose Morgan."

Rose extends her hand. "So nice to finally meet you, Ozzy."

Ozzy takes her hand to his lips instead of shaking it. "Well, aren't you a delicate flower, Rose. You must have some special pollen to tame Manchester here."

Frowning, I yank her hand out of Ozzy's hand and interlace our fingers. "Keep your pollination metaphors to yourself, Martinez," I mutter, earning a guffaw from my erstwhile friend.

For her part, Rose smiles at the oversized oaf and responds, "I'm not as delicate as I look." I squeeze her hand.

"I bet you're not since you're with this guy." He nods toward me. "Come on, beautiful, what does he have that I don't? What will it take for me to pluck you away from him?"

"I'm standing right here, douchebag."

Smiling, Rose replies, "Come now, Ozzy, we've only just met. But I've heard a lot of stories from Cole about you, and I'm not sure I'm your type at all."

He winks at me, then turns his attention back to Rose. "Why don't you give me a chance to prove you wrong? I'm sure Manchester hasn't painted me in the best light."

"Oh, he's given me a pretty complete picture. You're quite the hell raiser, aren't you?" While she's speaking, Rose points to the tattoos that form a sleeve on his left arm. His nipple piercing is evident through his shirt.

"Don't let the tats scare you away, Flower. I'm really a pussycat."

It's my turn to chortle. "Believe me, you don't want to be anywhere near this tomcat, Ro." I wrap my arm around her shoulder as the three of us walk amiably to the pool area, where all of our other friends now are gathered.

"Tell me Martinez, how long is your break, or is your tour over?"

"I'm off to Vegas for a couple of shows soon, but I'll be back in LA for a while afterward."

"Cool. I'm glad you'll be around," I say, patting his back.

All of a sudden, Emma lets out a loud wail, and all eyes turn to her. I walk over to Suzanne, who's comforting her in her arms. "Is she okay?"

"Yes. Sorry for the disruption. She bumped her head on the table," Suzanne says, bouncing the baby.

"She gets into all sorts of things," Dan chimes in.

I reach out and rub her forehead, feeling a lump beginning to form. "Poor Emma." In response to my touch, Emma's cries become louder so I yank my hand away.

"Let me get my guitar. Maybe a song will soothe her."

"Please, Cole," Suzanne says. "You'll be a lifesaver."

I sprint into the house to grab my guitar. When I return to the patio, Emma's still screeching. Boy, that girl has a set of lungs.

Clearing my throat, I say loudly, "This is going to be my newest single, scheduled to drop in September. It's called 'No One to Hold.' I wrote it for Mom."

I take a deep breath and play the first chords. About a third of the way into the song, Emma stops crying. By the end, she's smiling at me as if nothing ever happened. She even claps with all my other friends at the end.

"Thanks guys. I'm glad you all like it. And now I'd like to show you the mock-up of the album cover."

I've kept this a secret, even from Rose, which has been quite the feat considering she's pestered me about it for the past few weeks. I'm proud of the cover art, which I had a hand in designing. I pass around copies of the cover to *Moving Forward Slowly*, arriving at Rose last.

With a big grin, I make a big show of handing the final copy to her. She grabs it and looks it over carefully. "Wow. I like it; it's different."

I puff up with her compliment. Everyone else is echoing her sentiments, but Rose's words settle deep within my heart. So far, so good for this album.

A while later, Ozzy joins me at the food table. "Manchester, that's going to be a huge hit for you. I wish I had met your mom."

He selects a steak and puts it on his plate. *Looks good.* I do the same.

"She would have loved you." I pause. "She always had a thing for the weird ones." I add some lobster mac and cheese to my plate.

Popping a deviled egg in his mouth, he continues, "I have an idea." I quirk an eyebrow at him. "Why don't you debut your song during one of my Las Vegas concerts?"

"Really?"

"Why not? Plus, it'll be a good excuse to hang with you in Vegas, baby," he says with a wink, bypassing the salads in favor of a heaping mound of grilled asparagus.

Scooping up an impressive mushroom risotto, I reply, "That could work. It could be sort of an underground thing. You know, advertised yet not."

"Let's pitch it to Platinum."

We share a label, so this might actually work out. "I'll discuss the publicity angle with Rose."

He nods. "I'll let my publicist know once everything is all squared away. By the way, bro, I think Rose is a cool chick. She's good for you. Never thought I'd see the day."

My gaze wanders to Rose, who sits over by the pool on the chaise lounge that we christened right before the party, chatting with Jessie and Amanda. "Me neither. But she means the world to me. It sucks that we can't be out in public."

"I could escort her places for you."

"No way, Martinez. Keep your grubby hands off."

"Jeez. I was just trying to be helpful."

Laughing, we take our full plates and walk over to join the others, I scoot in behind Rose. "Feel familiar, Ro?" I whisper in her ear.

She turns a nice shade of pink, which earns me a stern "Cole" from Jessie. I shoot her my best innocent look.

"So, have you found a new roommate?" Amanda asks Rose, diverting my attention from Jessie.

This has been a bone of contention between Rose and me over the past few weeks. I want her to give up that rental. Damn stubborn woman has refused. Her lease isn't up until March and she says she doesn't want to break it. She's been interviewing potential roommates, but none have been approved by Kates's team.

"Not yet."

"I don't know why you don't just break the lease," I grumble.

Rose continues, "I don't want to cause any trouble for my landlord." She gives me a look that clearly conveys her feelings on the matter. I return her look. I have my own thoughts about it. "Besides, with the new alarm system Cole had installed, it's perfectly safe."

"Any news on the robbery front?"

"Nothing concrete yet, Jessie. My stolen items haven't surfaced. There was another break-in a couple of blocks away, but thankfully no one was hurt."

"At least that's something. And have you had any more run-ins with your stalker?"

I clear my throat. "Rose got an email at work a week ago, which our PI and the LAPD is looking into."

"Wow, Rose. What did the email say, if you don't mind my asking?"

Dan already knows all about this, but it's news to the rest of our guests. I trust them to keep the information private, so I give Rose a nod to let her know it's okay to share.

I pull her into my embrace to offer her my support. She responds, "It's fine, Jessie. I know I don't need to say this, but please don't tell anyone outside this group about the stalker." All my friends nod their heads nod in assent, as I knew they would.

"Thanks." Rose looks around and says, "Suzanne, cover Emma's ears." I can't help but smile when Suzanne does just that. It's no laughing matter, of course, but it feels good to smile in the face of this ongoing disaster.

Rose continues, "The email said, 'I don't know what you're trying to prove with this Emilie shit, but back off my man. Get the fuck out of his house. This is my last warning, slut.'"

Twenty-Nine

"C'MON EM, LET ME SHOW YOU to your room." I lead her toward one of the guest rooms in my penthouse.

"Thanks again, Cole. I really appreciate your invitation to stay at your place during New York Fashion Week."

"Not a problem. I needed to come out here anyway to visit my dad and get some photos for my upcoming video." I show her to the room and adjoining bathroom, pointing out the great view of Central Park.

In her cute French accent, she exclaims, "This city is one of my favorites. I love the skyscrapers and this big park. It is always so full of life." Emilie gives me a true, happy smile as opposed to the practiced ones she uses for modeling.

"What's your schedule like?"

"This week is filled with fittings and practices. I am modeling for many designers, and I have already done the preliminaries. My first show is Thursday, and then I will have a show every day through next week."

"So, not busy at all, huh?" I ask with a wink.

"It is nice to be in one place for two straight weeks, but I will not have too much free time. Once the shows get underway, I will be working from seven in the morning until eleven at night."

"Let me know if there's anything I can do to make this easier for you. How about I have the kitchen stocked with your favorite foods?"

"Oh, that would be wonderful, Cole. When it gets really crazy, I do not even have time to eat."

"We can't have that, Em. Give me a list and I'll make sure you have all your favorites."

"*Merci.* If you do not mind, *monsieur*, I am very tired and would like to nap. We are still going out for dinner later, no?"

"Yes," I can't help sighing. "We're all set for dinner at Le Bistro. Afterward, we'll meet up with your friends at Twist."

"I have been to that nightclub before. It is fun."

"I'm sure you'll like the restaurant. It's a French bistro."

Emilie's whole face lights up. "Tonight sounds nice. Thank you for picking a French restaurant."

"No problem." As usual, Rose's ideas are well received. "I'm going to take a nap, too." We both head to our respective bedrooms to unwind after the transcontinental flight.

As soon as I'm alone, I grab my cell and call Rose. She picks up on the second ring. "Hi, Cole."

The sound of her voice makes me smile and my cock twitch. "Hi, Ro. I wanted to let you know we made it into my penthouse and I'm already missing you like crazy."

"I saw you less than eight hours ago, Tarzan. I seem to remember your making me scream." I hear her giggle.

"I wish you were here with me. I would be making you scream all over again."

"I'm sure. I'll be seeing you in a couple of days."

"Yeah, but you're not going to be staying with me. You should be here with me."

"It would be kind of difficult explaining that to your model girlfriend." She pauses. "Besides, I haven't seen Mom in ages. She's only thirty minutes from your dad's place, so we'll meet up there on Wednesday."

I growl in frustration. "How about we sneak away for one night in New York?" The Big Apple is the perfect place for us to have a romantic weekend. After all, we both went to college here. And had our first, first time here. I'll make a reservation at the Gramercy Park Hotel—I've heard it's very romantic. During our room service dinner, I can finally tell her that I'm head over heels in love with her. And then I can show her all night. Yeah, I like this idea.

Rose's voice brings me back to the present. "Our schedules are pretty tight. Let's play it by ear, okay?"

At least it's not a definitive "no." I'll work on her at Dad's.

Rose continues, "Are you all set for tonight? The New York paparazzi already know you're in town because the photos of you and Emilie at JFK are making the rounds. Well done, by the way. You look like her big boyfriend protector in the pictures."

"I'm sure Wills would love to have that title." My bodyguard seems more than a little smitten with the French model. "To answer your question, yes, I got your email with all the details for this evening. Em is excited to go to the French bistro, so nice touch."

"Thanks. I thought she might be missing her home."

"Well, now that you've got my fake girlfriend all hooked up here in New York, what are you going to do about me? I'm missing *my* home. Especially my bed with a certain flower-birthmarked babe in it."

I hear her low moan softly through the phone and my cock jumps to attention. "I would love to help you out," she whispers, "but I'm at the office."

"You're killing me here, Ro."

"Oh crap. I gotta go, Greta's motioning for me to go into her office.

"Gruesome has shitty timing."

"Well, I *am* at work. Text me before you head out to dinner, okay?"

"Sure thing. Remember to stick with Roberto." I hate that I'm not there to protect her, but our guards have given us no reason to doubt them.

"Will do. Bye!"

With thoughts of Rose dancing in my head, I give in to sleep.

I'm pulled out of my sensual dream about Rose and her birthmark by a banging sound. "Cole, are you almost ready? Dinner is at eight."

What? Huh? *The noise ends and I turn over. Rose takes off her bikini bottoms by the pool at my house and dances around naked in the moonlight for me. Her perky boobs bounce near my face, but when I reach out to grab one, she dances away to music only she can hear. She shakes her luscious ass at me.*

"Cole, can you please zip me up? I cannot quite reach." *Rose is smiling at me over her shoulder, her tongue licking her lips.* "Cole? Can I come in?"

The sound of a door opening brings me fully awake to see Emilie standing at the threshold. "Cole? You are not up?"

Disoriented, I glance at the clock and see it's already almost eight. My eyes travel southward, to the evidence that the proper response to her question is most assuredly yes. I'm up. Shit. I fluff the comforter at my waist.

Shaking my head to clear the cobwebs, I clear my throat and say, "Sorry, Em. I forgot to set my clock. I'll be ready in a few."

"It is all right. I thought you were awake when I knocked earlier because you made a sound." *I'll bet I did.* "Would you mind zipping me up in my dress, please? I cannot do it myself."

"Sure thing." I'm halfway out of bed before I realize I'm nude. "Ah, can you come closer, Em?"

She walks over to my side of the bed, offering me her back while pulling her long hair out of the way. I go to pull up the zipper, but it gets stuck on some material. "Shit, it's stuck. Give me a sec."

I carefully pull it back down and up again, but it snags at the same spot. "Damn, this is messed up. Let me try again."

Third time's a charm, and her dress zips. "Good to go, Em."

She turns and gives me a brilliant smile. "Thanks, Cole." She pauses a beat. "And your girlfriend is a very lucky woman." She winks and walks toward the door, leaving me alone with the realization that I lost the comforter in the zipper tug-of-war.

DINNER TURNS OUT TO be delightful. I do enjoy Emilie's company, and the food at Le Bistro is kickass. Maybe Rose will want to eat here; I'll have to remember to ask her.

On our way out, I drape my arm around Emilie's shoulders, remembering Rose's instructions. Sure enough, we're greeted by a flock of paparazzi out on the street. Even though it's well past 10 p.m., the flashbulbs make it seem like it's broad daylight.

"Doing okay, Em?" I whisper into her ear.

She turns and gives me her practiced smile. "*Oui*. It is as it should be."

Following Wills, we make it into our waiting limo, flashbulbs going off like crazy, paps spouting off insulting questions. Soon we're heading off for the nightclub.

Shaking my head, I say, "I'll never get used to this. When I'm on stage and performing, I get it. But, seriously, we're just walking out of a restaurant. Is it big news that you and I are human and we actually eat?"

Emilie laughs, and from the front seat, Wills turns his head. "They are just doing their jobs. Like us."

"I guess. So, are you ready to go clubbing?"

"Oh yes," Emilie says. "I have fun dancing." Well, that makes one of us. I only like dancing with Rose these days. Preferably naked and horizontally.

Once inside Twist, I head to the bar to get our drinks—seltzer with vodka and a twist of lime for Em, a cold beer for me. On my way back to her, a brazen blonde with huge tits walks up to me.

"Need a hand? I can take that drink off your hands." She undresses me with her eyes.

"Thanks, but I got it."

"Suit yourself. I'll be over there in case you change your mind," she says, nodding in the direction of the back corner. I offer her a tight smile and continue to make my way toward Emilie.

Someone pinches my ass. Stopping mid-stride, I work hard to maintain both my composure and the drinks. I turn my head and raise my eyebrow at another blonde, who is licking her lips at me. "Ma'am," I say and resume my beeline for Emilie.

Finally, she's about twenty feet ahead. Who knew the walk from the bar to my date would be fraught with so many hazards? Before Ro, I probably would have taken both chicks' phone numbers, but today I feel neither flattered nor tempted.

A tall brunette jumps in front of me from my right, barely avoiding an alcohol bath. "Sorry! I didn't see you there!" *Yeah, right.*

"It's okay darlin'. Nothing spilled." *Em, come over here and save me.*

Brunette giggles. The sound is too harsh, not the right octave at all. She places her hand on my forearm, saying, "Can I help you with that?"

Really? "I'm here with someone, darlin'."

"That's okay. I don't mind sharing."

While her offer might have intrigued me at a different point in my life, it falls flat now. Still, she's a fan so I can't be rude. "I appreciate the offer, but I'm a one-woman man nowadays." That's the truth, at least.

"Lucky girl."

"No, I'm the lucky man." I give a huge, dimpled smile as Emile walks up to me. "Have a nice evening," I tell threesome brunette, and walk off with Em, who takes the vodka and seltzer from me.

"I was wondering what was taking you so long with the drinks, Cole. I see you were ambushes by the brunette."

Her English mistake makes me smile, and I don't correct her. "And two other blondes before her." I chuckle at the look on her face. "I'm sure you get guys hitting on you all the time, too."

"No. Some yes, but most men are too intimidated by models."

"I guess that's because you travel in packs. But not every man runs from the challenge."

She shrugs and leads us back to the table her friends have snagged.

A couple hours later and a few more beers into the night, Wills comes up to me and whispers in my ear, "Rose is fine. Roberto didn't catch the unsub, but Rose wasn't injured."

"*What?*" I roar over the house music blaring through the crowd.

Heads turn in my direction, but I don't care. *What the hell is he talking about?* I pull out my cell and see ten missed calls, three texts and two voicemails. "Fuck!"

I open the text icon. All three are from Rose. The first one, about an hour ago says: *I'm fine. There was a scuffle with a flower delivery.*

The second one, about thirty minutes ago reads: *Don't worry about me. No damage.*

Ten minutes ago, the last one says: *Hope you're having fun with Emilie. I'll check out the pix tonight. Roberto's making me do a police report.*

I'm feeling so many emotions at once: anger, hurt, fear. Why do I have to be all the way across the country from her?

"Wills, stay here with Em and make sure she gets home okay. I'm going back to the penthouse to get to the bottom of this mess."

"Boss, I need to protect you."

"Wills, whoever this is seems to be targeting my girlfriend, not me. Stay here with Emilie. Tell her I had to go, that something came up with my girlfriend and not to worry about me. I need to call your boss and get the full scoop. I need to talk with Rose. And I need privacy." I stride out of the club, ignoring Wills's pleas and the many women in my path.

Finally, I'm in a car on the way back to the penthouse. I call Rose, but she doesn't answer. "Shit!"

Taking a deep breath, I check my voicemail and listen to my PI's message. "Cole, Kates here. Your stalker posed as a flower delivery person and accosted Rose on the street outside her office building. The stalker gave Rose a box, which contained a single dead red rose. Rose wasn't hurt, but Roberto was unable to catch the delivery person."

The next voicemail is from Roberto. "Cole, I'm so sorry that I couldn't tackle the unsub—er, unknown subject. Rose was dazed but not hurt. She refused to go to the hospital. I'm taking her down to the police station to file a report. I promise to protect her with my life."

A single dead rose? Ro refused to go to the hospital? This is my worst fucking nightmare. As soon as the driver parks in front of my building, I race out the car and up to my penthouse. Then I dial Rose again.

"Hi, Cole."

It feels so good to hear her voice. "Baby. Are you all right? Tell me what happened."

"Cole, I'm fine. I'm finishing up here at the police station."

"All I heard is that you were confronted by a flower delivery person who gave you a dead rose. And that you refused to go to the hospital to be checked out." The fear in my voice nearly strangles me. "God, if something were to happen to you . . ."

"I'm fine. I was knocked to the ground, but that's it."

"Why wasn't Roberto with you? What the hell was he doing?"

"Cole, Roberto was in the car outside my building. I was about to get in, but this happened so fast. It certainly wasn't his fault. Listen, I have to go back. Detective Mahoney took my statement and needs me to finish up. I'll call you later. I'm fine, don't worry."

"I worry, sweetheart." *Because I love you so much.*

I call Kates, who basically reiterates what Rose already told me. He also lectures me about ditching Wills in the club.

"Why the fuck didn't Roberto stop this?" I demand.

"He was following protocol by waiting in Rose's car in front of her building." That was my protocol to protect Ro from Gruesome's rules. *Shit.* Kates continues, "Your stalker has just upped the ante. It's good that Rose is joining you on the East Coast tomorrow. Roberto will be traveling with her."

"Nothing else better happen." I hate this feeling of impotence.

"We're on it, I promise."

"Do you have any leads?"

"We're having the note analyzed."

"Note. What note?"

"The flower delivery came with a note that said, 'This is my last warning, slut. Move out of my man's house or else end up like this.'"

Thirty

"**B**ro, how about this one?" Jayson hands me a great photo of Mom, pregnant with me.

"Yeah, that's a good one. Put it in Rose's pile."

"Rose's pile is pretty high. When's she coming over?"

"She'll be here in," I check my watch, "twenty minutes."

I can't wait. It's been agonizing to be apart from her, especially after what happened in LA. Rose has been staying at her mother's, laying low after the attack—our hopes of spending a night in New York together were toast—and I've spent the past day going through photos of Mom with Jayson and Dad.

"I'm looking forward to seeing Rose again."

"Me too, Dad." I also want to strip her naked and check every square inch of her body to prove to myself that she wasn't hurt. I don't care what she's been telling me, I want to see for myself. And then I want to make her scream, in a good way.

"Did your PI get a beat on the stalker?"

"Not much yet, Jayson. The only thing they're sure of is that it's a woman who probably lives in the LA area. But, she's like a ghost."

"And the cops? Have they found anything about the robbery?"

"Nothing. But they're going to have to fence some of their loot eventually. When they do, I'll be waiting."

"You've got a lot going on out in LA, son. Maybe you should both stay on this coast for a while."

"I'd really like that, Dad, but I'm off to Las Vegas they day after tomorrow to play 'No One to Hold' at Ozzy Martinez's show."

"How's Martinez doing?" Jayson pipes up. They met when Jayson came to LA to help decorate my house years ago. That fueled his interior design bug, which has turned into a flourishing career for him.

"He's good. He's finished the main part of his tour and is resting up in LA. I saw him recently at my house. Rose and I hosted our first party."

"Nice."

Our conversation is interrupted by the sound of the doorbell. I race Jayson to the front door, just like when we were kids. All my hours in the gym give me the edge, though, and I get to the door first. In my excitement, I nearly rip it off its hinges. Standing on the front step is Rose, looking more beautiful than ever. My breath catches as I drink her in.

"While my big brother stands there gawking at you, I'd like to invite you in, Rose," Jayson says while inserting himself in front of me.

She gives my brother a smile, which is the only encouragement he needs to pull her into his embrace. Stepping back from him, she crosses the threshold, and I reach out and cup her face. When she looks at me, her eyes seem different—somewhat guarded, maybe? But I don't stop to think about it; I need to connect with her. I lean down and give her a sweet kiss, pouring my heart and soul into it. I relish the shiver that runs up her spine.

"I've missed you so much, Ro. Welcome home," I whisper in her ear. Then I turn us both around to face my father, who has just cleared his throat.

"Rose, it's great to see you again. Please come in."

"Thank you, Mr. Manchester."

"My dear, we're way past those formalities. Call me Ken, please."

"Thank you, Ken." They hug, then dad leads the way to living room. Roberto came to the door with Rose, and I hang back to talk with him. Relief is written all over his face after I reassure him I don't blame him for what happened in LA. We shake hands, and I head off to the living room while he joins Wills out on the street.

Rose, Dad, Jayson, and I spend a couple of hours going through the "Rose pile" of photos, whittling it down considerably.

"Is that all of them?" I ask Dad.

He nods, then shakes his head. "No, wait, there's one more box. Let me get it."

He disappears into the back of the house. Jayson is on the phone with Carl in the kitchen, which means Rose and I are finally alone together for the first time since the incident.

Catching her hand, I pull her toward me. "I've been so worried about you."

"I'm fine."

"Something's up." I caress her arm, trying to get her to relax a little. "You're wound tighter than a monkey's nut."

My phrasing makes her laugh. *Success.* "Let's see what I can do to make you feel better." I move in closer to her, closing the distance between our lips.

Something's off. It's like a wall has been erected between us in the three days we've been apart.

"What's going on, Ro?" I ask, kissing her neck.

"Your father is in the next room."

"He's happy for us, Ro. Believe me."

I slant my mouth over hers, running my tongue across her closed lips. Soon, our tongues are dancing, imitating what the rest of me wants to be doing. Rose melts into my body. Much better.

In between kisses, I admit, "I've missed you. Missed this." Knowing that we have limited time, I try to cool things down, but my cock ignores me.

"This is the last box, Cole."

We spring apart like guilty teenagers. While I'm trying to regain a semblance of propriety, Rose responds breathlessly, "Thanks, Ken."

Dad places the box on the coffee table. "These were Julie's favorite photos and keepsakes. Every so often she'd take a photo and say that she wanted to keep it in her 'special place.' I came across this box about a month ago." He swallows.

Sitting down, Jayson asks, "Have you looked through them, Dad?"

"Yes. There are some good ones in there. While you guys are going through them, I'm going to order some pizza, okay?"

Sensing that looking at these photos again would be too tough for my father, I say, "Sounds good, Dad. We can't get good pizza in LA." He disappears into his study to place the order while Rose and I share a secret smile, remembering our trip to my neighborhood pizza joint.

"It's tough for him," Jayson says. "I can't imagine what my life would be like without Carl and we haven't been together a quarter as long as Mom and Dad were."

"I know, me either," I respond, squeezing Rose's hand.

"Are you ready to take a look at your mom's most important photos?" Rose says, squeezing my hand in return. "We don't have to do this now."

"I'm ready. Jayson?"

"Yeah, let's do this."

An hour later, we've gone through the entire box. All of us shed some tears and laughed a lot, especially at the hairdos and clothes. The potential pile for the video has expanded again.

"Are you sure you want to share all of these with the world, Cole?"

"I have to admit, I'm feeling pretty raw right now, so why don't we go over them again back in LA, Ro."

"I had a feeling you'd say that. Jayson, do you have any issues with Cole releasing these?"

"No. I don't want Mom to be remembered as just another lung cancer statistic or Cole's Grammy date. Although that evening certainly was a highlight of her life. I can't believe how many photos of Adam Baret there were in that box."

Rose giggles, causing a chain reaction throughout the room. Dad walks in with two pizza boxes in hand. "I got back here at the right time, I see."

"Stay with me tonight, Ro."

"I can't. I promised Mom some girl time."

Frowning, I say, "We haven't been alone for more than five minutes since you got here. You were attacked in LA. I just spent the past two days going through Mom's photos. I'm raw and I want to be with you. I need to be inside you."

She sucks in her breath. To sweeten the deal further, I offer, "Tell your mother that I'm giving you two a spa day tomorrow. The works."

"Well, she did look like she could use a massage."

"You do, too." I nuzzle her neck. "But only with a female masseuse. C'mon, what do you say? Stay here with me tonight?"

Before she says another word, her entire body sags against mine. Gently, I tuck her hair behind her ear.

Rose sighs and rests her head against my shoulder. "I have no self-control where you're concerned."

I bring my arms around her and hold her close, inhaling her scent. "Right back at'ya." We remain entwined for a long while.

"Let me call Mom and tell her about the change of plans. Why don't you make the spa arrangements while I'm on the phone with her?"

Reluctantly, I let go of her and we each take care of business. After hanging up with the spa, I walk into the kitchen. Dad's pouring a glass of scotch. "Hey, Dad."

He points to an empty glass, but I shake my head. "Is Rose leaving?"

"No. That's what I came to talk with you about. If it's okay, she's going to stay over here tonight."

"No problem. You know where the guest room is."

"Dad. Really?" I know this is a sensitive area, having been over this before, but I'm sure even Mom would let Rose and me share a bed together.

"Who am I kidding? Sure, you two can sleep together. You may still want to use the guest room, though. Your mom and I put a queen-sized bed in there a few years ago. More comfortable than your twin."

"Thanks, Dad." I go over and give him a hug. "I love you."

"I love you too, son."

Smiling at my father, I pour a couple of glasses of wine for Rose and me, and Dad and I return to the family room. Jayson and Rose are laughing it up.

"I remember my big brother, clear as day playing the leads in all our high school musicals. There was one night—"

"I'm sure Rose isn't interested in hearing about high school, Jayson."

She smiles up at me impishly. "I'm finding Jayson's stories fascinating. You weren't always this super cool, smooth guy, it turns out."

I shoot Jayson a "what did you tell her" look, followed by an "I'm going to kill you" look. For his part, Jayson gives me his "I'm innocent" look, which means I interrupted at precisely the right moment.

"Reminiscing is over. Rose is going to stay over here tonight, so we're going to retire now. Say goodnight, Jayson."

"Just when I was getting to the good stuff. Well, he won't be around all the time, we'll have to pick this up later. It was great seeing you, Rose."

"I agree, Jayson." Rose kisses his cheek and whispers something in his ear, causing him to bark in laughter.

"Ken, thank you for your hospitality. I'll see you in the morning." She gives my father a hug and a kiss on his cheek as well.

Lacing our fingers together, I guide her toward the stairs. "Night, Dad. See you, Jayson."

Finally, we are in my room, alone. "Dad's right, this twin bed isn't going to work. Let me grab some things, and we'll use the guest room."

"I thought we weren't allowed to sleep together under your dad's roof?"

"Dad relented. Besides, if he hadn't changed his mind, I would have gone to you anyway. I'm glad we don't have to sneak around, though."

Smiling, she looks around my room. "I like your teenage bedroom. Especially the posters."

"Well, I was a typical hormonal boy when I last lived here. Models and rock bands were my idols."

"Not much has changed. You're even dating a model."

"Ha, ha. Very funny. Look, I need to do something before we leave this room."

Determined to make sure she wasn't injured from the latest stalker incident, I silently start removing her clothes, kissing every square inch of skin as it's revealed. Once she's standing naked in front of me—the first woman *ever* naked in this room—I pull her arms to the side and eyeball her thoroughly. I let out an audible sigh. There's not a scratch or bruise on her.

"Perfect."

"I'm hardly perfect, Cole. Perfect is Emilie."

My girl needs some reassurance. I'm up for the job, in more ways than one. "Ro, you're perfect for me. I love your hair." I run my fingers through it, from scalp to tip, inhaling her floral shampoo.

"I love your collarbones." I lean over and lick the valley of her sexy collarbones.

"I love the way your boobs fill my palms." I demonstrate with both of them.

"I even love your cute knees."

Then it hits me square in the face. I have to tell her how I feel about *her*, not only her body. Sure, this isn't the most romantic moment, but it feels right.

I look into her blue eyes and say, "I love *you*, Rose Bloomer."

She sucks in a breath. "Really?"

"Yes. Let me show you."

I begin by kissing her beautiful mouth while pressing her to my body, my hands splayed across her ass. I press my thigh between her legs, causing her to ride up on her tip toes and clutch my shoulders. My tongue invades her mouth as I walk with her so that the back of her legs are pressed against the bed. Gently, I bring her down to a sitting on the bed and position myself on the floor between her parted thighs. I'm rushing her, but I have to hear her come. Now. While I'm nipping at her left nipple, I let my fingers explore her pussy. She's wet for me.

I leave her nipple and say, "Let me do this for you, Ro."

I lick her wet folds; exploring, sucking. Hearing her moan softly, I look up while my tongue remains deep in her body. Our eyes lock, and her back arches while I rhythmically stroke her clit. Her body tightens, and I know that her release is close. Her hands are in my hair, silently urging me to continue. Inserting two fingers into her, I increase my tempo. Soon she's shattering all around me.

Still on my knees in front of her a couple of minutes later, I say, "See? Perfect."

Thirty-One

IWAKE EARLY, LOVING THE FEEL OF ROSE BACK in my arms where she belongs. At some point in the night, we managed to leave my bedroom and make our way to the guest room. I had her moaning under me three times before we fell asleep, exhausted.

I look down at the woman in my arms, reliving every moment of last night. Even though it's only been a few days, I've missed her. I need to talk with her about dropping the whole Emilie charade and coming clean with my fans. Gruesome wouldn't dare enforce her non-fraternization policy if I raise the subject with her.

Did I really tell Rose that I love her? She never told me she felt the same way, but I'm sure she does. Maybe she needs more time. More reassurances that I'm going to stick around. Which is understandable because she doesn't have a relationship with her father, and her fiancé died.

She mutters something unintelligible in her sleep and turns over, presenting her back to me. Not one to miss a good opportunity, I spoon her, nestling my semi-hard cock between the cleft of her ass. I reach over and cup her boobs. She sighs in her sleep, and I close my eyes and fall back asleep, cradling my woman.

Whispering wakes me. I'm all alone in the bed. When I look in the direction of the noise, I see Rose curled up in the corner of the room on her cell. Not wanting to let her know I'm awake, I strain to listen to her side of the conversation. I hear her say, "Soon, okay?" And then, "Yes, according to plan."

What plan? I'm fully awake and getting more confused by the second.

Bewildered, I sit up in the bed, announcing my return to consciousness. Rose smiles at me over her shoulder. In a louder voice, Rose says, "I gotta go now. I'll be home in a couple of hours and then we'll head out to the spa. Bye, Mom."

I push down the blankets to make room for her. Rose stands and walks toward me, wearing yet another T-shirt from my first concert. Mom must have single-handedly bought all of the remaining inventory.

"I was trying to be quiet. I didn't want to wake you."

Running my hands up her body, I reply "No worries. What did your mother have to say?" My hands stop their ascent at her ass, pulling her closer to me.

"She was annoyed that I didn't go home last night." Rose looks down and sequentially touches her fingers to her thumb.

I frown. "Everything okay, Ro?"

"Yeah."

"What 'plan' were you talking about?"

"Our spa day. It's Mom's first."

Relieved, I tease, "I was starting to get worried, babe." Her features are tight, so maybe she needs some more Cole magic. "Come back to bed so we can start this day over the right way."

"As much as I want to, Cole, I have to take a shower and get back to my mother's."

"Fine." She raises an eyebrow at my quick capitulation. "Let me get you a towel."

In the hallway, I open the linen closet and hand her a towel. I grab one for myself, then follow her into the bathroom.

At the sink, she turns and says, "Cole, we shouldn't. Your father is down the hall."

"Ro, I wouldn't care if the Dalai Lama were in the room, I'm going to wash your back."

She stares at me like I'm nuts. I'm feeling as if I just hit the stage without a set list. *Is this because I told her I love her?*

An hour later, we're showered, dressed and waiting for my Dad's pancakes. We needed the shower sex. We're both much more relaxed now.

"Is everything on track for Ozzy's show?"

Rose nods at my father. "Yes. All the advance work has been done. Rumor's out that Cole may take the stage at one of Ozzy's Vegas shows to perform his new single."

"That's great. I'm so happy my son has you on his team," he says while he's placing the pancakes on the table.

Rose smiles at my father. "Thank you, Ken. And thanks for letting us borrow your photos. I promise to return them to you in good condition."

After our pancake breakfast, Rose texts Roberto to let him know she's ready to leave. We walk together to the car. It pains me to leave her, but I say, "Have a good spa day, sweetheart. I'm looking forward to meeting your mom at dinner." I lean down and give her a passionate kiss. "I'll see you tonight at the restaurant."

Rose strokes my cheek with her hand. "I'm looking forward to it." She gives me another quick kiss and ducks into the car. Roberto drives my girlfriend away.

I wander back in to the kitchen.

"Rose is a good match for you, son," Dad says.

"Thanks, Dad. I agree."

"She seemed a bit off this morning, though. Is everything all right?"

So Dad noticed something too? "I asked her, but she said she was fine."

"I'm sure she's just preoccupied with the stalker. Plus, juggling her visit with her mother and trying to keep your career on track."

"Yeah, you're probably right. Not to mention Jessie's and Brandan's careers, too."

"She sure has her hands full." He slings the kitchen towel over his shoulder. "C'mon, help me clean up and we'll spend the afternoon at Jayson's."

I PULL INTO A PARKING space, cut the engine and reach for the bouquet of roses sitting on the passenger side. While I'm accustomed to mounting a stage and singing in front of thousands, I'm nervous about meeting Rose's mother without anyone for backup. Must be all of Rose's prior warnings about her mother. Guess it didn't help that Jayson heckled me nonstop about Ro this afternoon. At least Dad and Carl were totally on my side. Jayson was too, he just likes to tease me, especially since he doesn't get the chance too often.

Thankfully, it seems like Ro and her mom enjoyed the spa day. Her texts sounded increasingly relaxed as the day progressed. Yeah, I got this. I need to remember to give her a spa day again soon when we're back in California. Or I could always give her a massage myself. Naked, of course.

With that enticing image in my head, I get out of the car and head to the front door of the restaurant. It wouldn't do to be late, not when I want to make a good impression. I walk up to the hostess stand and ask for Rose's table. Realizing who I am, the hostess does a double-take and promptly drops a stack of menus on the floor.

Bending down to help her retrieve them, I say, "Slippery, aren't they?"

The hostess laughs self-consciously, but to her credit, she regains her composure. "Thank you, Mr. Manchester. I'm not usually such a klutz."

Glancing at her nametag, I smile and say, "No problem, Loni. No menus were hurt in the making of this video."

She smiles back and tells me to follow her. Around the bend, I spy Rose and my heart skips a beat. She's glowing from her trip to the spa. To her left is an older, attractive woman. She, too, seems relaxed. The two are deep in conversation.

Stopping at the table, I thank Loni and bend down to kiss Rose. She turns her head at the last second, so I end up kissing her cheek. In response to my questioning look, her eyes dart from left and right, as if to remind me that we're in a public place. This shit has to end really fucking soon.

But now's not the time to have a throw down about taking our relationship public. I turn to Rose's mother, conjure up a smile and offer her a dozen peach roses. The color symbolizes appreciation. *I'm seriously becoming an expert on the meaning of colors.*

"Ms. Bloomer, it's a pleasure to finally meet you." She takes the flowers, gives me a half-smile and replies, "Mr. Manchester. Sit." She places them on the empty chair next to her.

Whoa. There's something in her tone that communicates that she disapproves of me. And it hasn't escaped my attention that she didn't even say thanks. Taking my seat between the two ladies, I smile at Rose and try to lighten the mood. "So, how did you two enjoy the spa today?"

Rose returns my smile, although without much heat. Her mom responds, "It was lovely, Mr. Manchester. Thank you."

There it is again, that thick understated disapproval. I can also sense it in the way she said my last name. Time to turn up the charm. "I'm glad you enjoyed it. And, please, call me Cole."

"It's not often that I get to spend the day doing nothing but having other people wait on me."

Wait, what? I shoot a look over to Rose, but she's staring into her iced tea. What's going on?

I clear my throat and start over. "So, Rose tells me that you're a daycare provider. You must have nerves of steel."

I offer her a smile. She doesn't return it. "It's an honor to help people raise their children. The precious little ones didn't ask to be brought into this world, but I do all that I can to make sure they are well-cared for on my watch."

I can't seem to say anything right. Rose studiously stares at the menu. Bewildered, I grab her hand and kiss it. Our eyes meet and her mother continues, "Do you have any children, Cole?"

Turning my attention back to her mother, I respond, "No, not yet. But I look forward to becoming a daddy one day." I smile, thinking of my goddaughter.

Rose finally pipes up and says, "Cole is wonderful with Emma, his goddaughter. He's the only one who can get her to stop fussing."

"Yeah, she always quiets down when I sing for her. Her parents even use my albums to calm her." Rose and I share a smile.

Her mom doesn't seem impressed, though. "Music is a sure bet to soothe a baby. Sounds like you have some experience. Are you sure you're not hiding a baby from my daughter?"

Rose gasps. *Shit.* What does her mother think of me? "Ms. Bloomer, I can assure you that I don't have any children running around."

She harrumphs.

"I wasn't a saint before I met your daughter, but she means the world to me. I wouldn't hide anything from her, especially something as monumental as a child."

"What if you had a child, though? What would you do?"

I'm confused. What is this woman getting at? "I would make sure the child is well cared for, I suppose. I wouldn't be an absentee father. But, seeing as I don't have one, there's no need to discuss this further."

We eyeball each other for what seems like an eternity. I can't figure out why she's pushing, but I bet it has something to do with Rose's deadbeat father.

Rose jumps into the tense abyss. "Mom, Cole is getting ready to go on a world tour. He's going to Europe and Australia."

"Yes, you mentioned that before, Rose. Will Emilie be joining him, like she is here?"

"Ms. Bloomer, I'm not 'with' Emilie. Rose set us up for publicity purposes."

"Yes, I know. Emilie's quite convincing, but then you play your part extremely well, too."

Throwing Rose a quizzical look, I respond, "When I'm with Emilie, I'm playing a role. The media and public want to think they know me, and Rose orchestrates parts of my life to give them the perception that they do. What I want, however, is your daughter. I'm in love with her, and I want to shout it from the rooftops." *There. I said it.*

Rose's mom gives her a hard stare and then turns to me. "Are you aware that Rose's first boyfriend stopped by to see her the other day? Now there's a steady man. Marco has a secure, normal job. He's not the type who'd leave her behind to go globe-trotting."

Rose's first boyfriend has a name. *Marco.* This is all sorts of messed up. She didn't even mention him to me at Dad's yesterday. All the color has drained from Rose's face.

"Clearly, Rose didn't tell you about Marco's visit."

"No, she didn't, but I'm sure she has her reasons." I refuse to let this woman derail our relationship. "I may not have a traditional career, but I can provide for Rose. Our lives will be filled with new adventures and experiences."

Whoa, I'm getting ahead of myself here. I'm totally out of control, careening around like a ball in a pinball machine.

"Rose works for a living and her life is in LA," her mother snapped. "For now. Her job is not to gallivant around at your beck and call like some sort of Gal Friday."

"Mom, I work for Greta's clients. I'll be traveling with Cole on his world tour from time to time, when my job requires it."

"And will your bodyguard be accompanying you?"

"She only has a bodyguard—" I begin, but her mother cuts me off.

"Because of you, Mr. Manchester."

Guess we're back to formalities.

We sit in silence that's finally broken by Rose's mother. "I'm going to the ladies' room." With that pronouncement, she leaves us at the table.

I can't control myself any longer. "Holy hell, Rose. What the fuck is going on?"

"She's just overprotective of me because of my father," she says in a quiet voice.

"Why didn't you tell me that you saw Marco?" His name comes out as a sneer.

"He stopped by the house the other day. I told you before that his mother and my mom are best friends."

"Has he been in touch with you all these years?"

"Off and on, mainly through our mothers. Although now he says he'd like to stay in touch."

"Are you going to? I take it he's not married," I snipe. I don't like the sound of this, especially since he was her first love and her mother clearly approves of *him*.

"No, and yes, he's single."

I grab her hand. "Rose, I don't understand what's going on here. Your mom obviously hates me, and you seem distant."

Leaving her hand in mine, she replies, "Cole, I don't want to lose myself in you and your larger-than-life career. I'm a publicist, and I'm good at what I do. I need to work with all my clients." She pauses. "Your tour is going to last at least eight or nine months, and that's a long time for us to be apart."

Is she trying to break up with me? Did I scare her off by telling her I love her? No, no, no. This can't be happening.

"Ro, you're too important to me. I would never want you to give up your career for me. I know how amazing you are at it. Plus, I already told Gruesome I want you to manage my publicity on the tour, so we won't be apart at all." She does want to go on tour with me, right?

Her mother returns to the table, and our conversation thankfully turns to much more innocuous topics such as movies and local sports. Shortly thereafter the waitress brings our meals, so chitchat is kept to a minimum. No one wants dessert, and before long, I'm walking them back to Rose's mother's car. I want to spend more time with Rose before my flight to Vegas tomorrow. I need to make sure she knows how much I love her. What she means to me. Her mother can't derail us. *She can't.*

We stop in front of a white mid-sized sedan. "Ms. Bloomer, it was nice to finally meet the woman who made Rose the woman she is today." That is the truth. I refuse to say it was a pleasure meeting her, though.

"Cole," she sticks out her hand. After shaking my hand, she marches over to the driver's side and tosses my flowers into the backseat. She never invited me to call her by her first name.

"Ro, come back with me. We need to work this out," I say.

Simultaneously, her mother calls out from the car, "C'mon Rose, let's get going."

Raising her index finger at her mother, she replies, "I can't, Cole. I'm only here one more day and I have to spend more time with her. My mother really is wonderful. I'm sorry that you didn't get to see that side of her."

Frowning, and wishing I could raise a different finger to her mother, I say, "I wish you were coming with me to Vegas."

"Rose, let's go!"

She sighs and looks up at me. "You know I can't. Greta will be there. I'll see you in LA, okay? Do great at Ozzy's concert."

"Damn. Yes, we'll talk then." I pull her in for a kiss, but the car's horn blares. Really? Thank God this woman lives on the opposite coast from us.

I walk Rose around to the passenger side and open her door. Once she's settled, I bend down and give her a chaste kiss, say good-bye to her mother and close the car door. I jump back to avoid being run over by Momzilla, who peels out of the parking lot.

What. The. Fuck.

Thirty-Two

"**B**YE, DAD."

After giving my father one last hug, I leave my childhood home and slide into the backseat of the car that's waiting to bring me back into the city. Watching the scenery change from residential to the chaos of the New Jersey Turnpike, I keep replaying yesterday in my head. What was up with Ro? At least she texted me last night to let me know she got back to her mom's house in one piece.

Scrolling through my text messages, I open her last one and reread it: *Thanks again for the spa & dinner. Make sure you go out with Emilie tonight to the Gramercy Hotel.*

Where is the teasing, sassy woman that I love? Her mother had to be filling her head with all sorts of crap. But why did she take such an immediate dislike to me? She didn't even give me a shot.

Finally, we arrive at my penthouse and I head up to my bedroom. As I'm placing the last of my clothes into my suitcase, the front door opens. "Hi Em," I call out.

Emilie wanders into my room. "Oh, hello, Cole. Welcome back. How was your visit with your family?"

"Good." I don't feel any need to share my girlfriend issues with her. "And you? How's the modeling biz?"

Emilie gives me a tired smile. "It is going well. I have a break for the rest of the day, but there are more shows tomorrow."

"Rose says that we should be seen out in town tonight. Are you up for it? You look pretty beat."

Please say no, please say no. My nerves are stretched like a new guitar string, and I don't want to play a part tonight before heading out to the airport. Especially given all the shit that's going on with Rose.

"If Rose says we must go, then *oui*, I will go."

My shoulders slump. "Such a trooper. Why don't we do something low key? That way, the paparazzi can get their photos and spin their own story about us wanting alone time before I head out to Vegas."

"But do you think Greta will approve? What did she have arranged?"

At this moment, I don't care whether Gruesome, or more accurately Rose, will approve or not. The irony of her selecting the restaurant at the very same hotel I had considered booking for us is not sitting well with me.

"I'm sure she can improvise. So, how about a stroll through Central Park? We can get dirty water dogs."

Emilie's reaction is priceless. Her face draws back and scrunches up. "What?"

Chuckling, I explain the local name for hot dogs from a street vendor. She looks relieved, as I'm sure whatever she suspected the phrase meant scared her shitless. She offers, "How about I get a pretzel and you get one of those dirty dogs?"

"You're on. Why don't you go change and I'll meet you in the living room in half an hour?" She nods and leaves my room.

The more the minutes tick by, the angrier I'm getting. Not just at Momzilla, but at Rose. Why didn't she stand up for me at dinner? Or at least try to explain our situation? Why did she hide Marco's visit? *And why hasn't she said she loves me back?*

I walk into the living room and pace unseeingly in front of the floor-to-ceiling windows overlooking Fifth Avenue. I pull out my phone and text Rose. *Em & I are going to Central Park now & that's it for tonight. She's beat & I'm not in the mood. Flying out on redeye—will see you at home on Sunday. We need to talk.* I hit send as Emilie crosses my line of vision.

Despite my frustration with Rose, I appreciate Emilie's professionalism. "You look beautiful. The paps are going to eat you up."

"Thank you, Cole. Is your bodyguard joining us?"

A light bulb goes off in my head. Maybe she returns Wills's attraction? "Yes, if that's okay with you."

"*Oui*, that is good. He makes me feel safe."

"Is that all he makes you feel, Em? Should I be jealous?" A slight blush steals over her cheeks. Bingo.

Em is saved from further torment by a knock at the door. "Em, can you please get the door? I need to get something from the other room."

She nods and heads toward the front door to greet Wills. At least I can help them out this much. Wandering back into my bedroom, I call out from the threshold of my bedroom, "I'll be a few minutes. Make yourselves comfortable."

Once in my room, I sit down on the bed and check my messages. Rose has responded: *k*

Seriously, is that even a response? With a huff, I press "send" on my phone. She picks up after a couple of rings.

"Hi, Cole."

"Ro, what's going on?" No use beating around the bush.

"I'm hanging out with my mother." Great, Momzilla's within hearing distance.

"Tell her I said hello." I hear Rose relay my message, but her mother's response is garbled, like a Peanuts cartoon. I can only imagine what her mother said.

"Are you okay with the change in plans? Emilie and I don't want a long evening, plus I have to catch the plane tonight anyway."

"Yeah, that's fine. I'm sure the paparazzi will snap shots of you two in Central Park. Make sure to give them some good photo ops."

"I know the drill. Frankly, I don't give a shit about this charade we're creating. I need to talk with you. What is going on between us? It's like you're a million miles away from me."

"I'm working out a strategy for when Fashion Week ends and Emilie returns to Los Angeles."

"Wait, what? Go to another room so we can talk privately."

"I wish I could, but that's impossible. But I'll make sure your Facebook, Instagram and Twitter accounts are updated."

"Ro, I'm going insane over here. Give me this. Tell me we'll talk about whatever's going on when we get back home." I still don't know why Gruesome is insisting that she personally attend my "surprise" concert in Las Vegas. I would much rather have Rose with me. Especially now.

"That's fine." I am starting to hate professional Rose. Momzilla says something and Rose responds, but she must have put her hand over the receiver, because I can't make out their words.

Sighing, I realize this conversation is going no further. Just two more days. Then we can get to the bottom of her weird behavior.

"Ro, I know how you feel about me. And I love you. We'll work this out, whatever this is. I will see you Sunday." I don't wait for her to reply before disconnecting the call.

I splash cold water on my face in the bathroom. Time to put on a show for the media.

When I return to the living room, Wills and Emilie are sitting on the sofa, laughing and enjoying each other's company. At least that makes one happy couple. I clear my throat and they both stand up.

"Ready to go?" I extend my hand toward Emilie. She nods and we follow Wills to the front door.

A FEW HOURS LATER, I'm seated on a plane with Wills in the seat next to mine. I pull my baseball cap down lower to try to avoid being recognized as people file past us. I need to work out whatever the hell is going on with Rose. And I also have to mentally prepare for performing "No One to Hold" live.

At least the outing with Em went well. She even tasted my hot dog. I grin, remembering the look on her face after she took a bite. Some reporter took a photo of my wiping mustard off her lip. It was fun, but certainly no comparison to my experience at Pink's with Ro.

I lean over to Wills. "Are you okay with the situation between me and Emilie? You know I'm committed to Rose, and I do believe Em is falling for you."

"You're out of your mind," he said, raising his brows. "She's a supermodel."

"I think she's into the big protector types. I'm going to have to figure out a way you can take her on a date."

"You're nuts."

"Anything for love." I give him a wink. He punches me on my arm and turns away to get some shut eye. I do the same.

Thankfully, we land in Las Vegas without attracting too many gawking fans on the plane. The flight attendants were pretty good and not overly solicitous, either. I did overhear someone mention how hard it must have been for me to leave Emilie behind at Fashion Week. At least I can let Rose know that her publicity plan is working like a charm.

An airline rep escorts Wills and I directly into a VIP lounge with a special exit to the car. It's nice to have this privacy. "Wills, Roberto is flying with Rose to LA tomorrow, or I guess later today, right?"

"Yeah. He'll see her to your house safely, then go into the office to work with Kates and the police about the latest incident with your stalker."

"Sounds good." It reassures me to know that Rose will be safe. "I don't know about you, but I'm looking forward to crashing as soon as we get to

Caesars."

THE SOUND OF AN alarm going off rouses me from my fitful sleep. It's noon, and I need to get my head on straight before tonight's "impromptu" concert. Once my room service-provided French toast and sausage are lodged in my belly, I check my phone and send Rose a quick text: *Have a safe flight. See you at home.*

No use continuing to ask her what's wrong since I'm going to see her tomorrow and we can get to the bottom of it. *Together.*

My final text is to Martinez. *Yo, Martinez. When do you want to rehearse or are you too good for that?*

His response is instantaneous: *Just finished with twins. See you in the practice room at 2.*

I shake my head. Not long ago, I would have been with Martinez and the twins. Now the thought has lost its allure.

I take a quick shower and make my way to the practice room Martinez reserved. Sitting down at the piano, I play "No One to Hold." By the third go-round, I'm as comfortable with the song as I can be.

To change things up before Martinez arrives, I play "Taboo." Pictures of Rose run through my head. Of her on the beach in Santa Monica, of her fighting with me over the blue convertible, of us making love in my pool. Of her flower birthmark. I frown as more recent memories of meeting her mother take over, and sing the final lines quietly:

> *Will you always be here?*
> *I know I will*

Clapping brings me out of my fog. I turn to see Martinez walking up the aisle, his hair still damp.

"Sounding good, Manchester."

"Thanks, Martinez. Nice of you to join me. Did the twins leave you with any energy?"

A grin steals over his face as he fist bumps me. "They were fucking amazing. Too bad you're off the market. They're just your type. Nice asses and no inhibitions."

I give him a smirk and reply, "I'll leave the whoring to you, buddy. Rose gives me everything I need."

At the mention of her name, he looks around. "Where is she? I thought she'd be here with you."

I shake my head. "She's not coming."

His eyebrows go up. "Everything okay between the two of you?"

Now that's a loaded question. "Things are a little tense between us right now. I met her mother and we didn't hit it off." That's putting it mildly.

"Dude, that sucks. But if anyone can charm a skittish mom, it's you."

"I hope so." I don't want to get into this any deeper. Plus, what can I say? We're on really shaky ground and she won't talk to me? I'd sound like a real pussy.

I continue. "Rose wasn't supposed to be here, anyway. Greta the Gruesome pulled rank. But that didn't prevent her from making Rose do all the legwork for my appearance."

"Speaking of which, we should get to work. I want to get another round in with the Amazing Twins before show time."

Shaking my head, I grab my guitar and we begin to rehearse the song that I'm going to sing with him onstage before I perform my newest single. Eventually, we move to the stage and the show's director does a walk-through of how I'm going to "surprise" my buddy onstage. Following sound check, we're finished.

Clapping me on the back, Ozzy asks, "Dinner?"

I check my watch. "I'd love to, but I think Gruesome has me scheduled for some press stuff."

"Well, enjoy. I plan to. See you onstage, killer."

He leaves the stage, presumably in pursuit of the twins, and I return to the piano in the practice room. After playing a few more songs, I close the fall board and motion for Wills to join me. He's been lurking in the background all day.

"Hey, enjoy the rehearsal?"

"It was interesting. Got a good handle on the room's layout."

I nod. "So, did Rose's flight take off on time?"

His eyes shift from side to side. He looks . . . uncomfortable. My heart begins to race. He says, "She wasn't on the flight."

Is Rose sick? "What do you mean she didn't wasn't on it?"

"From what I understand, a guy showed up at her mother's and she was delayed. Roberto said the guy's name was Marco."

What. The. Fuck. Marco? The man her mother considers the paragon above all men? Her first boyfriend? Just how were they "delayed"?

"There you are, handsome."

I swing around to face Gruesome. Her tall, lithe frame is poured into a red jumpsuit, her collagen-injected lips stained to match. "Greta." Wills melts into the background once again.

She looks me up and down, clearly without a thought for her non-fraternization policy. "Ready for your surprise performance?"

I'm ready to punch out a prick named Marco. Then I need to find out what's going on from my girlfriend. At least I think she's my girlfriend.

"Cole?"

Swallowing my feelings, I respond, "Yeah."

"Good." She takes my arm and leads me toward the door. "Let's go whip the press into a frenzy."

Thirty-Three

FROM BACKSTAGE, I WATCH MY friend perform. He's really cranking up the crowd. They're eating him up. "Good for you, buddy," I mutter under my breath.

I take one more peek out into the audience. "You're going to do great, Cole," Gruesome says from behind me, rubbing her bony fingers up and down my arm. "The press is all abuzz."

"Thanks," I reply, extricating my arm from her talons by fiddling with my guitar.

"I wouldn't have missed this concert for anything. It's like old times." I don't remember Gruesome being around all that much at the beginning of my career. Whatever.

Martinez starts to chat up the crowd. I tamp down my feelings about Rose, letting the adrenaline take over. It's been a while since I've taken the stage, and this venue's the perfect size.

"I'm going to let you do your thing. See you afterward. Rock on." Gruesome squeezes my bicep and then disappears backstage. The stage manager taps me on the shoulder. "Ready to jump on the stage when he hits the chorus?"

Nodding, I close my eyes and count backward from ten, banishing all thoughts about Rose and that fucker Marco. My eyes slowly open again, and I'm 100% in the zone.

Within a minute, the stage manager hands me the microphone and says, "Go." I walk onto the stage. The audience's excitement crescendos as they recognize me; I need to adjust my earpiece to accommodate the racket. I hit my mark and start to harmonize with Martinez. He introduces me while I play the song's guitar riff, throwing the crowd a nod and a smirk. We finish his song to thunderous applause.

"Hope you don't mind, I was in the neighborhood . . ." We begin our rehearsed lines, making them sound as off-the-cuff as possible. Surprisingly, I'm enjoying myself.

"Say, Martinez, mind if I try something out?" Squeals rise from the audience.

"Buddy, whatever you want. I got all night." He looks out and blows a kiss to a young lady in the front.

Shaking my head, I continue. "How about I play my new single? It drops next week, but I thought since I'm here . . ." I let my voice trail off.

"Well, I don't know about that. What would our label say?"

I pretend to search the audience. "Don't see anybody from the label in here."

The audience claps like crazy. It's fun working them into a frenzy. All of my problems are gone. I've missed this.

"What do you all think? Want to hear this guy's new song?"

He pauses to listen to the shouts from the crowd. I hand my guitar to a roadie and walk over to the piano.

"I don't know, Manchester. They don't sound all that excited to me," he says, grinning at me.

I hit a few keys on the piano, more to test out my fingers than to gain attention. "Well, if they're not interested—"

Screams and clapping fill the theater. A smile passes between us. I take my seat at the piano.

Waiting for the noise to quiet down, I begin. "I hope you like this. It's dedicated to my mother. It's called 'No One to Hold.'"

I begin to play the introduction and a hush falls. All of sudden, the enormity of this moment hits me. I'm raw and exposed, and all my emotions about Mom and Rose are being poured into the song. It's just me and the piano. During the chorus, I look out into the audience and see a sea of cell phone lights swaying in time to the beat. I can feel Mom sitting beside me at the piano, lending her support as my fingers fly over the keys. I knew performing this song live would be difficult, but I never anticipated how utterly profound and naked I would feel.

As I sing the last note, all of the emotions welling inside me collide with the outpouring of positive energy from the audience. The song ends and there's a split-second hush, followed by an eruption of applause.

Taking a deep breath, I turn my head and see that everyone is standing. Looking up to the heavens, I whisper, "For you, Mom." Wiping a tear, I stand up and am immediately enveloped in a bear hug from Martinez.

"Manchester, that was magical," he whispers.

"Thanks, man." We both turn around, giving the crowd our backs.

"You okay?"

"Yeah," I reply a bit unsteadily. Clearing my throat, I repeat, "Yeah."

Pull it together, Manchester. I nod at him and we turn and walk to the front of the stage. The applause has not diminished.

"Isn't he fan-fucking-tastic?" More clapping.

"Thanks for letting me crash your party, Martinez!" Even more noise. "Now I'm going to let you get back to your concert."

"Everybody, don't forget to download Cole Manchester's newest single when it drops next week. But don't tell our label you heard it here first!"

I take my bow, wave at the crowd and return backstage, completely drained. Martinez strikes up another one of his hits.

"Great job."

"Thanks." I take a bottle of water from Wills and walk out the back door, straight into a crowd of well-wishers. In a daze, I fake a smile and sign whatever is handed to me.

Every woman here reminds me of *her*. A tween sporting a ponytail. A grandmother with glasses. A co-ed brunette. I keep signing and posing for photos.

Gruesome's familiar talons rake up my arm. "There's someone here who wants to meet you."

Bracing myself for more fakery, I do a one-eighty and come face-to-face with some Italian-looking guy. Who has his arm around Rose. *My* Rose.

Open-mouthed, my eyes dart from Rose to that fucker with his arm around her. This must be Marco. Smarmy prick. She refuses to look at me, but her hair is down, her contacts are in and she's wearing a sexy black mini dress with fuck-me pumps. Definitely not work attire.

Keeping his left arm around Rose, The Fucker extends his right hand to me, saying "Marco Ricci. Nice to meet you. I've heard so much about you."

I shake his hand, offering a bone-crushing grip. I can't force myself to utter a word.

"Rose and I were at her mother's, and I talked her into flying out here on my company plane for a quick weekend getaway."

He pulls Rose tighter to his side. She smiles at him, touching each of her fingers to her thumb repeatedly.

Clenching my teeth, I manage, "How nice for you. Both."

This can't be happening. When did Rose get back together with him? She's supposed to be on her way to LA, to my—*our*—house. I love her. I can't believe this. It's high school prom all over again. Rose has closed her eyes. So, that's how it is? She can't even bring herself to look at me?

Gruesome interrupts, "Now that you've met Rose's boyfriend, it's time for you to get back to your adoring fans."

She physically turns me around to face a tween girl who is looking adoringly up at me. *Rose's boyfriend.* But I must do my job and tend to my fans, no matter how much I want to punch out The Fucker and grab my girl away from him. All of my muscles tense in the desire to do just that.

Sucking in a pained breath, I muster what I hope resembles a smile and sign the girl's concert program. As I hand her paper back, I'm surrounded by a small handful of women. Again. I sign their programs, T-shirts, pose for photos, whatever, as quickly as possible.

About halfway through taking care of the group, which seems to be growing, Rose follows Gruesome out of the room, arm-in-arm with The Fucker. I look on in disbelief.

How the hell could this have happened right under my nose? No wonder she never said she loved me. Unbelievable. Martinez has the right idea; fuck 'em and leave 'em. I need a drink. Or twenty. Now.

The last person in the cluster is a blonde woman, and after I sign an autograph for her, she says, "Care to join me at the bar, Cole?"

She's familiar, but I can't place her. Whatever. She's going where I want to be. "Perfect. Let's go." I grab her hand and stalk out of the backroom.

Why did Rose come here with that douchebag? What is she doing with that Italian dick right this second? How can she do this to us? I come to a halt at the bar and catch the bartender's eye.

Blondie stops behind me, puffing. "You sure do walk fast, Cole."

I grunt in reply. I didn't walk fast enough to catch Rose, that's for sure. About ten other women from backstage, including Gruesome, join us at the bar. I order a round of shots for everyone. Rose doesn't even deign to make an appearance. She's probably too busy with The Fucker. Real nice.

After a couple of drinks, Gruesome comes over and says, "Congratulations, Cole. Your song was a big hit. Your surprise comeback is going to be all over the media tomorrow. Just like I planned."

Comeback? I didn't realize I had gone away. I force out, "Thanks."

"Listen, I need to run. Everything's covered here. Be a good boy." She kisses me on both cheeks and pinches my ass. Ugh. At least she's gone. Given my less than welcoming vibe, all the other women have wandered off too, except Blondie.

The bartender comes up to me and Blondie quickly says, "A bottle of

Dom Pérignon." My eyebrow rise at her, but I nod toward the bartender, putting up two fingers. I can get drunk off champagne, no problem.

Both bottles are put down in front of us, accompanied with two flutes. The bartender opens the first with a little flourish. I grab both bottles and head toward a secluded table in the corner. Blondie follows me, carrying the glasses. Taking the glasses from her, I pour generous amounts of the bubbly and hand her one. Quickly downing mine, I pour myself a second.

Before I can bring this one to my lips, Blondie says, "A toast to the successful launch of your newest single."

God, it's like my performance was days ago instead of only an hour. I'm incapable of speech, so I clink my glass to hers and down this one. I pour a third.

"You were amazing up there. Your voice was pitch-perfect. Were you nervous? You haven't performed since, well, months."

I look at her. She's taller than average, of average weight and looks. Nothing extraordinary like Rose, with her gorgeous mane of brunette hair, expressive blue eyes, perfect ass. I close my eyes.

Blondie repeats, "Were you?"

I clear my throat. Thinking about Rose isn't going to make her appear here, especially since she's with The Fucker.

"Excited."

Blondie nods in appreciation of my one-grunt response, smiling as big as if she just won the lottery. I chug my third glass of champagne, then refill both our glasses, putting the empty bottle on the floor and motioning for the next one to be opened. The server comes to do that, and I ask for a bottle of scotch. Somehow that liquor seems appropriate; it's my drink of choice for mourning, and it feels like something died inside me.

Following my sixth—or is it my eighth?—glass of alcohol, Blondie starts to run her hands over my chest. She leans into me, nipping my earlobe and breathing deeply. "You smell divine, Cole."

"Thanks, er." Shit. I don't know her name. "What's your name, darlin'?"

"Starr."

Again, bells go off in the dark recesses of my mind, but things are too foggy. "Have we met before, Starr?"

"We have," she whispers in my ear. "You gave me my name. At The Ice Lounge." She giggles.

I sort of remember meeting her. Didn't we dance? Whatever.

I finish my latest round and go for another glass. Her hand moves down my chest, descending toward my belt. I'm just drunk enough to enjoy Starr's touch, but not that far gone that I want to betray Rose like this. Even if she did leave with that prick Marco. I grab Starr's wrist and place it in her lap, shaking my head. She pouts, but moments later she's smiling up at me and rummaging through her purse.

"Selfie?" She asks while handing me her cell phone.

I take her phone and figure out where the camera button is. My fingers feel like lead, but I manage to get off a couple of photos before returning the phone to her. She reviews them and smiles again. "One more. I'll take it this time."

Shrugging my shoulders, I look at the camera she's holding out. Right before she takes the photo, she kisses me on my lips. "Hey!"

Giggling, she deposits her phone back into her purse and reaches across me for the champagne bottle, her tits brushing against my thighs as she does so. "Shall I top you off?" What a question. Although I'm quite drunk, the sting of Rose's defection still prickles. Betrayal. I down the remnants of the liquid in my glass and essentially shove it at Blondie-Starr, motioning toward the bottle of scotch.

Leaning over to me, she kisses that sensitive spot on my neck that always makes me hard. The alcohol has slowed down my usual response, but I'm getting turned on. Especially when her hand makes its journey southward once again.

"Let's get out of here," she purrs.

Why not? Rose is off with her *boyfriend*. Shit, Starr's biting my ear lobe. "Yessss."

We stand up, grab the open bottles of champagne and scotch, and head for the elevators. I don't want to take her to my suite, though. I had it prepared for Rose.

"What floor are you on?" I ask.

"Why can't we go to your room? Rose looked awfully busy with that other guy tonight."

How does she know about Rose? This is a bad idea. I'm about to call it all off when she says, "Never mind. I'm not in this hotel. Just a short taxi ride away, right around the corner from the Lasso the Moon Wedding Chapel."

She grabs my hand and places it on her tit, looking up at me meaningfully.

I sense someone behind us and turn to see Wills. "I's got it from here," I tell him, my hand still on her tit.

He purses his lips and says, "Rose is—"

I cut him off. The last thing I want to do is talk about Rose. I spit out, "You can goooo." Wills closes his eyes and walks away from us. Good.

Starr and I quickly make our way to her hotel. I down another glass of scotch and force the memories of Rose to disappear. Starr takes off my shirt, then strips, standing before me in only her fuck-me heels. There's nothing wrong with her. She's just not the woman I want, even if the right one's with another guy. My cock is sound asleep.

Looking southward, Starr says, "Cole, let me take care of you."

She plants kisses all over my naked chest and works my jeans and underwear down my hips. On her knees, she tries to coax my limp dick to wake up.

I reach down and put my hand on her cheek. "Slar," I slur. She pauses and looks up at me. "'S not you. 'S me. This—" I motion between her and me—"isn't gonna happen. C'mon, stand up."

She stands and presses her bare form against me. "Why not? I'm here and willing. I want to be with you." She rubs against me. My body doesn't react.

I pull away from her, keeping my hands on her shoulders. "Darlin', I'm shitfaced. Not gonna happen." *Not to mention I'm in love with my girlfriend. Who is off with The Fucker.* I frown.

"What did that bitch Rose do to you?"

That comment gets my attention. "How do you knows about Ro - Rose?" I smile, hearing the rhyme. I return my jeans and underwear back into place.

"Let me get you another scotch."

I should follow up with her about how she knows about Rose, but I can't seem to hold any thoughts. I take the drink and swallow about half. I'm so very tired. It's been a fucking long day.

"Come over here," she pats the bed.

A quick nap sounds good. I kick off my shoes and lie down. Starr wraps her body around mine.

Thirty-Four

I WAKE UP TO THE SOUND OF THE shower running and sunlight streaming through the multicolor curtains. Where the hell am I? I turn my head on the pillow and feel queasy. Shit, I'm still drunk. And I'm in some random hotel room.

It's a dick move, but I quickly right my clothes and head down to the lobby. I ask the front desk to call for a taxi, which thankfully pulls up within a minute. Ten minutes later, I open my penthouse door.

"Rose?"

Of course she's not here. Images from last night flood my alcohol-saturated brain. She left me for The Fucker, Marco.

In under sixty seconds, I'm in the shower. Soaping up, I try to remember last night, after Rose left with *Marco*. I recall drinking at the bar with Blondie. What was her name? Moon? Sky? Something celestial.

Scrubbing furiously, I also recollect the look on Wills's face when I told him to get lost. Then back at Blondie's hotel, where she tried to seduce me. I passed out in her room. How much did I have to drink? I remember some shots, two bottles of champagne and a bottle of scotch. No wonder I'm still drunk.

Wrapping a towel around my waist, I walk over to the bed and check my phone for the first time in hours. The screen shows a bunch of texts and missed phone calls. I'm surprised to see one from Rose: *I'm sorry about Marco. We have to talk.*

Does she want to rub The Fucker my face? How did my life get so messed up?

The phone rings in my hand, startling me. It's Gruesome. Great.

"Hi, Greta."

"Someone was a naughty boy after I left last night." I grimace as her voice pierces my skull.

"Listen, Greta, I'm in no shape to play guessing games. What do you mean?" I rasp, clasping my throbbing head in my hands.

"I thought I would have at least gotten an invitation to the wedding, Cole."

"*WHAT?*"

Instantly sober, I collapse on the bed.

"Or at least let me handle the public disclosure of your marriage. Now I have to deal with Emilie's people, too."

"What are you talking about? *I'm not married.*" I check my left hand to verify that there's no ring.

"That's not what the marriage certificate on the Internet says."

"*WHAT?*"

"It says here that you and Starr Nelson were married at three a.m. this morning."

I was passed out in Blondie's hotel room at three a.m. That's her name—Starr. "I most certainly did *not* get married last night, Greta."

"And there are photos. One of you two kissing, and another where you're both smiling and holding champagne flutes. Another of you two getting into a taxi. And one that's clearly of you two in bed."

"Greta, I don't know what the fuck this is all about, but *I'm not married.*"

"I remember this Starr hanging out at the bar last night."

"She was there," I whisper.

"What aren't you telling me?"

A whole hell of a lot. "I spent some time with her last night. But we did *not* get married. You're my publicist. Fix this."

"You're sure?"

"I've never been more sure of anything in my life."

"Okay. Let me see what I can come up with. I'll strategize and have Rose give you a call with the details shortly." Greta disconnects the call.

My heart stops.

Rose.

Fuck.

Fuck, fuck, fuck.

To be Continued . . .

Read the next installment of Rose and Cole's story in *Hard To Hold*, Book #2 in The Hold series, available now! For information, go to http://bit.ly/NoOneToHold.

Bonus Scene

Cole at 22

I TURN MY GAZE OUT INTO THE audience as I strum the last chord on my guitar. Good night. Over one hundred people here.

"Thank you," I say into the microphone, looking directly at a cute brunette. She holds my stare, licks her bottom lip and catches it between her little white teeth, prompting me to quirk a small smile in her direction. My last set for the night at Above The Bar is over, and it looks like I've found my fun for afterward.

"Great job, as usual, buddy." This from Dan O'Connor, my best friend since the first day of freshman orientation at NYU.

"Thanks, Dan. Hey, why don't you go and get us a couple of beers while I chat up that little brunette over there." I nod toward her table. "She's been sending me hot and bothered signals all night. I want to hear all about your job prospects, so I'll tell her to sit tight and wait for me." I hand him a couple of bills for the beers.

"Think you're going to get lucky tonight, huh?"

Quirking my brow, I make no response. I've filled out in college; I'm no longer that scrawny guy I was in high school. Not to mention that NYU's gym is very well appointed, both with equipment and a never-ending stream of cute co-eds eager to help me with whatever exercise caught my fancy. Fully clothed or totally naked. Yeah, some really good times were had in that gym. I'm going to miss it.

As I make my way over to her table, three sets of eyes greet me. "Good evening, ladies. I hope you enjoyed the show."

Not waiting for their response, I lean down toward my evening's entertainment and whisper in her ear. "I need to catch up with my buddy, and then I'm going to rock your world. Wait for me." With a nip on her earlobe, I walk away.

Dan joins me at a table, depositing beers in front of both of us. "All set?" My crooked smile is his reply. He bursts out laughing. "Seriously, dude, how long did that take? What the hell did you say to her?"

"I told her the truth."

"You're one lucky bastard, you know that? I'm going to buy me a git-ar so women fall down at my feet, too." We both chuckle.

Changing the subject, I ask, "So, have you heard back from any of your interviews?"

"Yeah." He takes a long sip of his beer. "I got two offers. I think I'm leaning toward the one in LA, but the opportunity here is tempting, especially since you're going to stay in the City." He hands me a cigarette and we both light up.

Dan and I both are majoring in business with a special emphasis on the entertainment industry. I also have a second major in performance arts, while Dan's interests lie in television production. He's been interviewing with a bunch of networks here on campus, and even had callbacks in Hollywood as well as in NYC. His dream is right at hand, and I couldn't be more excited for him. We discuss both offers in detail. In the end, we both know that the better fit for him is in LA.

Dan helped me with my decision to stay in the City to work on my music career. Since I've been singing at Above The Bar for the past year, I'm pretty confident about my career choice. I fucking love singing in front of an audience with my guitar or at a piano. Even though I have been the lead in most of the musicals at NYU, I don't feel the same connection to performing other people's material. I know, without a doubt, that this is the direction I am meant to take.

When my parents were less than thrilled about my decision, Dan was my sounding board. Dad wanted me to use my business degree to get a corporate job in the music industry. He told me that I could continue to sing "on the side," as if music were some sort of hobby to me. Music is as necessary to me as air, food and sex . . . though perhaps not in that order.

With Dan's help, I explained all this to my parents—minus the sex part—and we struck a deal of sorts. I have the next three years to make my mark in music. If I don't, I promised to seek out a job as a suit in the industry. I'm positive that I'll never have to purchase that suit and briefcase.

"I'm going to miss you, buddy. Don't forget your poor, starving singer-friend when you're the head honcho of that television station of yours," I joke.

"Fuck that, Cole. I'll create a TV show around you and your sex life. It'll be top ten forever."

"You'd better go to a premium channel for that, buddy. I don't want my sex life watered down for mainstream television consumption." We clink the necks of our bottles and take swigs.

"I can't believe that we're going to be on different coasts after graduation." I shake my head.

We've been through so much together over the past four years. He was there when I picked up my first guitar. I found it surprisingly easy to transfer my knowledge of the piano to the guitar. However, that doesn't mean that I played great at first. Oh no. He suffered right along with me through some excruciatingly bad practice sessions. It took some hard work, but now I consider myself a pretty good player. Piano is still my first love. When I write songs, I come up with the lyrics first and then the melody sort of pops into my head in the form of piano music that I then adapt to the guitar.

Keeping the mood light, I ask, "Who's going to write songs about all the stupid shit you do out in LaLa Land?"

I wrote "Prowling" after he left me a drunken note during freshman year. I still have it, and it makes me laugh every time I read his barely legible handwriting:

Please, please, please, I'm begging you to go prewl prawl prowling around campus for women with me—and bring that guitarr cause they loooove it.

While he didn't appreciate his song the first time I played it for him, he seems to score whenever I perform it. His opinion of my mad writing skills went up a few notches once he realized the correlation.

"Yeah, well who's going to be your new wingman here?"

I've been Dan's wingman more times than I can count. And vice versa, although I haven't much needed his efforts in that department. I've kept a steady diet of women, but none I would call a "girlfriend." That's not to say some haven't tried their damnedest to get that title. With so many willing women in the City that never sleeps, why should I tie myself to just one?

I check the time. It's getting pretty late and I have that brunette waiting for me. I glance over to her table. She seems to be in deep conversation with her friends. It's time to indulge in something other than beer.

"Yeah," I say, "it's going to be crazy not living together anymore. I'm going to miss your cleaning skills when my parents come over."

"Guess you'll have to learn how to wash a dish, man."

"Not tonight, I won't. Are you going to stay here or head back to the apartment? I think it's time for me to put that chick out of her misery."

Rolling his eyes, Dan replies, "I'm heading out. Have a good night, stud."

Oh, I intend to. Graduation isn't for another month, so I don't yet feel the urgency to cram in more time with Dan before he heads out to LA. We give each other a half-hug and he leaves.

I take a few steps toward the brunette's table. It's empty.

Stopping in the middle of the bar as if hitting an invisible wall, I scan the room for the girl. She was on board with being my date tonight, I'm sure of it. Maybe she went to the ladies' room? But I glance over, and she's not in the line. A woman has never before backed out on me like this. *Well, shit.*

The bar still is filled with plenty of chicks, but now I'm fixated on that brunette. She must be inside the bathroom. There's no other explanation. While I'm holding up a wall near the bathrooms, no less than three women come over and try to chat me up. I'm on a mission, though, and they all give up.

When a girl I saw in line leaves the bathroom, it hits me—I've really been ditched. This sucks. And not in a good way.

I'm making my way to the bar for a shot of something—anything—when I spot the brunette walking into the bar from outside. Changing course, I stride over to her. "You left?"

She looks up at me while her fingers play with her earring. "I, uhm, it was getting late."

Reaching out, I extricate her fingers from the hoop. Pitching my voice lower, I say, "But you came back." She blushes and nods.

For some reason I find her behavior endearing. Kissing her hand, I stare into her intoxicating blue eyes and ask, "Do you still want me, darlin'?"

What the hell? I never ask twice.

"I've been looking forward to meeting you for a long time, Cole." She swallows. "I don't want to miss out on tonight."

That's more like it. Time to change the status of this party to private. "Do you have your own apartment?"

"No, I live in the dorms."

I nod my head in understanding. "Are you in Hayden?"

"Yeah."

That one simple answer tells me a lot about her. She's a freshman at NYU and there's no way in hell I'm taking her back there. Been there, done that. I hate the lack of privacy. One time I was literally thrusting into some redhead when the door opened and her roommate walked in. Of course, her roommate joined us for a threesome, so I can't really complain. But I prefer to choose my partners ahead of time. Nope, not going back to the dorms.

"I have the perfect place for us to get to know each other. Intimately." I whisper the last word into her ear and feel her shudder in response. That's more like it.

I lead her upstairs to the room that I use to store my guitar. It's small but clean, and there's a sofa and a private bathroom.

Given my rather heavy conversation with Dan tonight and this cute brown-haired chick's almost defection, I'm not interested in small talk. I want to focus on something a lot more pleasurable. Like getting inside her. As soon as we enter the room, I spin her around so that her back is to the door.

Bracing my arms at either side of her head, I lean forward and stare at her lips. She tilts her head and closes her eyes. That's all the invitation I need. I swoop down to kiss her with an intensity driven by lust, beer and the knowledge that my college years will soon be over. My lips cover hers. This is not a gentle kiss. She moans as I thrust my tongue into her mouth and part her legs with my knee. Her hands climb my chest and encircle my neck.

I break away from her mouth and start kissing a trail from her neck up to her ear. "I think we're both overdressed for this party."

Hearing no objection, I reach down and remove her shirt.

"Rose."

Wait, what? Does she want me to give her flowers? My eyes raking over her lacy ice-blue bra that matches her eyes, I say, "Excuse me?"

"My name is Rose. Rose Bloomer. I just thought you should know . . ."

Smiling, I undo her bra with one flick of my fingers and take a pert nipple into my mouth. "Nice to meet you, Rose. Rose Bloomer." Just then her name registers. I try, unsuccessfully, to suppress my chuckle.

"My mother had an ironic sense of humor."

"Perhaps she was a frustrated florist?" Grinning, I look at her standing against the door, half naked. Her hair smells faintly of flowers. "I like your name. It suits you."

Kissing her again, I bring her flush against me and cup her ass. Her very nice ass. Not breaking contact with her, I turn us both and walk over to the sofa. I undo the zipper at the back of her skirt, and it drops to the floor in a puddle of fabric. I'm fully dressed; she's only in an ice-blue thong and black heels.

"Sexy," I whisper in her ear. "Leave the shoes on."

I put some gentle pressure on her shoulder, then follow her onto the sofa. Her hands work the buttons on my shirt and I let her take it off me. Her eyes dilate as they roam over my chest and abs.

"You're ripped. I didn't know. Wow."

All those hours at the gym were worth it to get this response. "For you, darlin'," I reply, while looking down at her body. Something at her hip catches my attention. "What is this? A tattoo?" I ask as I lave it with my tongue.

"Birthmark," she replies breathlessly.

"It looks like a flower. How perfect for you, Rose."

Soon I'm distracted from her birthmark by her scent. Pulling her thong down and off her body, I begin to explore her wet folds with my tongue. Her breathing increases as my fingers join the exploration.

Lightly blowing on her, I lick her clit and demand, "Come for me."

After a few more strokes, she clenches around me and moans. Nice.

My lips wander back to her nipple as I remove a condom packet from my wallet, placing it on a nearby table. I shuck my jeans and hear her suck in a breath. I don't have time to look at her before she's pulling my head to hers, devouring me with her lips, tongue and teeth. It's my turn to moan as I relish our bodies' contact, skin on skin.

God, this girl feels so damn good. Her tits are the perfect size, with their beautifully distended pink nipples. And that ass. I knead it while she wraps her hand around my cock and begins moving it up and down. Involuntarily, my hips thrust into her. For her part, she's writhing under me, moaning my name over and over.

"Do you want me, darlin'?"

"Cole. Oh God, Cole."

I take that's a "yes." I grab the condom and quickly roll it over my throbbing cock. With a quick thrust, I enter her to the hilt. Fuck, she's so tight and wet.

"Yes, darlin'," I breathe into her ear.

After I give her a moment to adjust to my size, I start pumping into her welcoming pussy. I slowly pull back and push forward, over and over. Her back arches perfectly, offering her pink nipples to my mouth. Who am I to refuse?

Deciding that I would like to see her tits bouncing, I change our position so that she's riding me. With my hands at her hips, I caress that cute birthmark and guide her into the perfect rhythm. She has one foot on the floor for balance, and the sight of her fuck-me pumps drives me crazy. I'm quickly getting close, so I stroke her clit. She falls apart. I love the look on a woman's face as she comes for me. Her climax sends me over the edge, and I come with a loud, satisfied groan.

When sanity returns, I pull out of her body. Lightly smacking her gorgeous ass, I go to the bathroom to get rid of the condom. Cupping my hands, I rinse my face with cold water and look into the mirror. My green eyes have a well-sated glint, and my brown hair is messy from all of her attention. No one would doubt that I just indulged in some seriously glorious sex.

Smiling, I walk naked from the bathroom to see her pulling her shirt on over her head. Her brown hair's red highlights glint in the dim light. Otherwise, she's fully dressed. "Now who's underdressed for this party?"

"Cole, that was . . . wow. There are no words."

"I had a great time too, darlin'."

She reaches up and traces my dimple with her pink fingertip. Her nail polish reminds me of her nipples. She brings me in for a kiss and then turns toward the door. With her hand on the door knob she says, "I'll never forget tonight, Cole."

Stopping her before she can leave the room, I bring her back to me for one last, long, passionate kiss.

"It was a *very* good night, Rose Bloomer with the flower birthmark."

Acknowledgements

I want to thank so many people for their encouragement and help along my first journey to publishing.

First, my #1 fan, my husband. He has given me so much support, listened to too many plot variations and loved me through it all. A great big shout out, too, to my mother, family and friends.

My critique partners, Noella Phillips and Michelle Bond. I am so lucky to have found these ladies who have laughed and cried with me, and suffered through agonizing storyline changes. Their honesty and support is humbling.

My behind-the-scenes plotting partner, Wendy Hamlin. She sat through many dinners (and drinks!) listening to me ramble on and on about crazy plot possibilities.

A great big thank you to my professional team! I was so fortunate to have found the amazing Angela Polidoro, whose edits made this book sing. With a huge heart and red pen to match, Jen Leisenheimer of Beyond the Pages Editing applied her skills to proofread this manuscript. The always upbeat Cassy Roop of Pink Ink Designs formatted the pages with practiced ease. And cover designer Kari Ayasha of Cover to Cover came up with the most amazing cover design, even though I couldn't articulate what I wanted. Thanks to each of these fabulous ladies for your patience in helping me produce my debut novel.

My betas – Maria Dema, Freddie Bonaire, Frances Rosa, Chip Cavill, Carrie Sutton, Sarah Robson, Renita van Dam-Jacobi and Lee Thomas. This has been a very long road, and their good humor through it all (can I say "what about this cover or this one?") means more to me than words can express.

My rock star go-to Greg Merkle. Thanks for all your insights into the music world!

Huge thank you to everyone who has supported me throughout my journey, especially Anne Walradt, Lilly Wilde, WT, Rekha Dave, Candice Benson, Nancy Herkness, Judy Kentrus and all of the wonderful authors in the NJ chapter of Romance Writers of America.

And finally, to all the ladies of the Playroom. You gave me the ludicrous idea that I really could write the story of my heart. I will love each of you forever for that.

To everyone who picks up this novel, *I hope you fall in love with Cole and Rose*. And if you do, please tells your friends and write a review.

About the Author

For as long as Arell Rivers can remember, she has been lost in a book. During her senior year in college, she picked up a Danielle Steele novel … and instantly was hooked on romance.

Arell started writing her first novel because the characters were screaming at her to do so. The story started coming out in her dreams and attacking her in the shower, so she took to the computer to shut them up. But they kept talking.

Born and raised in New Jersey, Arell has what some may call a "checkered past." Prior to discovering her passion for writing romance, she practiced law, was a wedding and event planner and even dabbled in marketing. Arell lives with a very supportive husband and two mischievous cats. When not in her writing cave, Arell is found making dinner in the crock pot, working out with Shaun T or hitting the beach.

Arell is a member of the New Jersey chapter of Romance Writers of America.

Want to keep up to date with Arell? Sign up for her newsletter at http://bit.ly/ArellRiversSignup.

Also connect with her via
Facebook: www.Facebook.com/ArellRivers
Twitter: @ArellRivers
Website: www.ArellRivers.com
Email: Arell@ArellRivers.com

Other Books by Arell Rivers:

Hard to Hold (Book #2 in The Hold series)
To Have and To Hold (Book #3 in The Hold series)